THE SHADOW OF LOTHAN

The Last Shadow Epic, Book Two

by

AJ Cooper

THE EMPIRE

SKY MOUNTAINS
PALADIUM
R. ISTER
R. SULIS
Arctos
Pallister
Thinai
Kersepoli
ELOESUS
Korthos
Imperiopoli
R. HYPER
Xanctum
Paladris
Northern Geats
The Northern Wall
GAD
R. GAD
Brilium
Bregantium
Norwood
Latera
BLESSED ISLES
SPICE ISLANDS
TEN CITIES
Megaris
RED MOUNTAINS
Haroon
KHAZIDEA
IMPERIAL SEA
Mekari Barbaricus
GOLDENHORN MOUNTAINS
Paradise Gardens
ANTHANIA
Rimi
Floridium
IRON MOUNTAINS
Imperial City
Larmathaun
Nichaeus
Isle of
Serpents
Amaroth
Perzgosh
Carta Mega
Zoar
KHEROE
100
200
MILES

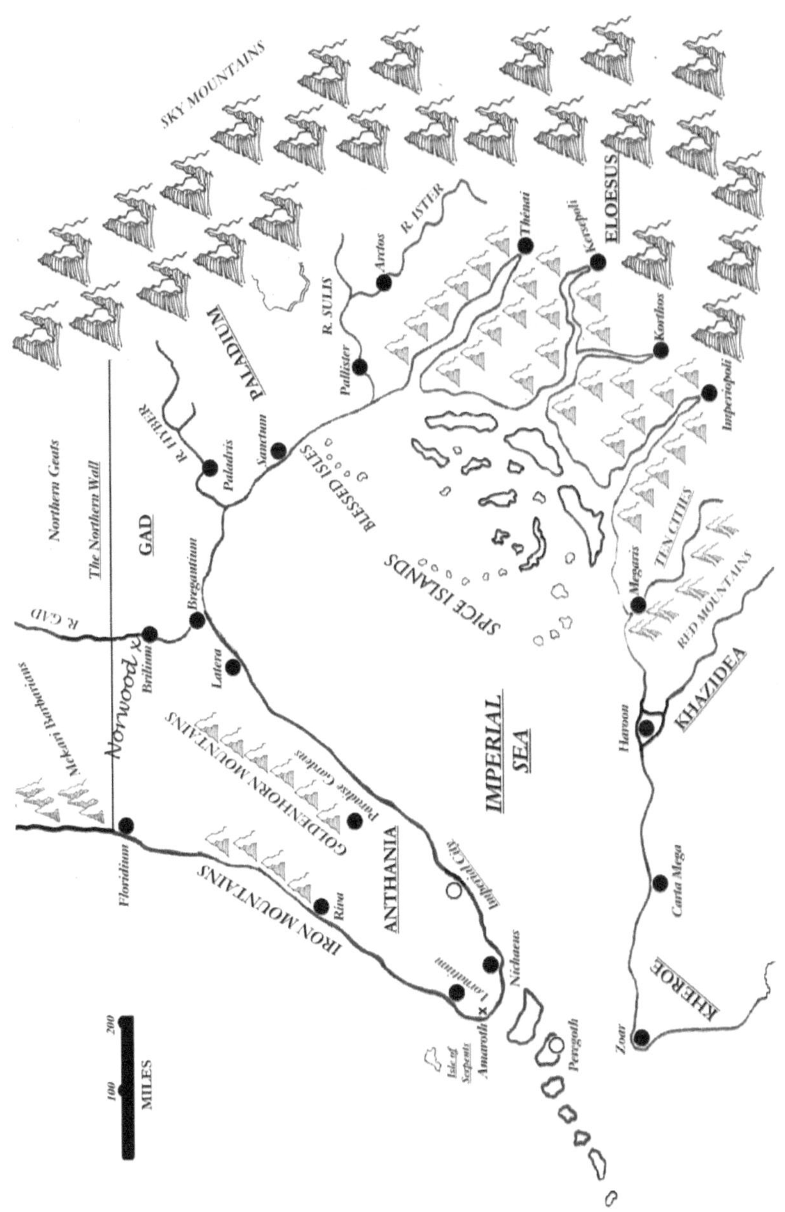

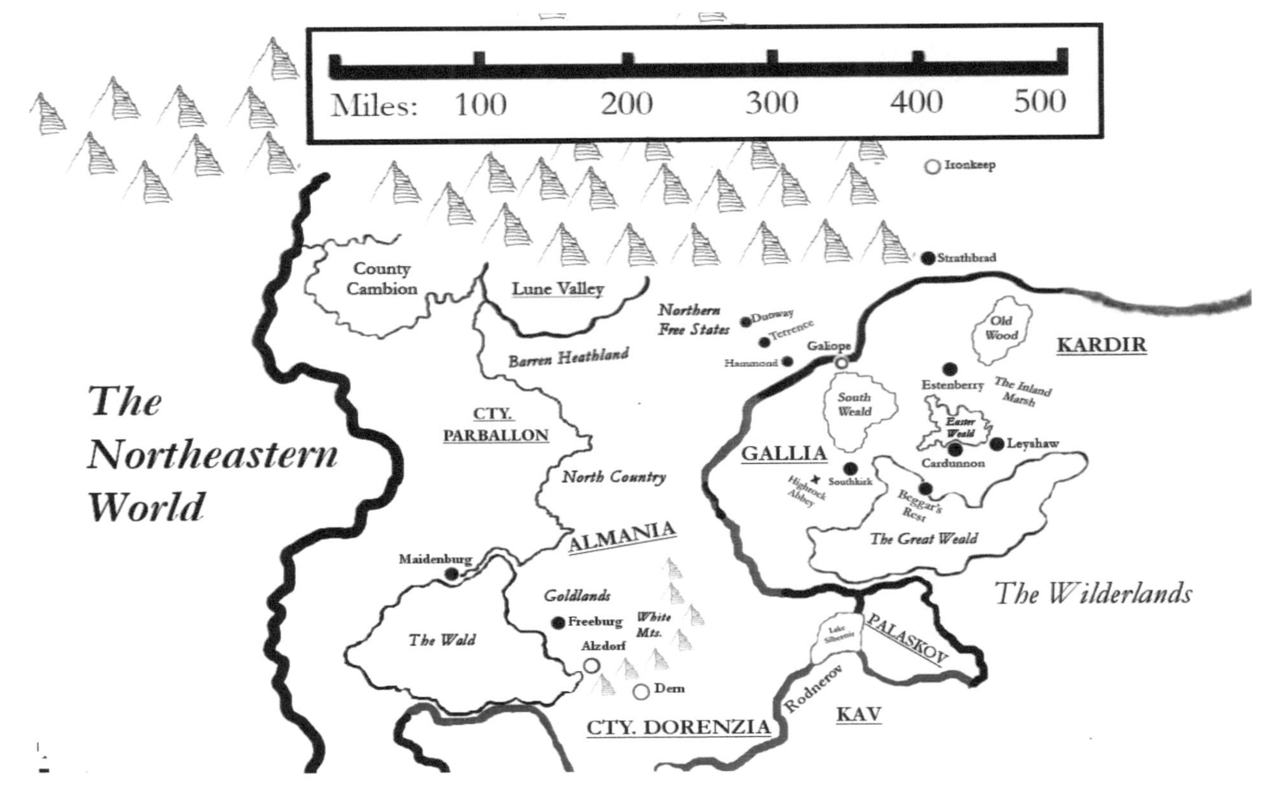

Miles: 100 200 300 400 500
The Northeastern World
Ironkeep
Strathbrad
County Cambion
Lune Valley
Barren Heathland
Northern Free States
Dunway
Terrence
Hammond
Galiope
Old Wood
KARDIR
Estenberry
The Inland Marsh
South Weald
Easter Weald
Leyshaw
Cardunnon
GALLIA
Highbrook Abbey
Southkirk
Beggar's Rest
The Great Weald
CTY. PARBALLON
North Country
ALMANIA
Maidenburg
Goldlands
Freeburg
White Mts.
Alzdorf
The Wald
Dern
CTY. DORENZIA
Rodnerov
KAV
Lake Silbermit
PALASKOV
The Wilderlands

GALIOPE

Garrick's Gate
THE ELVEN QUARTER
MARKET DISTRICT
SELWYN'S PARISH
Hawk's Keep
Strathbrad Gate
Tower of Pythor
Horn Keep
MIDDLETOWN
WODENSCROSS COURT
LONEN TOWN
GREENWATER
Bridge O'er Galios
RIVERSIDE
CATHEDRAL DISTRICT
Godsgate

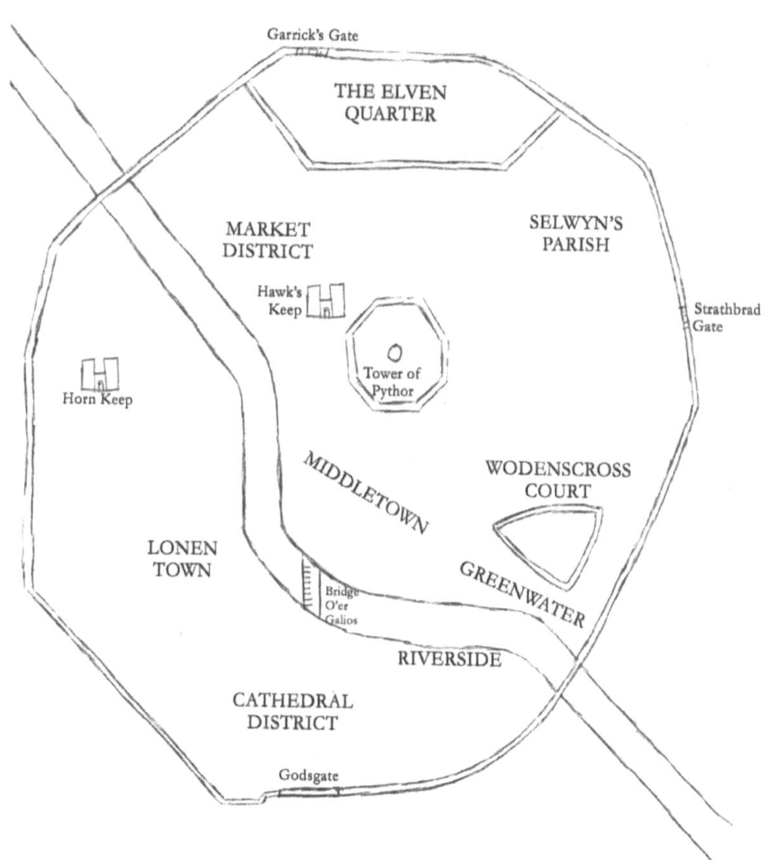

Chapter One:
The Proposition

Reev Nax galloped down the road with a purpose, and his purpose was to get home.

The two ratlings he had known as his foster parents had been given a proper burial and Norwood, the place of his birth, where he had been raised and reared, was now behind him.

At least, that was what he hoped.

Cobalt, his horse, eventually began to slow until his gallop was a canter and his canter was a trot. Even Elvish horses, Reev Nax supposed, could get fatigued.

The road hugged the banks of the River Nor, and if Reev followed for long enough he could expect to leave Noricum entirely and eventually find himself on the great highway that joined the north and the south. He had once been of Norwood, but now he was of Galiope, the Great Queen of the North. And he was eager to get back, for as he rode, the long shadows of the oaks and maples began to disturb him. A wind was picking up in increasing gusts, and clouds were blowing in from the west.

Few travelers were on the road. He had heard from idlers rumors of war, in the north and the south, of unrest in the east, and a pestilence in the air. But Reev had his sword, Doomblade, and he had on the armor of the city he had worn during the Battle of Galiope. There seemed to be an ill wind plaguing the hot summer air, but, Reev Nax reminded himself, he was well prepared and well protected.

It was dusk when the town of Tancreda appeared. In his youth he had been there, the greatest and largest town of Noricum. Its buildings were of stone, and its red-bricked piazzas were said to resemble the great cities farther south. In the ignorance of his youth he had thought it an immense city, but now, with experience, he knew it was little better than a village. About a dozen buildings circled the piazza, one of which was an inn he had stayed at long ago, an inn called the Blue Tabard.

He did not feel safe, but amid the small crowds gathered in the piazza, Reev knew that though he would stick out, he was in no danger. The agents of Seymus had been defeated. The Shadow, which had once threatened to engulf the world, was beginning again to retreat, and daylight was spreading once more.

The inn was small, much smaller than the Dragonpaw in Galiope. The servants attended to Cobalt and saw him into the stables, though they did so with sour faces and complaints on the tip of their tongues.

And when Reev entered, he thanked the gods the innkeeper was no one he knew, no one he recognized. He would be as anonymous as he could be.

"Your name," the innkeeper said, and there was a harshness to her tone, one he recognized, a tone the people of Noricum used for the "other," of those who did not belong. Though Reev had grown up in this region, he had never felt of it, nor was he treated so.

"Reev Nax," he answered. What use was there disguising one's name when the agents of Seymus were forever defeated?

"Say it again," the innkeeper said with a puzzled look on her face and a pen at the ready.

"Reev Nax," he said, more slowly this time.

"What sort of name is that?" the innkeeper grumbled, a point of rudeness he hadn't expected even in Noricum.

But in truth, he didn't know the answer. His name had been a mystery to him, his name, first and last. He'd never met another boy named Reev. He knew no one else with the family name "Nax." And so she did have a point, even though it was wrong to belabor it.

Eventually the transaction was made; for the price of three

silver denara, Reev had a room, a meal, and one last unfortunate night in Noricum, a place he couldn't wait to be rid of forever.

A lyrist was on the stage who had no business being a lyrist, and a singer who had no business singing. But the song was enchanting, telling the story of a wife whose husband went off to war.

And as Reev sat there at the table, still in the armor of the city, the rude innkeeper emerged from the kitchen with a smile on her face, and placed before him a great platter. On the platter was a meat pie together with mashed turnips, bread slices smeared with horseradish, and a steaming cup of tea.

He said a prayer and then took to his dinner.

The singer was dancing now, twirling about and hitting a tambourine.

"Brave Eustace, Eustace, home again

"Brave Eustace, Eustace home…"

There was a garland in her hair and her green gown billowed. The dagged edges of her sleeves just barely graced the ground.

No doubt they were local people, poorly trained, but their passion even now was evident, pulsing through every note.

It was late when Reev decided to retire. He was trying not to think of the journey ahead of him, a journey that would take many days and weeks, which would sap his strength and wear on his soul.

The innkeeper walked up to the plate, the rude innkeeper from before, and she took it from his hands. She bent down to Reev and said at a whisper, "Be warned, Master Reev, and I do not mean to alarm you, but that man in the corner's been staring at you all night."

Reev looked about in a frenzy, trying to find what corner she meant. As she walked away with the platter in hand, Reev caught sight of him, a man in the far side of the hall to his left. He was in a booth, and almost completely enveloped in darkness. In his mouth was a pipe that would occasionally flare, lighting in his black eyes.

I have my sword. I have my armor. I am safe…

Quickly and quietly he got up, making sure not to look at the man, whose attentions and interests were unwanted. He headed up to his room, Room 3, he remembered, and opened the door.

Within was a small room, spare and unornamented, with wooden floors and a ceiling that was partially sagging, a bed, a table and a few chairs. As he began to undress, he locked the door and tried it twice, then propped a chair against the knob. No one could come in or out. No one would come in or out.

But as he changed into his smallclothes, he couldn't help but remember those black eyes, and the fires that seemed to glimmer within them. He could not forget. He would not forget.

~

The great white road that cut across the hills, many wagons across, was well traversed and well tended to. Its white pavestones gleamed in the summer sun, and great crowds were walking in either direction when Reev joined it.

It was called the Path of Tidus, named after a forgotten emperor. It joined the remote north to the Empire, connected to disparate regions, and it was the path that would best take Reev back to Galiope. He knew wherever he went from now on, he would be well supplied, and there would be an abundance of places to sleep, and the protection of many thousands of guards.

What a change it was from before, in the dark times of just last year, when the agents of Seymus threatened to unmake the world. What a change it was from then, when now Reev no longer felt he had to hide his identity or conceal his movements.

He rode by his lonesome, mounted astride Cobalt. The sun was withering hot, and Reev—though he had lightened his load—again found he had dressed too warmly. In the distance, the oaks and maples were like dark shadows. The road was well traveled, with hundreds before him and ahead of him.

But Reev knew that he was making progress, though he was exhausted. He knew that though he was already weary, every day took him a little closer to his destination, a little closer to his new home, Galiope.

As the sun began to set, Reev began to inquire of inns on the road, and heard from an Imperial traveler that an inn was just a mile north. And so he rode, and there he found it, a three-story building, colored green with a tile roof, and a sign: The Fattened Goose.

Food he had: wine, bread, and cheese, and skewers of beef. He listened to pipers and watched dancers on the stage. It was a reminder he had left the small-mindedness and provinciality of Noricum and was in an entirely new place.

And then, with a heavy stomach, and no cares left in the world, he fell asleep in a feather bed lined with Khazidean cotton. As soon as his head hit the pillow, he had escaped into the land of dreams.

~

Thunder awoke him. Lightning flashed and illumined a dark-whiskered face. Outside rain was pouring and the wind was searing in its intensity. The firmament seemed shaken, and Reev, unprepared, knew his sword Doomblade was across the room, away from his reach.

Lightning struck again, and he knew those dark eyes; he had seen them. The blue light of the lightning told Reev all he needed to know.

"Who are you?" he said simply. He noted his own hands were not trembling, though his breath felt shallow, though he wondered if this was the moment he might die.

As Reev's eyes adjusted to the light, he could see twin sabers tied to the man's back. His eyes seemed black as the abyss. He was wearing over his body a coat of animal skins.

"Xandrast," he said. "Ivan Xandrast."

For a long moment there was an uncomfortable pause, and neither said anything.

"You've been following me," Reev stated.

Lightning flashed, and Reev saw that Ivan Xandrast was smiling. "Yes," he said. "Yes, I have.

"I have seen your nobility, Reev, your honor. You returned to your hometown just to see your foster parents given a proper burial."

Reev shuddered at the thought of Ivan Xandrast watching him from the bushes as he dug his parents' grave. But that was what had happened.

"Who are you?" Reev said again, and this time he meant it in a general sense. "Why are you following me?"

"I have a business proposal," Ivan Xandrast said. "I work on behalf of a powerful patron. A very rich man who can help you—"

"A rich man," Reev said. "I have no need of money. Who is your patron?"

"Lothan is his name," Ivan Xandrast answered. "He has taken a keen interest in you. He has observed your movements closely. He believes that if you go into business together, you can serve each other mutually."

"Leave me, Ivan Xandrast," Reev said, more forcefully than perhaps was wise.

"Please call me Xan," he answered. "That is how everyone who knows me addresses me."

"I do not know you," Reev said. "I want no part of this. I want to be left alone."

The storm seemed to have slowed; the rain had gone from a downpour to a steady shower. The wind was not blowing as hard as it had.

"You do not know me, you say," Ivan Xandrast answered. "You do not want any part of this. You do not want to even hear

Master Lothan's offer."

"No," Reev said. He sat up fully on his bed, and felt his muscles tense, ready to spring.

"Then," Ivan Xandrast said, "you must die."

And as he drew his sabers from his back, Reev dived across the room, grabbing his sheath in his hands, and swept Doomblade out of it. "Help!" he screamed. "Help!"

Doomblade met saber, so strong that sparks were formed.

Doomblade met saber again, and Ivan Xandrast seemed to be backing away.

Footsteps echoed across the hall. Guards and help were coming. A death had been thwarted, the death of Reev.

And Ivan Xandrast, with a loud cry, barreled past the guards as they ran into the room, then turned and gave chase.

From now until he reached Galiope, Reev would keep on his guard. Every door would be locked. Every path would be well thought through.

And perhaps, in the end, he should not take the main roads at all.

Chapter Two:
A Dance by Firelight

Where was she, and who was she?

Ambrass was weeping softly in her room in the Dragonpaw. The memory of last night still stung, the memory of she and Fortunato's parting.

On the battlements of the city wall, Fortunato had professed his love for her. And she had told him no. For though she was growing older, though she had rejected her former betrothed, Gaius, still she was not sure, of what to do, of who she was, of where she was going. She could not give Fortunato her all if she did not understand herself, if she could not look deep within.

On her bed she wept into her hands, and her sobbing was waxing or waning. She had lost Fortunato, now; he had been insulted and he would never take her back. He was an Imperial, with a strong sense of pride, and she had wounded him.

"What have I done?" she said softly. "What have I…"

The door to her room opened just a crack. Standing there was Glenda the innkeeper, Glenda the Half-Elven, Ambrass's employer—but she had become more than that, a mother figure, an older sister. Everything Ambrass was going through Glenda knew. She had told her everything, about last night, about how she felt… Glenda had been understanding.

I have made a mistake… I have made a terrible mistake!

"Ambrass," Glenda said, "why don't you get to work? You may find a little sunshine in your rainy day…"

Were her motivations selfish? Did she just want the Dragonpaw swept clean? Ambrass supposed, in a sense, that it did not matter.

~

The hearth was unlit, and the remnants from the winter logs had not been cleaned; Glenda thought the ash and debris was a good decoration. The room was sweltering with summer heat, and in the tables and booths patrons were fanning themselves or drinking copious amounts of water. It seemed in Galiope one was either deathly hot or deathly cold, and very little in between.

But Galiope was all Ambrass had ever known.

Fortunato was not from Galiope; he had seen the world. He was an Imperial, a son of the Empire.

And at the thought of him, regret sprang forth anew from a deep well in her heart.

Oh, to go back in time, to not say what I had said, to not do what I have done.

She crossed the room, grabbed her broom, and began to sweep the floor. It had been several hours since her last sweeping, but she supposed it was best to keep busy, like Glenda said, to distract herself, to ensure that nothing was out of place. It would help her take her mind off things, to help her forget the terrible thing she had done, the irreversible outcome she had engineered.

"Fortunato," she said softly under her lips. "Gods let me forget… gods let me forget…"

~

The day wore on. Patrons came and went. They arrived, sometimes to eat, sometimes to drink. Dusk came and the windows sparkled from Ambrass's cleaning. The floor was so immaculate Ambrass would eat off it. The sun began to lose its light; the day began to darken. Outside, the skies began to take on the colors of twilight. And through the doors, there was a commotion.

A man walked in, flanked on all sides by elves in dreary brown clothes. He had on black breeches and a doublet that was scarlet in color. On his head was a broad-brimmed hat as dark as pitch. Tied to his belt was a sheath where a rapier hung.

He was swart, with blue eyes and a brown moustache. There was an arrogant bearing about him, a certain swagger that filled Ambrass with disgust.

"Miss," he said, and at that moment Ambrass knew he was from the west, from Zarubain, and these elves were his slaves. "A room, please."

Glenda approached from the corner of the room. By the look on her face, she was no less disgusted by the sight of him.

Glenda, whose father was an elf, no doubt was disgusted by this slave-owner, a rich man, a noble from a foreign land who no doubt demanded to be worshipped wherever he walked.

"A room," he said, fixing his attention now on Glenda. "I hear this is the best inn in all the city. I will have you procure me your best room for myself, and lodgings for these churls of mine."

Though Glenda was disgusted, she was a shrewd businesswoman, and an opportunity had been presented to her. "A room, you say. My best. Five pence for you, and fifteen for these 'churls' of yours."

It was an outrageous price, Ambrass knew. There was no five-penny room in all the Dragonpaw, perhaps none in the city.

But this man put on a brave face; he'd never be seen a pauper. "Very well. Twenty it is. Have it."

"And your name?" Glenda said.

"Armande."

Ambrass, watching from the corner, knew there were certain laws in place. There was no slavery in Galiope or in all the Gallian League. The freeing of slaves was not normally done; if someone from Zarubain or the Empire arrived with their chattel in tow, they were normally left be. It was wrong, though, and as Ambrass stood there with her broom in hand, she envisioned herself waking Armande's slaves and running away with them in the middle of the night.

Armande idled there, and Ambrass could not help but stare daggers at him.

"Miss—"

"Glenda."

"Miss Glenda, what shall we be having to eat?"

"In the Dragonpaw, all are equal," said Glenda, "and everyone receives the same delicious, home-cooked meal. That will include your 'churls,' Master Armande."

Armande puckered his lips slightly. "A strange land, backward," he said. "What did I expect?" He turned. "Did you hear that, churls? No slop from the stables for you tonight."

There were scattered grumbles from the elven slaves. Perhaps they knew just how to behave, at the end of a switch. They were like a group of goslings following the mother goose, and Ambrass felt for them, yes, she felt for them strongly. Slavery was a burden not easily borne, though even she could not imagine truly how it felt, and what it meant. As a gypsy in Galiope, she had been ever the outsider, but what was it like to be owned by another, to have no agency, to be considered an object and not a soul, a tool and not a being with the divine spark?

~

Night fell and food was served: gravy laid over a bed of biscuits, with sausage stew. Armande and his elven slaves took up most of the room, and they drank freely. Up and down Ambrass ran from the cellar, ferrying up as many mugs of ale as they would pay for. Despite the repulsiveness of his company, Ambrass knew that Glenda Half-Elven would profit well from keeping her mouth shut and serving him in whatever manner he wished.

In the flickering light of the hearth, in the heat of the summer night, Ambrass walked to the corner and tried to regain her bearings. It had been an exhausting evening with a guest who demanded to be treated like a king. She could not imagine the wealth Armande must have. He had spent more money than Ambrass was like to see in a year.

"One more thing!" Armande cried from his booth. "One more thing to make this night most pleasurable! I shall see your lovely serving girl dance."

Glenda looked at Ambrass as if to gain her permission. In response, Ambrass gawked in amazement. How could she even entertain the thought, dancing for this rich cur? That had never been part of her job. To sweep and clean, to serve ale, sometimes to cook, that was her calling in life. To live out her days in quiet anonymity—that was what she wanted.

"If our guest wants a dance," said Glenda Half-Elven, "then he shall have a dance."

It was so insulting, yet pressure was building by the moment, by the second, and the longer time drew on the more unseen forces seemed to converge around her. At last she walked forward, unsure what to do, driven forth as if by a ghost.

And one of Armande's elven slaves pulled out a recorder, another a shawm, another a horn, and a group of them began to drum on the tables.

The music began, a furious and delightful tune, and before Ambrass knew it she was tapping her feet and twirling her arms, spinning, then leaping, then circling around the room.

Armande began to clap, and the looks on the elven slaves' faces were ones of delight, and spurred on by those looks Ambrass danced more furiously and more freely than ever before, tapping her feet, twirling her body, leaping up and down.

And eventually the music quieted, and the elf stopped playing his recorder, the others their shawm, their horn, and the only noise of the night was the crackling of the hearth and the faint clapping of Armande's hands.

"A job well done," Armande said. "A better dancer I have not seen in County Nis, and I daresay if you come with me you will have a place in my father's court."

"Never," Ambrass said firmly. "My place is here, in Galiope, at the Dragonpaw."

Chapter Three:
The Fight

The night on the battlements of the city wall still stung Fortunato.

It lingered with him even now, the sting of it. He had thought Ambrass loved him.

Now, in the tavern, he was thinking of his next best move the way he best mulled over things, a cup of wine in his hand, and a friend sitting with him, one who had latched on to him like an eager puppy—Wrinn.

The former slave of Reev Nax liked ale more than wine, and by now, they'd both had a lot to drink. It was late afternoon, and as Fortunato sat there, he remembered his resources were not unlimited, that eventually, he'd have to find some new job or some adventure to make ends meet. The life of a rogue was not easy, and it did not provide steady employment.

"You will forget her someday," Wrinn said softly amid the faint noise of the tavern.

The Green Girdle was mostly empty. It was one of Fortunato's favorites, a watering hole in Middletown, a place to get away and be forgotten. Here, in better days, he'd received jobs and been assigned tasks and been paid handsomely by high-ranking people, even officials in the Galiopean government. His years in Galiope had been few, but they had been his most lucrative.

But lucre was one thing, love and memories another, the stinging pain of rejection. He wondered if it was now time to leave. He could not forget the events of last year, the realization that Reev Nax was indeed the Sage, the Hand of the Gods, as so many had thought his father was.

He could not forget the siege.

But the Shadow was fading, and sunlight was spreading over hills and valleys. There was talk now of a long peace, of hope and tranquility that would last.

Fortunato's sword had put an end to the lives of hundreds of rokahn. Was his purpose served? Was it time now to depart, to seek his fortunes elsewhere, to say goodbye to the wizard Gastreel and all the friends he'd met along the way?

He looked around. Eventually the tavern would fill up, its empty spaces accumulating with people. That was when he would leave. The taste of wine was good on his tongue, but he wanted no part of the drunkenness, the carousing, the violent fights. His body was pocked with scars. He had seen much in his life. He wanted a quiet night, a stroll through the city perhaps, to think things over. His life was still ahead of him, and there were mountains to climb. There were, as poets would write, still dragons to slay.

~

In the gloaming light of twilight, Fortunato walked the streets of Galiope, and Wrinn followed along after him. The wine was still on his tongue, the harsh gall of Ambrass's words still about him. He remembered the days of his youth, of the Empire, the town of Ríva. Would he go back? He doubted it now.

But a shadow was approaching—no, many shadows, and as they drew near the shadows turned to faces. A man was walking toward them, a man in black breeches and a scarlet doublet, and a hat whose brim was wider than a saucer. Now Fortunato could see those behind him were elves with collars around their necks, the marks of slaves.

Wrinn wouldn't like the look of that.

They were in Middletown, not far from the Dragonpaw. The streets were eerily quiet save the group walking toward them. And Fortunato had a bad feeling he couldn't explain, a feeling of portent, a wind of change.

And so despite himself he drew his sword, Amenhir. Wrinn, following suit as always, pulled his quarterstaff from its brace.

"What is this?" the man called out. "Am I to be robbed in public, in the very daylight?"

His accent marked him as from the west, from Zarubain. And Fortunato did not like this man. No, not one bit.

"You will not be robbed," said Fortunato, "and you will be left be if you leave us be."

"What is this?" the man said again, and growled some indistinguishable curse. "And who is this? Your slave? I thought the pointy-eared dogs were treated like people in this wretched land."

At the words Fortunato wanted to touch Wrinn, to restrain him, to make sure he didn't do or say anything stupid.

"Speak!" the man said. "Can the pointy-eared dog talk? Are you this man's slave?"

"Watch what you say!" Wrinn shouted. "You might regret your—"

"Regret!" the man laughed. "That is funny. Perhaps I will purchase you and take you home to become my jester."

The man swept his weapon out of its sheath, and Fortunato saw it was of thin make, one of those dueling swords Zarube nobles were wont to carry.

"Get out of my way!" the man went on, "or it is you that shall regret your words. I am on important business in this backward land."

Fortunato knew this was not worth their trouble. "Come on, Wrinn," he said softly. "Let this go."

But Wrinn wandered out in the middle of the street, wielding his quarterstaff in both hands. "Apologize," he said. "Beg for my forgiveness. Or you're going nowhere."

"Wrinn," Fortunato wanted to say, but he knew Wrinn too well. There was no going back now. The rage was already building and it couldn't be stopped.

The man brandished his sword. "Get out of my way, pointy-eared dog, or I will slice you cheek to cheek."

And with a cry of rage, Wrinn charged him, and Fortunato watched what he had always known was coming.

The man struck with his rapier but was not Wrinn's equal. Wrinn pivoted and stepped in, stabbed down with his quarterstaff, and sent the man hurtling to the ground.

Aghast, the man writhed, but Wrinn showed no mercy. He pummeled the man with his quarterstaff even as Fortunato shouted, "Stop this!" and even as horns were sounded and the noise of galloping hooves rose in the night.

Guards were approaching by the dozen, town guards in Gallian dress. And like that, the consequences of Wrinn's short temper came into focus, though whether he would ever learn from it Fortunato had serious doubts.

The man on the ground was a shambles, a weeping thing, beaten and bruised by Wrinn's quarterstaff, no longer the brash and arrogant westerner from before.

"He struck me!" he wept, now playing the part of the beleaguered victim.

And the looks on the guards' faces indicated it was working.

"Fortunato. Wrinn," one of the guards said. "The heroes of the Battle of Galiope. How it is come to this…"

~

In the light of torches, the sentence was pronounced.

"Fortunato and Wrinn," said the Captain of the Guard in Middletown High Court. "You are from hereon exiled from the city of Galiope, and you are not to return. Consider your ties to the city severed for the remainder of your natural lives.

~

The morning dawned on the first day of Fortunato's exile. They had been thrown unceremoniously outside the city, and its walls loomed in the distance. The sun was rising, and they were forbidden to enter.

"Look," Fortunato said, "at what you've done."

Wrinn, stirring awake, showed no sign of regret and every sign of recalcitrance. "You heard what he said to me. He deserved it. I'd do it again."

"And look what you've done to me," Fortunato said. "No longer welcome in the city I fought for."

At that Wrinn had no answer, and he made a face Fortunato had never seen before. His brown elven eyes looked away from the city, farther south, and seemed to sparkle in the morning sun. "Over there—what's that?" He was pointing now, pointing south, and Fortunato turned to look.

There was farmland, fields of wheat and beans and mixed pastures for cattle. "Farms," Fortunato said, "for the people of Gallia to eat."

"No, farther beyond it… a sea of green."

As an elf, Wrinn could see more keenly than humans; his sight was perfect and far better than human sight.

"Go farther south enough," Fortunato said, "and you'll find the South Weald. The great forest that dominates most of Gallia."

~

The day wore on, and the cold of the morning evaporated. The sun cast long shadows over the farmers' fields, and Fortunato and Wrinn—with only a few coins left to spare—found themselves plotting their next move. On a green hill Fortunato sat, and as he sat there he could feel his stomach growl. The coin was barely enough for one night's meal, and Fortunato—who had brought his bow—knew what this all would soon come to.

"We will go hungry," he said, "if we are left like this for much longer."

"Perhaps a farmer has need of help," Wrinn said.

It was as good a suggestion as any, but doing back-breaking work for little pay did not entice Fortunato at all. In his earlier adulthood he had learned lessons of living in the wild, by the best tutors available. Perhaps, he'd soon tell Wrinn all of it.

Still, from farm to farm they went, but none had work for them. But as they wandered from house to house bits of information began to escape from the farmers' and farmhands' mouths, that what they called a Blight was swallowing up the South Weald, and that they feared it would soon swallow up their crops.

By the time night fell and they had spent their last few coins on a meal at a roadside inn, Fortunato knew just what they would do: they would live in the wilds as he had done before, and they would uncover the source of this Blight.

Chapter Four:
Night Walker

For days, Bala had slept outside.

The streets of Galiope had many places for him to rest, and when he rested at night he could see the stars and the moon. When everyone was gone to bed except him, he could rummage through the garbage and find something to eat, a bread crust, a bone with just a little meat on it, or a little hunk of moldy cheese.

His dada Reev was gone, and Wrinn had replaced him. But Wrinn was no dada, and he treated Bala harshly.

Bala, five years old, had thought to turn matters into his own hands. And he had left the Dragonpaw Inn a week ago today.

It was night and Bala was in the alley. Up ahead was a trash heap he hoped to pick through, and as he squatted down he listened and he perked up his ears. As a rule he'd wait ten seconds before picking through the garbage, for fear a town guard would come by and enforce the curfew and bring him home.

One, two, he counted.

Three… Four…

He scurried over and found the garbage pail. He began to pick through it.

His clothes had gotten dirty and his top hat was now crowned in slime. But he didn't much mind, and during the day he tucked himself out of sight to make sure no one could see him, or find him.

In the light of the moon his eyes adjusted. He could see papers wet with slime, documents he couldn't read, and a few disregarded apple cores. Ichor had formed over everything, and yesterday's rain had spoiled it all.

Bala grumbled.

He loved life outside, but he didn't much like this. On days when his hunting went poorly, he wondered if he should go back to the Dragonpaw and listen to Wrinn's harsh words.

He hopped down, growling softly to himself. And as he walked away, he heard something fall, and a skittering noise he didn't recognize. He turned and before he knew it, the dark shape was ahead of him, a black shape as large as his shoe. And he screamed and wanted his dada all the more, even his first dada, Nocturne.

And as he screamed the rat reacted, leaping into the air, and landed on him.

Bala struggled against it for what was a second but what seemed like a minute. And the rat bit him with its dark yellow teeth, and he screamed and howled in pain, desperate, weeping, crying.

Bala felt something surge through him. He shot his hands out and there was a purple flash of light. The rat fell limp, and its body hit the ground. The tiny black body was smoking. It was withered and shriveled up, and patches of hair had been burned away.

Bala looked at his hands, which were white in the moonlight, and he wondered exactly what he had done, and where that violent flash had come from.

Then he looked again and examined the rat that had bitten him, which even still was smoking, and he turned it over and picked it up. Its head seemed to have shrunken, and parts of it were hairless, and the moonlight was causing a gleam in its black eyes.

Like that, fear seized Bala and he hurled the dead rat to the ground. He wondered if dada was home yet. He promised he would come home.

He hurried through the streets, half waddling, half running, hoping against hope that he'd make it back to the Dragonpaw Inn in one piece. But why was he afraid, and for what reason was he running? He guessed he wasn't sure. Perhaps, he was afraid of the bright purple flash, or of the rat itself, or of the way the moonlight gleamed in its dead eyes. Perhaps he was afraid something else lurked out there in the night.

He was crossing the bridge, and the moon was white and full, and its light was glittering in the waters of the River Galios below. A voice echoed from behind him, "Bala Rabaam."

And when he turned he saw it was someone he recognized, that powerful wizard-man from before. What was his name? Gastreel! And he was riding on a horse, and his horse was packed with all manner of luggage. Gastreel had left, he remembered, but now he returned.

"Heading back to the Dragonpaw, are you?" he said. "It's terribly late."

"I... I... I sorry," Bala said.

"No need to be sorry," said Gastreel, and his eyes seemed to sparkle with interest. "Wait one moment, there, Bala."

He dismounted from his horse and led it by the reins, over to Bala. He touched Bala's cheeks with his fingers. "I sense... I sense..." The kind smile vanished, replaced with wonderment. "Bala Rabaam, five years old. You didn't just use magic, did you?"

"I... I... I don't know," Bala said. "I was in the alley and I saw a rat and it bit me and then there was a flash and then it was dead."

"Magic," Gastreel said. "In a child your age, it normally does not manifest so strongly. It is an interesting turn of events, for certain. I'll take you to the Dragonpaw, Bala. Here, I'll help you... up, up onto my horse. Come on!"

Chapter Five:
The Whisper

It was a cool morning when the South Weald appeared on the horizon. It abutted a farmer's field, and Wrinn and Fortunato were walking through the rows of wheat, stepping gingerly so as not to crush anything underfoot. The trees towered in the distance, mighty oaks and maples and hickories, and between the trunks a darkness that seemed profound.

On and on they walked and it seemed they were making no progress. The trees were towering in height and Fortunato realized that though the wilds were his purview, that he had never been in this forest before, and talk of the Blight, whatever it might be, alarmed him.

Yet from forests one could derive a living, with the gods' blessing and a skillful eye at the bow. Yet the vastness of the trees was daunting, and Fortunato wondered just how Wrinn had felt, if he was still supremely confident like he had been just hours ago.

Wrinn was running up ahead of him, and Fortunato joined him at a light jog. The wheat fields passed them by, and soon they took their first step into the wood.

With the sunlight vanished from them, the canopy overhead and a carpet of fallen leaves on the ground, Fortunato saw no sign of the path through the South Weald that humans took, nor of any other sign of human habitation. But as he scanned the primal woods, the hills up ahead and the creases and valleys, he recalled stories of holy men living solitary lives in the forests. Hermits, they were called, men and women who separated themselves from society entirely in the name of the gods.

"You say we can live out here," Wrinn said. "What is there except trees?"

Fortunato smiled and removed his bow from his back. "Ah, Wrinn, there is so much for you to learn. So much for me to teach you."

He had about a hundred arrows. More could be fashioned if necessary. Who knew how long they would be gone, or how difficult their exile would become.

He walked on, and this time Wrinn was no longer ahead of him, no longer overeager, no longer the one leading the way. Wrinn had been the one least perturbed about the exile, but now, perhaps, he realized that meant living off the land like a wild man. He was lucky to have Fortunato, supremely lucky, and someday he would realize it.

"Deer and elk can be found," Fortunato said, "if we wait for them. We can make fires ourselves, and a tent from animal hide."

"Animal hide," Wrinn said as if in disgust.

All he knew was the city, the urban life. He had ventured far from his elven origins, who—even in their great settlements—had some working knowledge or close connection to nature. But he would, with Fortunato as his guide, go back to the basics, back to the most ancient way of doing things. It was his task; it was both their tasks.

"What did you just say?" Wrinn said.

Fortunato turned to look at him. There was puzzlement and not a small amount of fear in his blue eyes.

"I didn't say anything," Fortunato answered.

"Yes you did. Don't lie to me," Wrinn said. "What did you just tell me? You whispered something…"

"I didn't whisper anything to you," Fortunato said, "and I do not lie. It is not in my nature."

Wrinn's indignance seemed to soften, laying bare the worry. Fortunato could envision what was on the tip of his tongue: "I want to leave." But Wrinn was not going to speak his heart. Even now his pride was too strong. He'd never admit he was afraid, nor would he admit he'd done wrong in causing their exile.

In olden days, when civic pride was at its height in Gallia, exile was considered worse than death. But for now, Fortunato was happy he still had his life, and as for Wrinn, he would teach him how to live in nature and bring him back to his elven roots.

Yet in the low light, obscured by the canopy, there was still worry writ on Wrinn's features. Who had spoken to him? Perhaps, it was just his fear speaking.

Chapter Six:
Vampires

Ambrass, the daughter of Kunakil and Gaida, was again in her room.

The crowds in the Dragonpaw had thinned out. And Ambrass was beginning to wonder just what she was doing in Galiope, and what her people were doing here as well. For centuries, the gypsies had wandered from place to place in their colorful wagons, finding no acceptance in Zarubain, no acceptance in the Empire. But at last their wagons had reached Galiope, a city that welcomed the refugee, where the outsider and the foreigner were invited in and allowed to become Gallians.

Now she was without the one she loved. He had vanished from her, and it was her fault he was gone.

She tried to breathe free. She tried to summon within herself her strength. She thought of going back to Selwyn's Parish, where the gypsies of Galiope lived, but there were challenges and worries there as well. For in gypsy life, a woman was a man's property, and among the gypsies a young woman Ambrass's age was supposed to be married. If she went back she'd see Gaius again, whom she had foresworn.

And at that moment, Ambrass decided she would never go back. Her place was not among her people. She was a Galiopean, now, and she would remain so. Gone were the colored wagons. Gone was Selwyn's Parish, the place she had known. Gone were her brothers, her uncles and aunts and cousins. Her place was in the Dragonpaw Inn now.

~

In the great hall of the Dragonpaw Inn, Ambrass was at work sweeping. Glenda was behind the desk, but the booths and tables were empty. Armande, that cur, was gone, and so too were the gaggle of elven slaves he had mistreated, whom he had flaunted in a city that rejected slavery entirely but was too cowardly to free the slaves of foreigners that entered its gates.

She looked about the hall. Up the stairs, among the rooms, she heard the loud squeak of the floorboards. And a dark shape emerged, waddling, a little form in a top hat that was far too big for him and oversized clothes, the urchin Glenda had taken under her wing and whom Ambrass hadn't seen in many days. What was his name? Ah, yes, Bala.

"Hello, little one," she said, "are you hungry?"

Bala smiled, and his snaggle-toothed grin unveiled a fang. She recalled the legends she had heard, the rumors told under the light of a moon, the race of people who drank the blood of sentients in the dark of night… the vampires.

Bala began to stumble down the stairs, and his oversized trousers dragged so much on the floor it was a wonder he didn't trip.

"Milk," he said. "And bread!"

"Coming right up," Ambrass said.

The milk, ferried in every morning from Gallian farmers, was already likely to spoil, but Glenda had found a cool place in the kitchen to store it. As for bread, several loaves were already in the oven being baked. The young urchin, whom Glenda doted on and had given a home free of charge, would be well fed and given the best that could be offered.

Ambrass poured into a ceramic glass a heaping portion of milk, then set it aside. She watched the oven as the dozen loaves took on a crisp character. She began to prepare a plate.

When she brought the bread and milk to him, Bala was sitting in the booth by himself.

" 'Tank you," he said, and Ambrass smiled in return.

She sat down across from him as he began to gobble the bread. The milk he had a hard time reaching, but with Ambrass's aid he managed to wrap his hands around it and drink.

By the time he was done, the young child had a white moustache of milk over his lips.

"You," he said, "remind me of my mama."

~

Hours later, when the night was done and the guests of the inn were sleeping in their beds, Ambrass pulled Glenda aside.

The light of the great hall was scant, and the fire in the hearth had faded to dim embers.

"About Bala," she said. "What do you know of him? Who are his parents? Who is his mother?"

And Glenda grew quiet, though there was no one to hear. "His mother, I do not know. She must be human," she said. "But his father... his father is someone you should pray to the gods you never meet."

"Tell me of him," Ambrass said softly.

And she felt the air in the hall change, though it was empty, though she and Glenda were alone. The name was on the tip of Glenda's tongue, but she kept quiet as if it were the name of a spirit whose attentions she wanted to avoid.

In the hall, the hearth's flickering embers caused the shadows of chairs and tables to dance.

"Let us not speak of him in the night," Glenda said. "Night is when he roams."

~

Ambrass dreamed that night of a cold embrace, of a land

swirling with snow. She dreamed she was left for dead in an icy and barren land, with a kiss of love lingering on her lips.

29

Chapter Seven: Not Safe

The road from the south to the north was long, and three days after Reev had left the Empire's borders he had begun to feel weary of traveling. He knew he was somewhere in the land of Mekara, and all about him were hills covered in forest, a monotony broken only by the occasional watchtower or high fastness. The Empire held sway over this land, but it was not their own, and Reev knew he had to be his own protector, his own defense.

Nightly, he would pray to the gods, hoping that strange man Ivan Xandrast had lost him, that somehow or some way he had been utterly confused and driven off Reev's trail.

Above him, scattered clouds hung uneasily in a blue firmament. In the sweltering air Reev had removed all but his light clothes. And when he rode, he knew he was in danger, but he knew he was as prepared as he could be.

Over the long days of traveling, memories returned. Of the night in the temple of doom, where the Servants of Seymus had trapped Gastreel, he had at first remembered nothing. But memories began to emerge, vague memories of his body filled with power, of light and of hope and of peace. But Seymus's servants and agents were defeated now, and the shadow was retreating, and light was coming in.

At twilight, Reev stopped for the day. He dismounted from Cobalt and got out his daily helping of road-bread and salted jerky. He drank copiously from his waterskin and then began preparing his tent, a tent he had purchased from the finest tent maker in Galiope.

As he was fastening the tent to its poles, he heard the sound of approaching hooves beating against dirt. And in a moment's span, he dropped what he was doing and drew out Doomblade, sure beyond surety that Ivan Xandrast had come to kill him.

But when the man became visible, and Doomblade was gleaming in Reev's hands, he saw it was not Ivan Xandrast at all, but an Imperial soldier girt in a glossy breastplate and a shining helm on his head topped with a red horsehair crest.

At the man's side was a shortsword, the kind of shortsword Imperial soldiers wielded, tucked neatly in a sheath.

"Hail!" the soldier said. "Where are you going, *signore?*"

"Must I state my business to you?" Reev said.

"It is not required," the soldier answered. "But it may be in your best interest. I am here to protect all travelers."

"Are there bandits about?" Reev said.

The soldier's face took on a grim expression. "We cleared out a few nests just yesterday. You should have nothing to worry about."

He paused, as if he wanted to say something but wouldn't.

"I am heading to Galiope," Reev offered, though he hadn't been pressed.

And the man's ears perked up, and for the first time there was a look of concern on his face. "Galiope," he said. "Why aren't you taking the main roads?"

"I have private business," Reev said in answer.

"Mind if I search your things?" said the soldier.

"I'd rather you not," Reev said.

But he knew at this point disobeying would mean arrest. Though Mekara was not a part of the Empire, still the Empire's soldiers acted like Mekara's policemen, arresting this or that person, confiscating whatever goods they saw fit.

And so Reev did not resist as the soldier dismounted and began going through his things, all of it, the armor of the city, the countless rations of food, and at last his sword, at which the soldier marveled.

"What sort of metal is this?" he asked, and as he held it up, the *estirion* blade seemed to glitter with twilight.

"It is my sword," Reev answered. "You will not take it from me, will you?"

"No, no," the soldier said. "I am no bandit. But tell me, what is its make?"

"*Estirion*," Reev said.

"Star-iron?" the soldier said. "Here… you may have it back.

"I will send word to the camp to fortify these back roads. The Empire's chief goal in Mekara is the maintenance of the roads, to ensure the safety of travelers. Commerce must be defended."

Commerce… that was what the Empire cared about most. Why would that surprise Reev? He was an Imperial citizen, born in a backward village in the Empire's hinterlands.

"Gods be with you," Reev said, now again with Doomblade in hand, and he waved off the soldier as he galloped away, feeling suddenly less protected and less safe.

He realized, at that moment, how alone he was in this wilderness, surrounded by low trees on all sides. He wondered how long it would take before he reached Galiope. Many, many days were yet ahead. But where the Empire held sway, there its soldiers would be. Bandits he would not have to fear. So what did he fear?

~

Days later, after a trek through much wilderness, the trees began to taper away. It was high noon and the sun was shining, and before him was a tunnel through a series of hills. Dangling from the tunnel were three soldiers in Imperial dress, their necks cinched with rope, their bodies steadily dripping with a foul ichor. They showed signs of putrefaction, their faces greenish and bloated. They had been dead many days.

And the first thing Reev thought was of Ivan Xandrast. He

wondered if his old foe had done this to frighten him. But then he realized it was preposterous.

The Mekari natives did not much like the Empire, and their roving bands of warriors loved nothing more than attacking the Empire's soldiers. It was the natives who had done this, no doubt, but it showed to Reev he was still not safe. No, he was not safe at all. Here where he rode dangers abounded, and the Empire's power could not keep him safe.

Perhaps, the Shadow had not fully retreated. Perhaps, the light was not yet here. Seeing the conflict first-hand, Reev wondered whether the world might spiral suddenly into war, whether the nations of Varda might rise against each other and—gods help him—the agents of Seymus arise again.

No, no, Reev thought. *I shall not entertain such dark thoughts.*

He had to get home, but there was something he had to do.

He cut the ropes from which the soldiers hung. He dragged the fallen bodies into the woods and gave them a light covering of leaves. Then he hopped on Cobalt and rode on, galloping ever ahead.

Every day took him a little closer to his destination. Every day took him a little closer to Galiope.

Chapter Eight:
Nature's Bounty

To hunt and succeed, three things were needed: a little luck, a lot of skill, and much patience. But Fortunato, crouching, waiting, knew that for Wrinn, patience was in short supply. And so he was alone, perched in the branches of a tree in view of a game trail, near where he thought some deer were bedding. Such a catch would feed them for more than a week, and with the proper preservation, for a month.

He had sent Wrinn on what he suspected would be a fruitless chase, to collect as many *sindomas* blossoms as could be found. *Sindomas,* which bloomed in autumn, would be difficult to identify and even more difficult to collect, but even now, before it was ripe, its tender stems were medicinal, and when brewed in a tea offered protections from all sorts of maladies.

He knew the South Weald abounded with animal life, but after hours in the tree little luck awarded to him: a coney running too far out of range, a roe deer getting wind of Fortunato and then bolting off…

Yet hunting required more than skill, it required luck. He had spent hours in the branches of the tree, waiting, wondering, hoping. He would not leave until his arrow was loosed and it found purchase. He would not leave until he and Wrinn could eat.

~

Wrinn stumbled through the forest around the camp, searching—as Fortunato explained—for tender unopened flowers with stems whose color "was like dark green or midnight blue." He had seen many tender shoots, and ferns the size of bushes. He had passed through clearings where the sun shone, and he could—thank the gods—see the sky. He had gotten down on his knees, picking through thorns and thistles and seedlings that were struggling to grow. But he had found nothing of what Fortunato had asked for.

He was pushing through a thicket, carving a path for himself crudely with his quarterstaff, casting leaf and vine and shoot aside, poking away the greenery in search of that unfindable *sindomas*. At last he broke free of the cloying vegetation and entered again a large clearing inset between two great hills, where he could again see the sun.

He remembered when he and Reev Nax had gone to the Old Wood, and been pulled into an adventure on the other side of the world. He wondered if Reev would have had better luck finding unopened flowers with stems of dark green or midnight blue.

Wrinn kept his eyes open, searching for just that. But here there was just grass that reached his knee, intermixed with large patches of dirt. There was no sign of *sindomas*, not here.

He waited in the clearing of the great wood, and the sun was shining on him. Only now did he feel any sense of regret; only now did he wish he had bitten his tongue. This was all that was left for him, trees, green shoots. From the wilds they would gain their living, or else they would starve.

Wrinn's stomach growled.

"Who are you?"

Wrinn shrieked at the whispered word. In a moment's span his quarterstaff was at the ready, prepared at any moment to strike whoever was foolish enough to strike him. He spun the quarterstaff around his wrists and then locked it in position. His bare feet were on solid ground; he would not be moved.

The wind picked up, and it was a warm and gentle wind. The blades of grass rustled in its path. Overhead, clouds were in their place and the sky was blue.

"Look," someone whispered.

Wrinn could not tell what direction the voice was coming from.

Fortunato, he knew, was hunting somewhere, perched in some secret place with his bow. Was he playing tricks on him, like he had before?

"Look," the voice had said, and amid the wafting grass, Wrinn did just that, searching the green blades resplendent with light. He scoured the whole of the clearing, and in the center found a stunted stem with a dark color, crowned with a white bulb.

He knelt down and plucked it gently from the dirt.

"*Sindomas*," Wrinn uttered. Fortunato didn't think he'd be able to do it. But Fortunato had been wrong before. It turned out, even in the wild, there were some things Wrinn did better than his tutor.

~

In the primeval forest, perched in a tree, Fortunato waited with his bow unslung, with an arrow at the ready. His eyes scanned the forest floor below. He knew the day waxed late, and that thus far his storied skills with the bow had not proven productive. He'd had many close encounters with deer of all kinds, but they'd been either too far off or they'd detected him too quickly. He had not expected such a challenge, but he supposed he had not used these skills in a long time, and gaining one's food from the wood was never going to be easy.

Far ahead, he saw movement, and his heart began to race with the thrill of the hunt. The bush had twitched and it was within range; whatever moved it was within his ability to kill.

From the green of the leaves, brown color emerged and Fortunato drew back his bow.

But in the wan light the shape of the deer became evident.

The deer was large but it was thin, and its ribs were visible. There were blackened spots on its fur and in some places the fur had completely fallen away, baring the skin beneath. Its eyes were pinkish and when it walked it stumbled.

The Blight.

Fortunato would not harm such a wretched creature. If it were in his power to heal it, he would do so, but he was not so skilled. Only elven magic could heal such a malformed being. As it staggered on, Fortunato felt his eyes water of their own accord, that there was such horror in this world.

He looked about and saw where it was coming from: the south. Was that where the Blight lay, where it had ravished and destroyed so many creatures?

Fortunato looked back and saw the deer take its last few staggering steps before collapsing into death. How quick was life, how short. Life's flower blooms and then so suddenly the winter rolls in and that bloom begins to wither.

He relaxed his bow. He decided to examine it further.

The deer was in its death throes, trembling. Its dark eyes seemed wild with fear and despair.

Fortunato crouched over it, laid his hand over its head, and its body seemed to stiffen, and some of the fear seemed to leave it. Its hooves' tremulous movements began to ease, and its lips stopped their fluttering.

"Easy," Fortunato said quietly, "easy there."

The deer had clearly witnessed something horrible, something beyond description. Fortunato wondered what this 'Blight' was that the farmers had talked about. It seemed his duty was to find out.

He looked up and saw that the light was waning. He knelt next to the deer as it fell into unconsciousness. He would not eat this deer, for fear of poison or disease. Instead, he would watch over it, try to ease its suffering, attempt to comfort it in its last moments.

The deer's trembling returned; its eyes bulged and it took a deep gasp, a great sucking-in of air. Then it was completely still; it was dead.

~

Fortunato walked toward the clearing empty-handed, expecting a haughty but disappointed look on Wrinn's face. In the end, the man who had spent many years in the wilds had failed to produce food.

He followed the contours of the forest as the last bit of light was leaving the woods. But in the clearing where they'd set up camp, Fortunato saw light anew.

Wrinn had started a fire. And by the fire were ears of wild corn and bulbs of wild garlic, leeks and cold peppers and even a mound of wild grapes.

"What is this?" Fortunato said.

"Care to eat?" Wrinn asked.

"How did you do this?" Fortunato said. "You weren't trained."

"Not trained," Wrinn said. "Let's just say I'm a good listener. And also, I found this."

He held up to the light of the fire a sprig of *sindomas*, whose night-blue stem was crowned with a bloom of virgin white. When Fortunato sent him on that errand, he had intended it only to keep Wrinn busy.

But a tea of *sindomas* could ward off sickness, and after Fortunato saw what he had, after witnessing the deer shorn of fur, dying as it lived, he supposed an ounce of prevention was in order.

Wrinn had somehow put together a wild bounty, and they would together eat the fruits of the forest. In the end it had been Wrinn and not Fortunato who was the hero of the day.

Chapter Nine: Night

Ambrass was again in her room, again thinking, again wondering, pondering the night she had bidden Fortunato goodbye. She wondered if she could change his mind, if she could convince him that she had not meant what she had said.

No... no... it can never be. It will never be.

The door to her room opened and in waddled Bala.

Over the days, the little urchin had latched on to her in a way she wasn't sure was healthy.

He toddled over to her.

"Ambirss—" he said her name in his own way—"I afraid."

Her room was not fit for children; her tabbac cards were scattered on the floor and her *hukpa*, her gypsy staff, was leaning against her closet door. She was an adult and Bala had only seen five years in his short life.

"Why are you afraid?" Ambrass said as she reached out to him.

Bala stumbled over. "I afraid," he went on, "because Dada is gone so long and I had a bad nightmare that he was dead."

"Don't worry yourself," Ambrass said. "Master Reev will be back soon, and I'm sure he will be thrilled to see you."

"No," Bala said. "Not Reev."

"Not Reev?" Ambrass said. "Who do you mean? You mean—"

Glenda had not wanted to speak of Bala's father. Glenda had not even dared speak his name, as if it were the name of some tormenting spirit.

"You mean—"

"I mean Dada..."

And like that Bala fell into a bout of childish weeping, and though Ambrass was alarmed at his words, she wrapped his arms around him and patted him and said, "There, there…"

As he wept uncontrollably, Ambrass realized that the situation wasn't right, that someone Bala's age shouldn't be left like this, that if his father was as troublesome as Glenda implied at least his mother should care for the boy. But his parents had not done their duty. No, his parents hadn't done their duty at all. They had left poor Bala alone like this, five years old and set free without supervision in the dangerous streets of Galiope. It wasn't right. It wasn't right at all, and at that moment Ambrass promised herself she'd do something about it, whatever it was in her power to set this right, to call on the authorities, to locate Bala's mother and give her a talking to, to do whatever it took to ensure Bala was properly cared for.

"There, there," she said softly. "It will all be all right."

"You miss your Dada, don't you?" she said, and immediately regretted her words.

His wailing seemed to rise, and thoughts began to percolate in Ambrass's heart. Someone needed to look out for this child, or else he'd end up on the streets as an adult, a pickpocket, a thief, a ne'er-do-well.

But his weeping quieted, and eventually he fell still.

"There, there," Ambrass said again.

I will do something about this, she told herself. *I will.*

~

Ambrass donned the finest clothing she possessed, a round red gown of pressed silk and a fine shirt of mixed leather and cloth. On her way out, Glenda took note. "Where are you going?" she said as Ambrass was pushing her way out the door.

She had in her hands the letter she'd just written, carefully, in ink on paper. "I intend to deliver this to the Lord Mayor," she said quietly. She looked about, seeing that the great hall was empty and Bala was nowhere in sight. "It is about Bala. His parents have abandoned him. They need to do their duty."

"A compassionate thing to do, or so it would seem," Glenda said in hushed tones, as if she too were afraid that Bala was in listening distance. "But Bala going back to his father… it wouldn't be in his best interest."

"He has a mother," Ambrass said. "We all do."

"Ambrass," Glenda whispered so forcefully it was almost a hiss, "come with me."

In the kitchen of the Dragonpaw Inn, it seemed Glenda wanted to give her a stern talking-to.

"I didn't take in Bala lightly," she said. "And as for his mother, I know more than I let on.

"Nocturne, his father—"

That was his name, Nocturne.

"—he is a dangerous man. He was on trial a while back but some people still think he is the High Street Slasher."

The High Street Slasher… Ambrass had not been alive for the murderer's reign of terror.

"But forget his father a moment. His mother has her own deficiencies. She is one of those people in this world that can scarcely take care of herself. And, I confess, I knew her as a girl. She lives in Greenwater. She is not fit to be a mother. She is weak willed and I suppose that is how Nocturne wormed his way into her life.

"Bala… is the product of that union, half human, half vampire. He is safest here, under my roof. He is as well cared for as he can hope to be… if that is the motivation for your concern."

"Of course it is," Ambrass said, insulted. Of course all she wanted for Bala was a safe home, a safe place to stay, a place where he could feel welcome and feel secure.

Glenda took the letter in her hands. "I will dispose of this," she said, and left with what was almost a glare.

~

On that night on the battlements of the city wall, Fortunato had attempted to kiss her and for the first time, Ambrass had refused.

"What is this?" Fortunato had said to her. "You are so hot and cold."

And she had not been able to disguise her growing doubts, her uncertainty.

Ambrass felt her eyes water at the thought of it. She was so burdened with regret at what she had done, and what she wouldn't give to see him again. Where was Fortunato? He hadn't shown his face in the Dragonpaw in more than a week now. It wasn't like him. Where could he be?

On her bedroom floor, with the door sealed shut, she invoked the gods of the gypsies and shuffled her *tabbac* deck.

"What," said she, "is my past…"

She laid the first card on the floor ahead of her.

"My present…"

Down went the second card.

"My future."

She laid the third and final card on the floor.

To take one's own fortune was to go against the rules of *tabbac*, it was supposed to be a service for the unsure, for the desperate, for those who needed it.

"Past," she said, and flipped the first card over.

The Lovers, showing a man and a woman in an amorous embrace.

"Present," she said, and flipped the second card over.

The Churl, depicting a man working in the fields of some lord.

"*Future*," she said, and the card she revealed next was *Night*, a woman reclining on her divan, a filled-up bowl beside her with moonlight reflecting in its water.

She shuffled the cards again, heartbroken by the outcome but unsure what the cards meant.

"And Fortunato's future…" She invoked the gods once more.

Down went the cards.

The Lovers was his past.

Night was his present.

Death was his future.

Ambrass swallowed a scream. She had to find him. She had to find him at once.

But how?

Chapter Ten:
The Adversary

Fortunato was stirred awake and for a moment, his mind was reeling, unsure of where he was, half expecting to be at home in his upper-story room in Galiope. But his eyes adjusted to the darkness and he remembered he was far away from there, in the primeval forest of the South Weald, here, exposed, among the trees and bushes.

Wrinn was fast asleep beside him.

And something had awoken him. He trusted his instincts by now, instincts he had honed among the Woodsmen of Brill. He scrambled out of his bedroll, grabbed his bow, and from his quiver, a fistful of arrows, and set one arrow to its string.

Then, crouching, he peered and waited.

His eyes scanned the darkness but he was no ratling or elf. In the darkness, he was at a disadvantage, and no matter how long he crouched here, his human eyes would never fully adjust to the dim light. And so he scooted over into the center of the clearing, using his ears rather than his eyes, ready at any moment to loose his arrow and put a length of steel into any foe's heart.

He wheeled about, listening for sound. There was a crunching noise to his left, the unmistakable sound of a foot crushing a twig. It would appear that Wrinn and Fortunato had company.

And so, with his bow still outstretched, he kneed Wrinn awake, who opened his eyes with a cacophony of complaints.

"What? Why?" Wrinn said. "You interrupted the most splendid—"

There was a crunching noise again, this time from behind, and Fortunato whipped around, bow at the ready, arrow nocked, prepared at any moment to shoot.

By now Wrinn had clambered out of his bedroll. Groggily, he grabbed his quarterstaff.

"We have a visitor," Fortunato whispered.

"A visitor," Wrinn repeated, his mind clearly still cloudy.

And like the presence of a phantom or some dark thing, Fortunato became aware he had lost. Someone was behind him.

He relinquished his arrow, dropped his bow, and put both hands above his head.

Wrinn shrieked and placed his quarterstaff into position.

"Fortunato," said a voice he knew all too well. "I have bested you again."

Fortunato didn't have it in him to smile. He turned around and saw a tall figure in a black cloak pointing a razor-sharp arrow directly at his head. In the darkness of the hood, a bloodless white face was partially visible, and two dark but keen eyes.

"Nocturne Rabaam," Fortunato said. "Only you would be here at this late hour."

~

They made a fire anew for the sake of hospitality, though it was deathly late and beyond any reasonable hour. Nocturne, after all, was an old friend, and when an old friend surprised you, one was obliged to offer him your company.

"How did you find our camp?" Fortunato said.

"I heard about your troubles," Nocturne said quietly.

The fire reflected on his pallid but handsome face and his close-cropped black hair. Wrinn did not know anything of him or of his checkered past, or that he was one of the vampires, those cursed elves with a thirst for blood.

"You did not disguise your tracks very well," Nocturne said.

"Nor did I try to disguise them," Fortunato said. "We are not running from anything. Or at least we weren't."

Wrinn, still dazed, seemed barely cogent, but he seemed to be sitting as far away from Nocturne as was politely possible. Was it his dark eyes or was it the bow he still had in his hands, or the prodigious fangs that were sometimes visible when he spoke?

"Am I to be the executor of your will?" asked Nocturne. "Will you leave everything you once had to me?"

"I am not dead," Fortunato said. "And I intend to get back in Galiope's good graces."

"And how would you do that?" Nocturne said. "After beating the emissary of a foreign land to a pulp?"

"So you'd heard all," Fortunato said. That meant everyone knew. His crime was now common knowledge.

"I will get back in Galiope's good graces," Fortunato insisted. "Somehow, some way, I will be back. You cannot take my belongings, Nocturne, if that is why you have come."

"I only came to bid you goodbye," Nocturne said in turn. "You are an old friend. I thought you would manage. Now I see that you will."

Wrinn seemed to have inched even farther away from Nocturne.

"You are welcome to stay at our camp for the night," Fortunato said. "But do not take what is mine."

But Nocturne shook his head. "I must get back to the city. I have things to do tomorrow evening. I must get my rest..."

"So be it," Fortunato said. As the vampire stood up, he repeated his words. "Do not take what is mine, Nocturne. Do not take what is mine."

Chapter Eleven:
The Hopeful

When Bala arose, Glenda and Ambrass had already made him his breakfast, oats and bran floating in a bowl of warm milk together with hot tea and dried plums. He was scarfing it down, bit by bit, but his mind had turned to blood. It had been several days since he'd drunk, and his gums were getting raw, and his teeth were getting sore.

The door to the Dragonpaw opened, and someone came in who Bala recognized, the wizard-man, Gastreel.

"A pleasure to see you, Master Gastreel!" shouted Glenda from the corner.

A smile grew on the wizard-man's face. "And you as well. It is good to see you all. But I'm afraid I've come for one Bala Rabaam."

"That's me!" Bala said, turning away from his oats and bran.

Gastreel's smile had faded somewhat as he began to walk over. "Come with me, Bala. Let us go for a stroll."

~

The daylight hurt Bala's eyes, and it was difficult to adjust to the light. But he followed the wizard-man just the same.

He tried to explain what happened, how he had been sleeping in an alley, how a rat had surprised him and leapt on him and attacked him, how there was a flash of light and then the rat sizzled and burned and then was dead.

"What color was this flash?" said Gastreel.

They were approaching an immense gate, beyond which was the tower that overlooked the city.

"Purple," Bala said. "It was purple."

"Purple," Gastreel said and he sounded disappointed. "That can mean any number of things. Perhaps, it is not the color that we should keep our eyes open for. Perhaps there is a different way to determine your *wyrd*."

"*Wyrd?*" Bala said. "What's that?"

"Every wizard has a power over something. For me, it is lightning. Others can cast jets of fire or of ice, or vault themselves over great distances," Gastreel said. "I can sense that you have magical talent even now. What you did in that alleyway is still about you, and it lingers on you."

Gastreel gave a signal and a shout, and the immense towering gate began to roll open, baring bit by bit a vast courtyard that surrounded the tower.

Bala and Gastreel walked on.

The tower was dark, but in alcoves along the long winding staircase, orbs of light glowed.

"What those?" Bala asked.

Gastreel, gripping his hand and helping him along, answered quickly: "Inside each of those crystal orbs, magic is laid. Only the finest starstones give light to the Tower of Pythor. Torches will last you but a few hours; these will glow for centuries."

There was a doorway on the seventh level and Bala peered inside. The door was open and in the room, also lit by starstones, were cages of bronze and gold. A wizard in green robes was tending to the creatures in the cages, feeding them with spoons.

"What those?" Bala said. The creatures were like tiny dragons, the size of his head, and their scales were pink and red and green and blue, every color of the rainbow.

"Faery drakes," Gastreel said, "which have long been gone from this world. Master Herman is trying to bring them back to health."

On the sixteenth floor, a door was also open, and beyond was a great space lined with mirrors. In the distance were several chests laid on top of each other. In a corner was a shelf crammed top to bottom with scrolls.

Before Bala could point and say "What those?" Gastreel answered: "The sorcerer Melcom was defeated five hundred years ago. His belongings remain in our keeping. And this door is meant to be sealed shut!"

He slammed the door closed and Bala could see the door was made of stone. Gastreel laid his hands over it, and like water spreading over low valleys, bright lines of light began to glow, the form of a door surrounded by vines.

"There," he said, "none but a skilled wizard can open this now."

~

It was on the thirtieth story that they stopped, and by that time Bala—haggard and exhausted—had climbed onto Gastreel's back. Through an opened door Gastreel carried him, and in the light of the starstones Bala hopped off.

"What this?" he said.

And he looked about and saw a great room with an emerald-green floor, brightly lit, with a window in the distance that overlooked the city below. Shards of crystal, some whole and some almost dust, lay scattered about the floor. There were statues of wizards throughout the room, surrounding its edges, some depicted with hoods over their heads and others with pointy hats or neat caps.

"This," Gastreel said, "is the Room of Determination. I already know you possess magical talent, Bala, but I must make it official.

"Surrounding you here are shards of mooncrystal, which even those of slight magical talent can move by their will.

"Now I ask you, Bala, look deep within yourself. Peer into your deepest essence, into your most inmost fibers. Shut your eyes and close out every distraction."

Bala walked to the center of the room, so that he was surrounded on all sides by the crystals and bits of crystal. He did what Gastreel said. He shut his eyes. He began to raise his hands…

~

Gastreel watched as his new young ward lifted his hands. He was a slight figure, only as tall as Gastreel's knee. He was the spitting image of his father except for his white-blond hair.

How strange is fate, how fickle she is, how quickly and how suddenly she turns and then leaves and places new people and new situations onto one's lap.

The crystals began to twirl and rise up, until it was like a storm of snow, small, white, glistening shards swirling about Bala as if he were the center of a blizzard, the very north wind himself.

What talent he had. Even Gastreel had not possessed this much power.

How gifted was Bala, how radiant with talent. What a weapon he would be if war ever came to Gallia. What a tool he'd be in the wizard order's hands.

Yet Bala screamed and fell, and his wailing was desperate. He shuddered and fell stiffly to the ground with tears in his eyes.

"What is it?" Gastreel said, rushing over to his young ward. "What is wrong, my boy?"

~

He tried, in as many words, to tell Gastreel what he had seen, though certain things he did not have words for, and certain things he could not comprehend or understand.

"I dreamed I was old," Bala said. "Old like Dada. I dreamed there were monsters behind me and they was listening to me. And

I dreamed I was bad, Gastreel. Bad!"

Gastreel was comforting him, patting him on his back, trying to make him feel better.

"And then I dreamed I was me and I was here, and I was in this room, and there was someone watching me, Gastreel, someone watching me. And then I looked up, and he was there, and he had black hair and eyes that were gray. And he is coming for all of us, Mr. Gastreel! He is coming for all of us!"

He did not know who the man was. He did not know where he came from.

"Who was this man?" Gastreel said. "Was it your father? Your, er… dada?"

"No," Bala said. "No, it was not Dada!"

What a terrible thing for the wizard-man to say.

"Was it Reev?" Gastreel said.

"No!" Bala said. "Of course not!"

"Who was it, then?" Gastreel said.

"He told me his name," Bala said. "But I can't remember!"

"Try to think!"

But he couldn't remember. He thought it started with an "L" but he wasn't entirely sure. The man said he would change him, that he would turn Bala into something bad, like he'd been in his nightmare. But who was he? Bala did not know. He couldn't tell Mr. Gastreel what he wanted to hear.

He wanted to go home, to the Dragonpaw. He wanted to see Mr. Reev again. Only with Mr. Reev would he feel safe again.

Only with Mr. Reev.

Chapter Twelve:
The Capture

It was late in the day and the forests of the duchy of Almania were all about Reev, hugging either side of the road. In the distance were the mounting foothills that led into the White Mountains. Ahead of him, not far now, a week away at worst, was Galiope.

And Reev, though he was glad to be safe and free from Ivan Xandrast's attempts to hurt him, and though the incident at the inn had become a distant memory, he was now beginning to dread Galiope. How would it have changed? Would the people receive him like a hero like they had before, or had they turned against him? Was Gastreel all right? Was everyone all right?

But he braced himself and tried to ignore those poisonous thoughts in the back of his mind, the poisonous thoughts that many people had when they returned from a long journey.

Reev had never traversed this road before, and he had passed by many villages and hamlets of gold-bricked houses, and seen cathedrals on hilltops that lay in the sun. The Grand Duke of Almania allowed the passage of travelers, as long as he knew where they were going and they did not arouse suspicion.

Now he was far from the Empire, far outside its control, where its soldiers did not patrol and were not welcome. Here he was free from the control of the nation of his birth, free from its power.

The day waxed late. Reev had spent almost all his money, and he had grown a little fat eating in inns along the road. Perhaps, it was time to rough it a bit, not to give in to luxury, to grant himself the chance to prove himself in the wilds.

He set up the tent underneath an alder tree. In a nearby meadow, daisies were blooming, and Reev wondered whether, if he searched long enough, he could find himself food. But instead he found himself opening his pack and grabbing the last of the dry road-bread, road-bread he'd had since he departed Norwood. The dry biscuits had been pulverized in his pack but were still edible.

"Seven more days, at worst," Reev told himself, "and then this journey will be all behind me."

By now he had grown saddle-sore; though Cobalt was an Elvish horse, and the best of his kind, though his movements were smoother and gentler than any other steed, still Reev's legs ached and his body had grown weary.

He did not bother building a fire, but instead watched the stars. He was beginning to drift off asleep when a sudden energy filled him, and he was wide awake. Still in his smallclothes, he hopped out of his bedroll. He grabbed his sheath and swept Doomblade out of it. The blade gleamed in the moonlight.

He peered into the shadows, seeing dark bushes and the black outlines of trees, the stars circling overhead in their nightly cavalcade. And against the night noises, the chirping of the frogs and crickets, the low gusts of wind, another noise distinguished itself, what sounded like a low growl.

In the darkness, Reev saw it: a giant black dog, its eyes gleaming in the white light of the moon. Its paws were the size of Reev's head.

But Reev steeled himself. He walked over to the growling dog, showing none of his fear. "Back!" he said. "Get back!"

And before he could strike the dog, the dog yelped and ran off, bolting into the distance.

As he watched the dog burst through the bushes, Reev could not help but note the unusualness of its gait. It ran at almost a stagger.

~

The journey through Almania continued over a period of days, and in inns along the road and from travelers passing by, Reev overheard that a great national enemy, a criminal of some war, had been captured and brought to trial in the duchy's capital.

Dark were Reev's dreams, and each day he passed through Almania he was tormented by nightmares.

Chapter Thirteen: "Bad People"

Fortunato was leading Wrinn deeper into the woods, and the farther from civilization Wrinn got, the closer he felt to nature. The trees and ponds and forests, the swamps and fens and marshes, became a part of his daily life, and Fortunato with his hunting and Wrinn with his gathering of vegetables ensured there wasn't a day they went hungry, a moment their stomachs growled.

How long had they been gone now? Wrinn had no idea. But they were walking due south, as Fortunato had wanted to, and the canopy above them was so thick it was almost like night; not a single ray of sunlight shone on the forest floor below.

In the darkness Wrinn wandered, quarterstaff in hand, and as he stepped over the carpet of dead leaves, in the great hollow spaces of the forest, he realized he was out of time and civilization, as far from his former life as he ever had been. The forest was vast and they had scarcely explored only a fraction of it.

In the distance was a dark shape. Fortunato shouted something indistinguishable and rushed over to it. Wrinn followed moments later.

A deer had collapsed on the ground, a deer with white spots on its back. It was panting and heaving, wheezing and choking. It was in its death throes.

Wrinn knelt over the dying beast as Fortunato prepared a mercy-stroke.

As Fortunato's sword came down, Wrinn gazed at the body and saw it had no hooves, but paws instead, paws like a wolf or a dog.

Off rolled the deer's head.

"Look," Wrinn said, pointing at the paws.

Fortunato circled around and knelt on the forest floor. His

hands touched the strange paws, paws that were of flesh but speckled with tender white hair.

"What devilry is this?" he said. "Wrinn, we are getting closer to the Blight. I assume we will find out more about what is plaguing the forest. But we will be in danger. What is happening isn't natural."

"If it's not natural, what is it?" Wrinn asked.

"I do not know," Fortunato replied. "But I fear this Blight… I…" He looked into the distance.

"What is it?" Wrinn said. He turned to look in that general direction, but only saw trees.

"I thought I saw something," Fortunato said.

"Another deer?"

"No, a black shape. Something almost as tall as the trees. It looked… It looked like a person."

Fortunato was not one to frighten easily. But there was a bit of worry in his eyes, the first time Wrinn had seen worry in all this time in the South Weald.

"Let's keep going," Wrinn insisted, and Fortunato gave a slight nod.

~

When they set up camp for the day, they split up as was custom, Fortunato to hunt and Wrinn to gather.

And as Wrinn wandered through the woods, there was a sickly feeling in his gut, a feeling he couldn't shake, an unsettled tingling in his stomach. How could he forget that deer whose feet were paws, struggling, dying, succumbing to whatever illness the Blight had given it?

"You."

There came the whispers again, the whispers he couldn't identify, the whispers only he could hear. Some might think he had gone mad, but it was those whispers that allowed him to find a bounty of vegetables most every day. He listened to the whispers, and they spoke the truth.

"You there."

He was in the sunshine of a clearing, enjoying the gentle warmth of the wind.

"You are going where death is," the whisper said. "Have you come to save us?"

Wrinn turned around, trying in vain again to find out who spoke, or where the voice was coming from. It seemed to come from everywhere. He looked up and down, into the sky, at the trees, at the ground, and though he heard the whispers for what seemed like the thousandth time he could not identify its source.

"Who are you?" Wrinn said aloud, but he had asked the question before. "Where are you speaking from?"

As expected, the answer was silence. The whisperer would not identify itself.

The silence dragged on from seconds into minutes, and at last Wrinn gave up hope of ever receiving an answer. So instead he busied himself with his task, gathering food, keeping his eyes open for berries or tender shoots or the tubers that grew in the sun.

~

He was descending a steep ravine where he'd caught sight of a mushroom patch. Some sun was filtering down as a wind rustled the trees. And Wrinn felt he was not alone. As he stooped down, hurriedly picking the mushrooms and shoving them into his basket, he kept looking up and around, hoping he was not in danger, hoping nothing was hunting him.

"Why do you hurt me?" the whisper came again.

Then another whisper floated through the air, harsher, almost a song, "Son of the Forest, where are you going?"

And another whisper drifted through the wind, "You must save us! Save us!"

Now Wrinn was beginning to grow worried. In human society, those called "touched by the gods" could be seen begging on city streets. Was he also mad? Was he losing his mind?

"You are going where the bad people are," the whisperer said.

"The bad people!" said another whisperer.

"They are coming! Run!"

And as soon as the words were spoken, there was a crunching noise up ahead, at the top of the ravine, and there were a few scattered human voices. Wrinn dropped the basket, and the tubers and mushrooms fell to the ground. He covered himself with his cloak and laid as still as could be.

"Yes, Son of the Forest," the whisperer went on, "hide. Hide yourself."

The human voices continued, a scattered conversation Wrinn could just barely hear above the sound of the wind.

He distinguished a word: "Lothan."

"Forge" was another word he heard.

But they were too far off to hear clearly. Yet now Wrinn knew he and Fortunato were not alone in this wood.

"Galiope," he distinguished among the distant conversation.

"Eventide" said someone, the Lord Mayor, the leader of Galiope.

The people, whoever they were, whom the whisperers called "bad," were now growing more distant from him. They were leaving the site.

But who were they and what were they doing so deep in the forest that civilization was countless days away? They had spoken in the Gallian tongue, but what they were doing this deep in the South Weald, Wrinn could only guess.

The wind was a gentle breeze, the warmth of the sun mild. The voices faded away into nothing, but Wrinn kept quiet far longer than he needed to, for fear the "bad people" would find him and do what "bad people" did.

~

"There are others?" Fortunato said in the light of the fire. "I saw no trace of them."

"I think one of them's named Lothan," Wrinn said.

Coney was roasting in a pot, together with the mushrooms and tubers Wrinn had found. They would eat well tonight after several days of meager fare.

"I've never heard a name like that," Fortunato said.

But some people did have strange names—Reev Nax came to mind. "Well, now you have," Wrinn said, "now you know someone in Gallia's name is Lothan."

The expression on Fortunato's face indicated disbelief, but that was his loss. As for the whispers, Wrinn still dared not tell Fortunato about them, yet they had led him to bounties of food. And now the whispers were warning him he was approaching not just the Blight, but death.

The whispers had called him "Son of the Forest." Whatever could that mean?

He hoped to the gods madness was not falling over him. He was too young for that. Let him babble and hear things when he was Gastreel's age, when he was white-haired and had a long, unkempt beard, and had children to take care of him.

"I will keep my eyes open, as always," Fortunato said. "I believe we are drawing near this 'Blight,' whatever it may be."

That was not a comforting thought, not to Wrinn and likely not to Fortunato either.

Dark and gentle was the night, and the sun's heat had long relented. Wrinn fell asleep with the memory of the whispers on his mind, and the memory of those "bad people" hovering over him.

Chapter Fourteen: The Return

The day was balmy, and the skies cloudy, when Galiope appeared on the horizon.

As Reev trotted over the hill, down the great Royal Road toward Godsgate, he realized his joy was not uniform, that anxieties lingered on the periphery of things. Had the city changed? Had the peace that many expected not come to fruition? Had the Servants of Seymus, whom divine power had smote to dust on the mountainside, returned to life?

No, it was not so. It could not be so.

But seeing the great city appear, the tower in its center seeming to scrape the sky, caused Reev to halt his ride. And for a moment he just stopped and stared at the gloomy grandeur of Galiope's gray walls, the high hill on which the city's mansions were built. Tens of thousands of souls made their dwelling in this city, this city on the banks of the River Galios. She was the queen of the north, and she had become Reev's home, at least for now.

The air was too foggy to see the Dragonteeth Mountains, but on better days, when the skies were clear, their snowcapped peaks were visible against the city walls. Only the mountains outdid the city's majesty.

At that moment it struck Reev how far he had traveled, though his journey was swifter than the first time he'd ventured here. The roads had borne him swiftly, though they had not been without their dangers, chief among them Ivan Xandrast whose black eyes he had not forgotten.

With a cry he coaxed Cobalt on, who took off at a gallop, bearing Reev swiftly toward the city. Reev was home. He was back home!

~

He rode through streets crowded with people, down winding roads and through narrow paths. He had decided not to go to the Dragonpaw but instead to a place his heart was leading him, the house of his mentor and friend, the wizard Gastreel. The people did not pay Reev attention or cry out his name. They seemed to have forgotten the Battle of Galiope already, and that was just as well.

In the city's richest, most exclusive neighborhood, on its highest hill, was Gastreel's home.

Soon enough Rosetree Manor lay before Reev, its gates wide open, overlooking the cobblestone street. A light was on in the window. Inside, the hearth was burning.

~

"You have returned," Gastreel said, the hearth fire casting red light on his face. In his mouth was a pipe and at odd intervals he would puff smoke. He seemed distracted by something.

Reev had expected Gastreel to be thrilled to see him, but his mind was elsewhere, and it was a dagger in Reev's heart.

He sat down on a wooden chair near the hearth, next to the man who had been his tutor, his guiding light in a dark and dangerous world.

"I've just returned from the west," Gastreel said. "I was on official business of the Council of the Twelve."

The Council of the Twelve reigned over all wizards and formed a nation-state of their own in the center of the city. Now Gastreel, as archwizard, was at its head.

"The west is crumbling, Reev," Gastreel said. "The things which sustained the west are beginning to crack and fade away like chaff. And a new enemy has appeared."

"Seymus?"

"Do not speak his name!" Gastreel's voice echoed with magical power; thunderous and final was the sound of it. Yet he was without his staff and whatever power he carried he carried within. "It is not the Dark One that threatens the west, at least not visibly so. It is mortal man that the west must fear. And it may be too late."

His gray eyes turned to Reev, and for a moment the turmoil in those eyes seemed to fade.

"I fear… I fear…"

He pursed his lips.

"Reev," he said, "we must prepare for the final battle."

"The final battle?" Reev said. "What are you talking about? The Servants are dead."

"Dead? No, they are not dead. They cannot truly die. Not until the gods' return…"

The Shadow is fading, Reev had told himself. *The light is already here…*

"You must come with me," Gastreel said, "into the mountains. The lost prophecies… they may be hidden there."

"In the mountains?"

"There is a great library sheltered in a mountain pass, an elven library where the ancients would store knowledge not widely known to non-wizarding eyes. It is called Dendérion," Gastreel continued. "There are books in that library, ancient books, scrolls of prophecy and wisdom. We must go there, Reev, and you must accompany me. Consider yourself my protection, my bodyguard."

A wizard of Gastreel's power did not need a bodyguard, unless there was some foe Reev did not know about.

"The elven libraries were built in secret places," Gastreel said. "They were built to store knowledge that could not fade. Wherever the elves ever held power, their libraries can be found."

"In Gallia?" Reev said.

"Once even Gallia was in the power of the elves," Gastreel said. "Almost the whole of the world was, in ancient days.

"Come with me… let us get ready. We must prepare quickly. We must go there at once."

Reev supposed he did not have a say in this, that whatever Gastreel decided would happen. Wasn't that how it always was? Wasn't that how things always ended up?

"Very well," Reev said. "I am your bodyguard, your protection, you say." And a faint smile formed on his lips.

"That is what you've always been, dear Reev," Gastreel answered.

~

Reev donned his armor and clipped Doomblade in its sheath to his side. Then, mounting Cobalt, he followed just a short distance behind Gastreel on Ivy. They rode swiftly, at a canter, through the city of Galiope. As they rode, a few idlers in the streets remarked on the "Green Wizard" going by.

Soon the city was behind Gastreel and Reev, the city with all its people and its troubles.

The mountains awaited.

Chapter Fifteen: Dendérion

The closer Reev and Gastreel drew near the mountains, the lonelier the roads became. Somewhere on the northern edge of Gallia was the mining town of Strathbrad, a place Reev had never been nor cared to go to.

As the ground ascended and they traversed hills and open streams, the air took on a crisp character, and soon the Dragonteeth Mountains were before them, the Dragonteeth Mountains that never failed to stun Reev and fill him with awe. Dark were their slopes, almost purple, and even now, in the height of summer, much of their peaks were crowned with snow. Gastreel said they ran through the entirety of the Northern World, serving as the border with the Elf Lands and preventing easy travel. But Reev knew humans lived in those mountains, humans living hardscrabble lives of mining or herding. They were called the mountain folk.

"Up here!" Gastreel thundered. He raised his hand and the wind whipped his robe about. He looked like a mighty man of legend.

The road branched off in two, and Gastreel veered left. Cobalt followed a moment later.

~

The ascent into the mountains grew steeper and steeper, and soon they were in the thick of it, the peaks before them, venturing up switchback after switchback. Soon bare rock faces met them, and meadows overgrown with wildflowers. Soon it was cold, and in places there were partially-melted patches of snow.

"This," Gastreel said, "is a forgotten path. Few know it and that is by design."

The rough path was leading them swiftly up toward one of the Dragonteeth's mighty peaks. They were so far from civilization. They had moved so swiftly.

"How did we get here so quickly?" Reev asked, "It is not even night."

"I have my ways," Gastreel said. And Reev knew in that instant he he had cast some spell of speed or quickness, or else magicked their way up into these high mountains.

"Here," Gastreel said, "we round the pass."

And the road became cloven between two high rock walls. There was snow on the ground, crunching against Cobalt's hooves. This path through the walls was clearly not natural; it had been chiseled away.

"If you do not look carefully for the pass," Gastreel said, "you will miss it easily, and you will not find the elven library of Dendérion."

The pass opened up to what appeared to be a large open air vault. Up ahead was the twilight sky, amber in color. To Reev's right was a deep pit, which appeared bottomless. And to his left... to his left... Reev halted Cobalt's stride and gasped.

The elven library was like a great basilica. The roof tiles that covered the three titanic domes were red, but they seemed ancient, having lost some of their color and weathered to dull shades. The library itself was twice the size of the largest cathedral in Galiope, and Reev was an ant before it.

At its fore, before the courtyard, was a copper fence and gate, which time had colored blue.

"Dendérion," Gastreel said in a low tone. "Few know about it, and that is how it must remain. Tell no one about it. The elven libraries of the world must be kept safe from those who would use their knowledge for evil."

Gastreel dismounted from Ivy and tied her to one of the fence posts.

Reev hopped off Cobalt and hurried toward the titanic building.

"Careful, now," Gastreel said. "Careful. There are protocols to be followed, protocols to keep the knowledge of the library safe from unwanted eyes."

But the stone-cut symbols along the edge of the domes, and the alien architectural style of the library itself, had drawn in Reev's fascination, and all caution in Reev had vanished. He wanted to see it up close, to wonder, to marvel. He hurried ahead, a few steps in front of Gastreel, beyond the open gate to a snow-swept courtyard of chipped stone.

There was a boom and the earth seemed to shake, drowning out the sound of Gastreel's screaming. The sun's light was gone… no, something was blocking it. Reev craned his eyes up and saw something crowding out the sun, and before he could react, he was gripped in giant fingers and hoisted aloft. Reev could feel metal wrapping him in a viselike grip, no — gauntlets as large as an oxcart.

He was half as tall as the library itself, a giant in armor, an elf as tall as a colossus, one whose skin was chestnut brown and whose eyes glowed violet. Reev squirmed within his grip as the giant reached for a sword fit for his size, strapped to his side.

"Stop!" Reev cried out as he was carried away. "I am an ally!" The giant elf in armor had pitched back his sword, preparing to behead Reev.

A burst of energy, a burst of strength, and Reev had wriggled out of the giant's grip. He fell to the snowy ground with a bruising thud and began to run, as Gastreel sprinted forth, calling out, "I am an an elf-friend! I am an elf-friend! *Sí quilenthi!*"

Reev turned. His pursuer went rigid, and those violet eyes seemed to sparkle in the waning sunlight. He pitched back his giant sword as if ready to strike.

"*Sí quilenthi!*" Gastreel said again.

The giant seemed to fade, his body to dim, and his violet eyes turned a shade of blue. He withdrew to the edges of the courtyard with trudging steps.

"I told you to be careful," Gastreel said with a sneer. "You could well have died."

"I'm sorry," Reev said.

"The library's wonders have drawn many people off-guard before," Gastreel said. "From now on, follow my instructions exactly."

Against the howling wind, snow began to drift down from the heavens, and Reev thought that a blizzard might come, even now, in the summertime, they were so high up.

They crossed the courtyard. With a cry of exertion, Gastreel heaved open the great double doors of the library, and into the library they went, a vast space lit by hundreds of starstones.

"You," Gastreel said in the vestibule, "stand watch. The rokahn of the mountain know of this place, but they are too stupid to understand its use."

"Guard duty?" Reev said, disappointed but still shaken. "Are they nearby, the rokahn?"

"The Olimnavon now knows you are a friend. He will help you stand guard, but he cannot protect us from all dangers," Gastreel said. "There is danger here, Reev, and not just from the outside world, not just from rokahn. There is knowledge here that is good, that can help us, and there are scrolls which record potent evil. I am going into the lower stories, where I hope I can find the lost prophecies."

Outside, the snow was swirling down. The double doors were creaking, and at last they slammed shut with a deafening boom. The library smelled of old must and mildew.

~

For the first hour, Reev remained still, a guardian as motionless as a statue, remaining in the vestibule. He could hear the winds outside and the occasional steps of the Olimnavon. He wondered why Gastreel had been gone so long. How difficult could it be to scour the lower levels and uncover these "lost prophecies," whatever he had called them?

He stepped away from the vestibule and through a set of doors.

And there he saw the inner chamber of the library. It stunned him beyond words, a great domed room the size of an entire town, bookcases that stretched toward the impossibly high ceiling. And the domed ceiling was painted with the leaf and vine symbol so common in elven architecture, laid down carefully in gilded gold.

The books were of varying age, some so old Reev doubted he could touch them without them collapsing and crumbling into dust. Most were scrolls of parchment or rawhide, yellowed by centuries. And Reev guessed that as long as he remained in the library, Gastreel would have the protection he needed. What use was he standing in the vestibule?

He found there was some organization to the library, that the shelves were labeled with Elvish words, but those words were ones he did not understand, *Indoren Hannen, Indoren Sirot…*

And Reev found himself walking the great space, past shelves and shelves of books crammed with scrolls. Occasionally there would be a modern form of writing, a codex that looked relatively recent, but these were few and far between.

He knew he could not read any of these books, that his knowledge of Elvish was basic and rudimentary. So instead he passed by the shelves, looking about, observing the wondrous architecture, the dome whose gold leaf markings were like the stars in the celestial vault.

And then he saw it: in the far corner of the room, a narrow door, covered in flaking, lurid red paint and missing a knob, and above the door a lintel. *Riven Velatoren Drasoren.*

"The Books of the Outer Princes," was Reev's best translation.

What does that mean? What were the outer princes? Were they princes who served on the outer marches of the Elven World? Guardsmen of the border?

He turned to head back to the vestibule, and found himself halted.

He turned back to the ghastly red door, the door whose knob had been removed, and curiosity won out. He entered the secret lair.

The room was small, and codexes rather than scrolls filled its two shelves.

But on a platform on the far edge of the room, a platform of stone, a book was already set in its place, a book whose leathern cover was red, and on which a face had been painted in black ink.

Reev walked up to it. He touched the cover. And the book opened up of its own accord.

The illustrations on the page seemed to dance, the images of elves, men and women, wearing crowns of flowers and leaves on their heads.

"The souls of nine philosophers bound their lives to this book," said a voice as clear as any voice in the mortal realm. "Do not turn this page. Do not look beyond…"

But the starstones in the room began to dim and lose their light. The room seemed to come alive, and Reev tried to scream but there was no voice left in his throat. He tried to turn and look away but his body refused. He tried to shut his eyes but his eyes remained open. And though he did not turn the page, a wind seemed to grow within the room, a wind created just for this.

And the page flipped open. A terrible face greeted him, a face with inky black eyes. He saw the name Lothan written on the page.

And the lights of the starstones winked out. The room went pitch dark, and Reev shut his eyes.

When Reev opened his eyes once more, they opened in another world.

Chapter Sixteen: The Trees

It was dusk, and Wrinn, again, was helping Fortunato set up camp, helping him cook the food he'd found, helping him like a doting servant.

Though he loved Fortunato like a brother, being alone with him for so long, Wrinn to had grown irritated with his habits, the way he talked, the way he spoke boastfully, the way he cooked the food they both worked for.

Simmering in the pot was wild corn Wrinn had shucked, together with goose Fortunato had dressed and prepared. Together, they formed a sticky mélange of fat, meat, and vegetables. As the day darkened, Wrinn's stomach growled, and he realized after all that he was lucky to have Fortunato. Wrinn would be hopeless alone.

And then a thought came to him, as the low light cast shadows over the trees, as the darkness grew and formed somber shapes in the hills. There was a shadow missing from this place, a dark outrider that could have been put to good use.

"Tyra Jade," Wrinn said, "your wolf. The one you ride. Where is she?"

And a smile appeared on Fortunato's face, that brash smile Wrinn sometimes liked and sometimes loathed. "*My* wolf, you say," he said. "It is debatable whether I am her master or she is mine. She is like a daughter to me.

"She will show herself when she wants to. I wouldn't be surprised if she is following at a distance. If I need her, she will show herself. That is how it has always been."

A low wind was blowing through the hills, and Wrinn smelled something like death on the air, the smell of rot, of putrefaction, of dead things that had been lying in the sun.

"Help us," the faint whisper on the wind said. "Help us, Son of the Forest."

Dare he tell Fortunato about this new madness he'd acquired?

Instead of saying anything to the whisperer, he stood up, and as the goose and wild corn sizzled, he stepped to the edge of camp, to the very edge of the fire's light and warmth. And he shut his eyes, and he tried to listen.

"Son of the Forest," the whisperer said on the wind. "We are dying. We are dying."

Another whisper carried by: "Three-score sunrises and sunsets has it been so, and now the death is spreading to our roots."

Our roots, the voice had said.

"Soon death will reach all of us if you cannot help, Son of the Forest." The whisper on his ear was like a cold breath. He placed his hand on a tree trunk.

"Why do you touch me?" The whisper was like that of a wizened old man. And Wrinn felt a presence behind him, one he knew all too well.

"What are you doing, Wrinn?" Fortunato said.

"The trees are talking to me, Fortunato… The trees."

Chapter Seventeen: Dark Majesty

Late was the hour, and Ambrass was dreaming of lying down on her feather bed, of sleeping until morning came. In the great hall of the Dragonpaw, traffic was light, and only occasionally would Ambrass have to stumble into the cellar to pour ale. In one booth were two human travelers, at a table three elven revelers, and in a corner booth, two Galiopean women. It was a night a serving girl dreamed of.

The musicians they hired for the evening were hard at work, a young woman cranking a hurdy-gurdy and a young man belting out a crisp tune. The stage had been erected near the hearth, and as the entertainers shuffled their feet to the tune, the fire cast shadows about the room.

Late was the hour, and as Ambrass waited for her next task, her next request, the next order from one of her patrons or from Glenda Half-Elven, her mind returned to the night on the battlements.

"So you have decided to leave me?" Fortunato had said, and his eyes had darkened. "You have decided to forsake our love?"

And she had not had an answer; she had stood there with a trembling lip until it was clear she had nothing to say, no way to put on a salve on the wound, leaving her statement unsaid, her intent obvious by her silence.

Why had she done this? She did not know why, though she'd looked within herself, though she'd asked herself countless times, *Why?*

"Oh, Fortunato," she said under her breath, "come back to me. Let me change my mind."

On the hurdy-gurdy played, eking out its eerie tune. The young man sang some elven folk song about a king who had sent his wives away, a somber song that nonetheless was given an exciting beat by the rhythmic thrumming of his tambourine.

The doors to the Dragonpaw opened and a shadow appeared.

Glenda gasped. The shadow had contours, yes. The shadow had a face. A man—no, an elf, his ears coming to slender points, his complexion as pale as the moonlight. Dark were his eyes, and his black hair was closely cropped. He was handsome and his form was tall but lithe, athletic. He wore a jerkin of black leather, and two knives dangled from his belt in a sheath.

Glenda stared at him in shock, as if she had nothing to say, too amazed by this man's arrival to speak.

"Glenda," said the man, "am I no longer welcome at the Dragonpaw Inn?"

"Of course you are welcome," Glenda said in answer. "Of course you are, Nocturne…"

And Ambrass's breath felt light, and of her own accord she was dizzy. When she thought of a vampire she thought of a vile misshapen beast, a thing with many eyes and a great maw of razor-sharp teeth, not someone like this, not someone like this at all. Not him, not someone of such dark majesty.

Yet Ambrass knew him better than he thought she did. She was not just any serving girl but the right-hand woman of Glenda Half-Elven, one to whom the proprietor of the Dragonpaw Inn shared secrets. Was Nocturne Rabaam the High Street Slasher? Ambrass did not know, but she thought he might be.

"I have come to collect Bala," Nocturne said, "if you have him."

Glenda stood there, still in stunned silence, no longer the dagger-tongued woman Ambrass had always known.

"I will go fetch him," Ambrass said, showing herself from the shadows.

Nocturne's eyes twinkled, and a smile came to his face. There in the light of the hearth she saw his white teeth, the two fangs prodigious indeed.

"And who is this fair lass?" Nocturne said.

"That is not of your concern." Glenda had snapped out of her shock. "Ambrass! Go bring Bala to his father at once."

~

Ambrass searched the rooms, first Reev and Wrinn's where Bala had been staying, but there was no trace of him there besides his bed. Then one by one she searched the other rooms, those not occupied by guests, then the kitchen, then Glenda's bedchamber, and finally her own.

She returned in defeat. "I cannot find him, Glenda," Ambrass said, but if Nocturne was bothered the smile had not faded at all from his face.

"Perhaps, Glenda Half-Elven," Nocturne murmured, "you are not a better parent for Bala than I. Perhaps I am not as negligent as you think." From his pockets he drew the letter Ambrass had written, and she was aghast.

She had not identified herself in the letter, nor given any indication of who had written it. She thanked the gods she had not signed the letter and told a dangerous man what she had done.

Where had he gotten it? Glenda said she had disposed of it.

His dark eyes turned to Glenda as he threw the letter on the door-side desk. "I will forgive this slight, for the sake of old friendship," he said. "I require one thing, however… I hear your serving girl is a masterful dancer. I shall have her dance for me."

"Never!" Ambrass said. "Never for you, Nocturne Rabaam." And this time her words were final, no wavering like there had been for Armande.

There was a look of surprise on the vampire's face, perhaps genuine hurt. "So be it. Glenda—" he turned to the one he had called an old friend. "—if you find Bala, bring him to me. That is my order as a father."

Chapter Eighteen: Lothan

Through shifting sand, beyond time and space, beyond history or the confines of imagination, Reev found himself sinking down and down, drifting unconsciously toward a destination he did not know or want to go to. Whether it was a moment or ten thousand years he could not tell, but at long last he inhaled, and his eyes opened, and his feet were shaken.

He breathed in what tasted like tainted air. He saw that he was in a great room faced with a window of transparent glass. Beyond the window was a landscape of black mountains erupting with fire, and in valleys, steaming yellow pools that glowed in the night. Every once in a while, a bolt of purple lightning would strike but no thunder followed.

Reev had begun to gain control of his hands. He wriggled his fingers. He wriggled his toes. He breathed in the poison air.

And he realized he was not alone.

On a divan whose cushions were red as blood, a man sat lengthwise, or what appeared to be a man. In form, he was like the spitting image of the human ideal, but his eyes were featureless and gray, like stone.

"Who are you?" Reev said, and blind panic was rising inside him. "Where am I?"

On either side of the divan were beasts that were like the spawn of a wolf and a monstrous jackal, with shaggy black manes and fur as dark as night. Their eyes were red and they were larger than the largest wolves Reev had ever seen. They stood as tall as his chest.

"Who are you?" Reev said again, and his panic was tempered only by his resolve to get out of here somehow. "Where am I?"

The fire in the beasts' eyes was like the fires of Hell, and there was intelligence behind them, deviousness, a sharp craftiness beyond most humans.

"Where are you?" The gray-eyed man's voice was like silk. He sat up and smiled. His teeth were like razors. "If I told you, you would be afraid, Reev Nax."

"I already am," Reev answered.

"Reev Nax, why did you reject my servant's proposal out of hand? Why did you not hear him out? Why did you force me to meet you here, where you do not want to be?"

"What are you talking about?" Reev said. He tried to will himself away, to break himself free of this, what was surely no more than a terrible nightmare.

"My servant was thwarted by the people you call the Almanians," the man said. "You may know him as one Ivan Xandrast. In this realm, he is known as Lamach."

"You…" Reev said, and he was sweating. Was the room warm or was he just afraid?

"You…" he went on, "are Lothan."

At the name, a concert of violet lightning erupted; in one of the distant yellow lakes, a jet of liquid shot up and sprayed the rocky ground around it.

"And you," Reev said, "you are not a man like I thought. You are… You are…"

"I am the forger of what cannot be forged. I am the joiner of what cannot be joined," Lothan said. "I am the maker of what should not be made. And I know you are the Master's mortal enemy. But know he is not my master. I am my own."

More thunderous violet lightning erupted. Reev's breath was like a cold wind.

The Master… that was what he called the Dark One. That had to be what he meant.

And the devious beasts were walking toward him, tongues lolling from their knife-sized fangs. And as they drew near, Reev took note of their feet, which were not paws but were like human hands.

"I can give you power," said Lothan, "unthinkable power. I can make you a weapon with which you may conquer. I can join you with what cannot be joined. I can make you invincible."

"No" was Reev's response. "No, you cannot. No, you will not. Release me! Release me!"

"I will give you aid and comfort," said Lothan, "and help you defeat the Master!"

"Release me!" Reev's cry was desperate now, a weeping, a wailing.

"Yes, yes," said Lothan, "I will make you into a mighty instrument. I will make you into what cannot be made. I will join you with what should not be joined.

"A mighty weapon you will be, Reev Nax! And a conqueror of the earth…"

"No!" Reev's cry was a scream. "Gods in Heaven! Gods in Heaven save me!"

"My forge is already at work and its fires are lit. You cannot stop my great work, Reev Nax! But you may join me!"

"Save me!" Reev cried, but could the gods hear him in this place?

What was this place, and where had he been taken? Where was this dream occurring, this strange state, this hallucination?

"I am the preparer of the armies," Lothan said. "Armies that can be yours!"

Reev was in agony.

But a noise was rising above the charred hills, echoing over the hissing yellow lakes, not thunder but a loud reverberance.

Lothan was approaching now, but Reev found he was paralyzed and could not move.

"Here," said Lothan. "Join me."

And he raised his hand as if to consummate a deal.

And Reev's hand was lifted of its own accord, and fiery was Lothan's grip.

The thunderous reverberance echoed again, and Reev could hear it was not just a noise but a word, a word that was indistinguishable.

The horrid beasts that Lothan had made were yelping now, baying and howling.

The reverberance was echoing fiercely, and the earth was shaking, and things were coming undone.

"Reev!" the strained noise was crying over the hills and lakes and mountains. "Reev! Wake up!"

The air wavered. Lothan's mouth was agape, and his tongue was like a writhing red serpent.

The world was shaking, the mountains were quaking.

And Reev was back in the Library of Dendérion, back in the room of the Books of the Outer Princes. He was sweating. His entire body was drenched, as if he had just dived into a lake.

Gastreel was above him; Gastreel's was the voice he had heard echoing in the hills and the mountains of his dream.

"I had a terrible nightmare!" Reev shrieked. "The worst nightmare I've ever had!"

Sadness was in Gastreel's eyes. "I told you not to leave your place. Now," he said, "we must go."

"In the night?" Reev said.

"We must flee this place," Gastreel said. "We must flee what you started."

Chapter Nineteen:
A Wizard's Wyrd

For hours now, Bala had been wandering the streets, hoping he'd escaped Dada, hoping Dada never found out he was at the Dragonpaw, never found out that he was with Miss Glenda and Miss Ambrass and Mr. Reev. And where was Mr. Reev? he wondered. He had been gone so long, and as Bala saw the Bridge-O'er-Galios appear under the light of the moon, a tear formed in his eye.

Where was Mr. Reev indeed?

The streets were empty. Bala stopped in his tracks. He remained totally silent, so silent he stopped breathing.

And against the silence, there was another noise, so faint he could scarcely hear it, a low growl, like a dog's growl. Bala turned to look, and under the lamplight there was a small shadow, moving toward him, a shadowy creature as tall as his knee.

And he screamed and went staggering toward the bridge under the light of the streetlamps and the light of the moon. He ran and ran; he ran until he was out of breath and he could run no longer. He was on the bridge now, again, and the moonlight sparkled in the water.

He looked back. He was free. He could see no one behind him, not even that tiny little shadow. And he wiped the sweat from his brow and keeled over, and panted. His stomach growled.

And then the noise rose again, the low moaning, the dull roar. He turned to look again, and the shape was there once more, inching toward Bala.

He took off at a run, heedless of his exhaustion.

The bridge was behind him.

He looked back and saw the shape was getting farther and

farther away.

Down Bala went.

He had struck something.

Two figures were there—two figures on horses.

Gastreel was there... and Mr. Reev.

"Mr. Reev!" Bala exclaimed, thrilled to see him, thrilled to know he was back from the long journey.

"Bala," Gastreel said. "It is good to see you, even at this late hour."

"It almost morning," Bala said. "Why you awake?"

Gastreel pursed his lips. He looked at Bala, then past him, then beyond him. And his eyes bulged, wide as saucers, and his mouth fell agape.

"Bala Rabaam," he said, "what have you done?"

Bala looked back. The shape had caught up with him.

It was the rat from before, the rat he'd killed with magic in the alleyway. It was upright, forepaws outstretched, staggering toward Bala, dragging itself forward with one leg. Its eyes had rotted away and its teeth dangled from swollen gray gums. Its body had putrefied and bits of flesh were hanging from open sores.

It was dead, but it was moving.

"Is this the rat you killed?" Gastreel said. "The rat you told me about?"

"Yes, it is," Bala answered.

And as the rat continued to drag itself forward, Gastreel shook his head and said, "Gods have mercy. Bala, undeath is your power. If you were to become a wizard, you would be a necromancer. Necromancy is your *wyrd*."

The undead rat was close now, just feet away, within biting distance.

"Bala Rabaam," Gastreel said, and his voice was overpowering. Everything but him seemed to darken and dim. "If you were ever to join under my tutelage in the name of the All-Seeing Eye, there is one thing you must learn."

The undead rat was inches away, but Bala found himself unable to move.

"Magical power must never be used lightly, and only in the most exceptional of circumstances and according to the laws of man should it be used to end a life," Gastreel said. "A good word must be used first, then a sword, and then and only then, the powers of wizardry."

The undead rat had stopped before Bala, waiting, stinking, and its scent was putrid.

It would not harm Bala; it was his creation.

"But this thing you unwittingly made must be destroyed," Gastreel said. "It is of no use, and it thinks not, and it feels not. A sword will not easily kill the undead, so if your life's path takes you under my tutelage, why, then, know what I do now is a deed of last resort."

There was a blinding flash, a sizzling spear of bright blue light. A bolt of lightning zapped the undead rat, and left it a smoldering pile of dust.

Bala wanted to cry at the sight of it, the ended life, even if it was not living.

"Bala," Gastreel said, "I know who it is you run from. Keep yourself safe and secure. Do nothing rash. Do not use your power in any way. I will find you and meet with you soon. The wizard order does not just let anyone of talent into its ranks, but I can see that your talent is great."

Chapter Twenty: Sí Quilenthi

It was the early morning and the colors of dawn were shining over the forest, red, gold, and orange. The air was crisp and clear, but as Fortunato walked on, the ground he trod on seemed looser, and the leaves did not crunch under his boots.

Wrinn said, "I fear—"

He had stopped in his tracks. Fortunato turned to look at him.

The prior night he had confessed that the trees had been talking to him, perhaps expecting that Fortunato would think he was mad. But Fortunato had been around the Elf Lands, to its great kingdoms that spanned a continent. He knew that among the woodland elves, of the tribe called the Umen, there were some who could speak to and shape trees.

He knew Wrinn was not mad.

"We are close," Wrinn said. "Close to the Blight… I can hear a million voices screaming out in pain. I don't want to hear it but I can't help it."

Could a Treespeaker shut his ears? Fortunato did not know.

"Come," he said, "perhaps if we enter the Blight you will hear them no longer."

And Fortunato continued his walk, up high hills and through steep valleys, underneath a canopy that blocked out much light. Wrinn followed right behind him with his quarterstaff at the ready.

He noted specks of brown on the ferns and vines in increasing frequency. The air lost its crispness. The whole of the forest air grew thick, and he began to feel queasy. Greater than his sense of queasiness was his sense of danger, and so he drew his bow, and nocked an arrow to it.

And then they were in the Blight so suddenly Fortunato did not realize it was happening.

The trees had shriveled; some had fallen, and others stood unsteadily, their leaves having turned brown and begun to drift downward. Ahead of Fortunato was a small pond surrounded by dead brown grass, and the pond's waters were murky black.

"What horror," Fortunato said, "what death."

He turned. Wrinn had keeled over, and vomit was dripping from his mouth.

He turned back to gaze at the Blight once more, awestruck and appalled by the sight of it. The hills were brown; everything that had been alive was dead. What evil could have caused this? What plague could these trees and plants have caught?

"Let's get out of here," Wrinn said, and in the sickly air there was no arguing with him.

Fortunato turned and Wrinn followed a step ahead, first walking, then running from the scene of such horror.

~

In the place where greenness remained and the air was not so foul, Fortunato relented his run. "What horror is in this world?" he said.

There was a flash of light to his right, blinding white. To his left, in the hills above, two figures were approaching, slender figures he could not distinguish because of the blinding flash.

He turned to the source of the light. He loosed his arrow at the white light but his arrow caught fire and dissolved to powder.

Wrinn reached for his quarterstaff but in a moment's span the two figures were upon him, overcoming him and knocking him unconscious with a sap. And as the light-clothed being approached Fortunato, he could see that those two figures were elves, dressed in green, that there were bows at their backs and sabers at the ready.

"*Sí quilenthi!*" Fortunato shouted. "I am an elf-friend."

Chapter Twenty-One: Ramona

The sun was shining on the steeples of the churches and the great towers of the monasteries in Cathedral District. And Reev Nax, now back in Galiope, having just returned, did not feel well. His experience in the Library of Dendérion was not one easily forgotten, and last night he had awoken in wild terror, fearing what he had seen.

Yet as he stood there among the crowds, among the travelers going about the way, the monks in their habits and the priests in their brown robes, waiting for something—he did not know what—he recalled the task he'd been sent here for.

A great council meeting was set to take place in the Galiopean Townhall, a meeting of what Gastreel called "exceptional importance." The rector, Bartholem, leader of the churches in Galiope and a stakeholder in Gallian affairs, needed to hear a summons, and who better to give it than Reev Nax, the son of Simeon? That was how Gastreel explained it, but Reev wondered if he were only lazy.

"Make way!" A voice rose above the crowd, but no one heeded it. "Make way for Her Excellency Ramona Nax Bensange!"

Nax, the voice had said. Who else was named Nax? Was it possible he had a living relative? Was it possible there were some in his family who were still alive?

"Make way! Make way!" the voice continued to shout, no doubt a herald sent by Ramona Nax Bensange herself. But the crowds did not disperse; it was as if they were deaf.

And yet eventually, Reev, standing there, saw some in the crowd veer off to the side. Two lines of armored men on horses rode through the street, and between them a woman was walking, a woman in a silver gown, whose raven-black hair was tied up in a caul. Near her was a young boy perhaps half Reev's age.

Out of excitement or recklessness, the hope he was not alone, Reev leapt before the procession.

"Ramona Nax?" Reev said. "Are you my kin? I am Reev…"

The look of disconsolate wrath on her face vanished as suddenly as it appeared, and her gray eyes widened. "Reev Nax," she said. "Simeon's son. Simeon, my brother."

And she met him in an embrace.

Reev never knew he had an aunt, or what appeared to be a cousin.

He was not alone in the world, after all.

~

By the time they reached Wodenscross Court on Galiope's highest hill, their destination, Gastreel had caught word of Ramona's return and met them. He kissed her gently on either cheek.

They were at the gate of Wodenscross Court and its many mansions were in sight. The men in armor had departed, leaving Ramona Nax Bensange and her son Asher alone.

"You are back," Gastreel said. "I wondered if I'd ever see you again when you married the count."

There was a long pause. Neither knew what to say.

"And you are back…?" Gastreel said with a nervous giggle.

"Elfraine and I…" Ramona said. "We have parted ways. The High Priestess does not easily grant divorces, but our marriage was annulled."

"Annulled," Gastreel said, sounding somewhat aghast. "Well, I am sorry, Ramona."

"Do not pity me," Ramona said, her voice harsh, her eyes stormy. And then a light in her eyes grew, and she smiled. The anger vanished from her voice. "I am back here. Back home. Where I belong.

"And Ash and I have kin… we have Reev. The Nax family endures."

Reev smiled at the sound of her words, at what they meant. He had so many questions, so many questions he did not know if Ramona wanted to answer.

~

And from one end of Galiope to another the news spread, what some called a miracle and others a reminder of dark days, that the sister of the hero Simeon Nax had returned from the west. All considered it a sign of momentous days to come, that the world was changing, that great or terrible times were ahead.

And Reev now had a connection to a forgotten world, the world that had existed before he had been born.

Chapter Twenty-Two: The King's Daughter

As Fortunato agreed, he walked blindfolded, and as he walked, sometimes staggering, sometimes stumbling, he wondered what elves were doing so far from their homeland—not Gallian elves who lived in the city and adopted human customs but true elves among true elves, sent from afar. He could only guess. He hoped they had not been sent to do harm. They had removed his sword, Amenhir, and they had removed his bow and his arrows. He was defenseless, save for his fists, and so it was a matter of trust that he had agreed to this.

"Sí quilenthi" he had said in the heat of the moment. "I am an elf-friend."

And those words, which were true, had likely saved his life. In the great city of Danarion, both Fortunato and Gastreel had been named elf-friends by order of the king. Wherever elves dwelled they were allowed to go, with only some restrictions.

But as for Wrinn, the elves who dwelled in the homeland would consider him to be foreign, not a true part of their race. He would be treated as a human, or at best like an outsider. Only those born in the Elven World were considered to truly belong.

There was commotion around Fortunato, scattered shouts in the light of the day. His walk came to an abrupt halt. The blindfold was rudely jerked away from him, and, dazed, his eyes only slowly adjusted to the light.

They were in a camp underneath the trees. Tents whose flaps were lined with the leaf-and-vine symbol surrounded the remains of a campfire.

And three elves were there in total, one blond, one brown-haired, and a red-haired woman in a white gown and veil.

"What is the meaning of this?" Wrinn began to shout. "Let me go! Let us go!"

The red-haired woman had a staff in her hands. It was she who had produced the blinding light that dazed Fortunato and caused his arrow to fail.

"Silence, *dra'datsi*," the brown-haired elf said, and walked around to examine them. "You are lucky we left you alive. We are on strict orders of the king that any living being leaving the Perishing be killed."

His blue eyes gleamed in the sunlight.

"I am Sinderion," he said. He motioned to the blond-haired elf. "This is Goni. We are captains of the Forest Regiment, sent on a mission by the king.

"And this… this is Nenré, daughter of the king himself. Lay your eyes on her and despair. A greater lightbearer you shall not find in the whole of the world."

"And what is this Blight?" Fortunato said. "What you call the Perishing?"

"Will you not bow before the princess?" said Sinderion.

"Do not make them bow." Nenré's voice was gentle but radiant with strength. "They are not my people."

There was a pause, and Sinderion's eyes gleamed once more and he repeated Fortunato's question. "What is the Perishing? Six months ago, our spies in Alonar witnessed battalions of rokahn entering this forest, carrying with them tools and materials for building. The king quickly sent us to investigate and bring back word of what had happened. And by the time we arrived, the trees were dying and the Perishing had spread.

"Life cannot easily survive in the Perishing, not even the healthy. The air is poison and whatever is causing it is beyond our reach. You are lucky to have survived. Those who spend any length of time within come out malformed and diseased and die within hours.

"The Perishing is growing at a rate of about a quarter-mile a day. Soon it will cover all Alonar."

"Alonar?" Wrinn said.

"Gallia, according to your language," said Nenré.

"I fear an evil power is at work," Sinderion said. "A name I dare not utter.

"We must stop the spread of this death. But I do not know how, not yet. Illunitari has not revealed the path to me."

~

There was a faint wind blowing, and Wrinn could smell death on the edge of it. A quarter-mile per day, these elves claimed, the Blight or the Perishing or whatever they would call it spread. So many trees were at risk, so many, every hour of every day. They cried out to him in desperation, thinking he could do something about it when he could do nothing.

He did not trust these elves like Fortunato did. He did not like their company. If the King of the Elves' daughter was here with them, she was bound to be haughty. And they did not see Wrinn as one of them, Wrinn, who did not know his parents, who was born in slavery and sold from one master to another until his emancipation, but who nonetheless was a son of Lumas and Luvé.

"We have brought food." Goni spoke for the first time, and his voice was deep. His blond hair was long, and his green eyes were keen. "I am sure that you are famished."

"Will you let us go?" Wrinn said, and if it was rude he did not care.

"No," Goni said, "not yet."

The cakes Goni brought forth were soft and tender, and they had been baked with honey in an oven on the outskirts of camp. Wrinn would be lying to himself if he did not admit he was thankful after so many weeks eating wild vegetables and gamey meat. The cakes were good for the soul, and they had brought not only cakes but many flasks of wine, not regular wine but the wine of the elves, what the Zarubes called *Gerusivel.*

"Will you ply us with cakes and then leave us for dead?" Wrinn said, but his voice did not rise above the roaring of the fire and of the chattering of Goni and Sinderion, and of the conversation between Nenré and Fortunato, who had ended up sitting next to each other.

Wrinn again felt alone.

Alone, he thought, *except for the trees.*

As the fire burned on and the twilight turned into night, Wrinn, with a cup of wine, wandered away from camp. If elves and humans would not be company for him, perhaps the green growing things of the world would.

On the outskirts of camp, in the forest, he laid his hands on one of the trees and spoke dully, "How can I help you? How can I heal you, if even I cannot enter the Blight without dying?"

The answer was not a whisper but words that echoed in his mind: *You will find a way, Son of the Forest, because you have to. You must rescue us, or we will all die.*

"How did it all begin?" Wrinn asked. "Where did the Blight start? Who made it?"

The tree seemed to creak in the wind, to twist and to turn. Gentle was the sound of its voice. *I do not know. But three score sunrises and sunsets ago, there was fire. And many turns of the seasons ago, that was when the bad people arrived.*

"The bad people," Wrinn said. "Who are the bad people?"

The tree did not speak. Instead, Wrinn sensed a presence behind him. A twig crunched.

He turned and saw, as he expected, Sinderion.

"A Treespeaker," Sinderion said. "Of the Umen tribe you must be. Such power is only seen among the people of the Forest Realm."

Sinderion's presence was not welcome. Wrinn had wanted to be alone. "I am not of the Umen tribe," he said, "I am of the Gallian League, and the city of Galiope. You think you are wise, Sinderion, but you have a lot to learn."

And Wrinn walked past him, back reluctantly to the campfire.

~

Wrinn twisted in his bedroll. "They aren't letting us leave, are they?"

"Why would we go?" Fortunato said. "Our goals are the same."

"I do not trust them," Wrinn said. "I do not trust them at all. They almost blinded you, Fortunato. They knocked me out with a sap."

"And yet they are servants of the king, sent by him," Fortunato said. "Their mission is grave. We must help them."

"Help them," Wrinn said in disgust. "I do not want to help them."

~

In the morning, he awoke, and it was still dark. Fortunato was snoring next to him, yet Wrinn could hear dull murmurs in the distance. And so, quickly and quietly, still in his smallclothes, he got up, gingerly opened the tent flap, and stepped out into the morning air.

It was brisk, and dawn was just making itself known among the hills and trees.

Goni was asleep, having collapsed near the remnants of the fire sometime last night.

Quickly and quietly, secretly but with haste, Wrinn made his way over to the direction of the voices. Perhaps he would hear these elves' real intent.

Nenré was in the clearing, already in her white gown. Her veil fell in a trail all the way down her back. She was without her staff.

She was speaking to Sinderion, and their choice of place indicated they did not want to be heard.

"Té veli," said Nenré, looking down and seeming somewhat bashful.

Sinderion appeared wroth. *"Bet inié indoren granaras dus héan?"* His tone was harsh.

What a strange world where Wrinn, an elf, could not understand the speech of his own race, but Fortunato, a human, could.

But Sinderion looked back, toward the bushes where Wrinn was hiding. *"Bet el?"*

And before Wrinn knew it, Sinderion was through the bushes and had tackled him to the ground.

"Stop this!" Nenré called after them.

As Sinderion pinned Wrinn to the ground, his eyes wrathful, almost murderous, she stepped through the clearing gracefully. Even now, without her staff and not seeming to call on magic by intent, her gown was brilliant white, seeming to give off faint illumination.

Sinderion would obey his liege. "We have a listener," Sinderion said. "An eavesdropper. A spy. Should we have killed you, boy, when we saw you fleeing the Perishing?"

"Enough of this," Nenré said. "There is a deficit of trust. He will learn to trust. He will learn our mission is grave. His quarterstaff may be put to good use in time."

Sinderion relented and scrambled to his feet.

"Sorry," was on the tip of Wrinn's tongue, but even now he couldn't bring himself to say it.

He hopped up, and Nenré's eyes glistened. A soft smile was on her face. Her red hair fell in locks down her back. Her blue eyes were like sapphires cut and polished, or like the ocean in dazzling sunlight. Wrinn considered himself a skilled fighter, but he was in awe of her. Wherever she walked, her power seemed to go with her.

~

Fortunato was not in the tent, and for a moment Wrinn panicked, wondering if some creature of the Perishing had wandered out here and snatched him in the morning darkness. But he quickly realized that was impossible.

He looked about the forest surrounding the camp, the towering maples, the mighty oaks, the stands of white-barked aspens. And on a ridge he saw his old friend standing there, cupping something in his hands.

"Fortunato," Wrinn said, "what is that? What are you holding?"

Fortunato turned to him. There was a slight smile on his face. It was a bluebird he was holding, and he was whispering to it indistinguishably.

"What are you doing?" Wrinn said.

Fortunato kept whispering a little while longer. Then he gently nudged the bluebird, and the bluebird soared away.

The sun was growing in strength, shining on Fortunato's black hair.

"When I was young," he said, "I went to the town of Brill, and there I learned the craft of the Woodsmen, the guardians of the forest. I learned the beast-tongue."

"You're saying you can talk to animals?" Wrinn said.

"Only in a certain sense," Fortunato said. "I can tell them the things they are capable of understanding. "And I... I am merely a novice. I was in Brill two years, and then... then I was called north."

"There is a lot I don't yet know about you, Fortunato," Wrinn said.

And as he stood there, he noted that the bottom of Fortunato's cloak had been frayed, torn off or crudely cut, as if by a knife.

Chapter Twenty-Three: To Walk By Night

Ambrass was in her bedroom, watching the rain trickle down.

It was falling in a drizzle, and her window was frosted. The day was a bit gloomy but she had hope the sun would shine, the clouds would part, and the brightness would return.

But against her frosted window, a dark shape the size of her fist appeared. Propelled by curiosity, she grabbed hold of the window frame and pushed it open.

A bluebird was there, a bluebird with brilliant feathers and bright eyes. With its orange beak it began to sing a song, and for a moment Ambrass felt she was in the wild, in a beautiful wood underneath the trees, and that sunny days and bright times were ahead.

Then the bluebird flew off, darting through the air. It was gone, and so was that thought, that hope on a rainy day.

~

It was the afternoon and the rain had stopped, and outside the sun was shining with just a few clouds in the firmament. Ambrass had swept the great hall so thoroughly that every contour of the floorboards was visible, and not even a speck of dust could be found. Glenda was in the kitchen preparing dinner for the night guests.

And Bala… Bala had not been seen in days, not since his father had walked through the front door.

Ambrass had begun to think on her future, whether she wanted to spend the rest of her days at the Dragonpaw. She supposed she hoped to marry, though Fortunato was now lost to her.

Glenda had told her the news the other night: that he and Wrinn had gotten into a fight with a foreign ambassador, beating him almost to the point of death. It was so unlike Fortunato, and Ambrass guessed Wrinn was the instigator, but they had both been exiled, and who knew where they had gone now?

The town of Beggar's Rest in the far south of Gallia offered welcome to brigands and those fleeing the law. Would they go there? Wherever they were, Ambrass hoped they were safe, and she hoped, in her heart, that they would return.

The door to the Dragonpaw opened. In walked a dark figure, who stamped his feet on the rug and just as quickly hung his cloak on the rack. And in that moment, panic rose up in Ambrass as she saw the pale white face, the closely-cropped black hair, the keen dark eyes, the square jaw.

"Nocturne," she said, instantly a stammering mess. "What are you—I mean, how can I help you?"

"Help me?" Nocturne said. Was there guile in his eyes? "I'm looking for my son. Have you seen him?"

"No, no, I… I haven't," Ambrass said.

"Don't be afraid," Nocturne said. "There is nothing to be afraid of."

Glenda walked into the main hall from the kitchen, her face covered with a powder of flour. "Nocturne," she said, "what is the meaning of this? Why have you come?"

Nocturne pursed his lips. "I just came back from the South Weald," he said, "from the great forest. I was looking for my old friend Fortunato."

"You know him?" Ambrass said, a silly thing to say perhaps, but she couldn't imagine a man of Fortunato's caliber befriending someone like Nocturne.

Nocturne's dark eyes turned to her. "Yes, Fortunato and I are old friends. We fought together in the wars of '41 and '42."

Ambrass remembered those years, though she had been a child, and they had been terrible years, the mountains vomiting forth rokahn in astounding number. It was only with great effort, and all the towns of the League banding together, that they'd been beaten back.

And in that moment, Ambrass realized Nocturne was holding something in his left hand.

"I went looking for him," Nocturne said. "I thought the South Weald was where he might be."

It was a length of cloth he was holding, a jagged piece of green fabric, partially stained with mud.

"And I found this," he said, "and by it there was blood. It's his cloak. I think the wild animals may have gotten to him... I think he is dead."

"No!" Ambrass said. "It can't be..."

And her eyes welled with tears, Fortunato, her hero, who had been her love. How could the gods be so cruel? How could fate have brought her here, to this moment? What agony, what an evil day.

But there was still hope, surely there still was, hope he was alive, hope—even if his cloak had been torn—that he had survived the ordeal.

"Are you sure it is his?" Ambrass said, drawing near to Nocturne. She took the green fabric in her hands and as she felt it she was convinced this was his, this had been part of his cloak, the cloak she had seen before, which she knew.

"This is all terrible news," Glenda said. "But he may still be alive. Fortunato has escaped many dangers before."

"Perhaps," Nocturne said, "but I doubt it. There was so much blood."

And like that, Ambrass began to sob. "It can't be," she said, "it can't be."

What a cruel world it was, and she did not know where to turn for comfort. What a cruel world, and now she would only wait and wonder, hoping against hope that he was alive.

Nocturne was gazing at her, Nocturne, dark-eyed, dark-haired. And as she stared at him she began to follow dark trails in her mind. How strange for him to find Fortunato, to chase after him. Some in Gallia had called him the High Street Slasher. Was it possible that, if he was capable of murder, he was also capable of murdering his friend?

No, no, and what a cruel accusation. It was not warranted. Ambrass had no reason to think Nocturne had anything but love for Fortunato, for his friend.

"May I keep it?" Ambrass said.

"Of course," Nocturne answered, "if having it will comfort you."

"Comfort me?" Ambrass said, aghast. "It will not comfort me. But it will remind me. It will remind me to look for him."

And there seemed to be a questioning look in Nocturne's dark eyes. That questioning look faded, and focus replaced it. "Ambrass," said Nocturne, "if there is anything I can do to help you, tell me."

"There is nothing you can do for me," Ambrass said. "There is nothing anyone can do for me now."

~

The rain had returned. The patrons had gone to bed. Ambrass had doused the fire in the hearth with water and then returned to her room. She was in her smock, still devastated by the news, but functioning.

Against the cascading sound of the rain, she was staring out her window. Though the news was troubling, she could not help but feel an inkling of hope. What if her love was still alive? What if he had survived? What if Nocturne had been mistaken?

Someone like Nocturne, after all, could never be trusted. From what Glenda told her of him, he could not be trusted at all.

In the light of her candles she examined the length of cloth, crudely torn, colored green, frayed along the edges. Fortunato had overcome rokahn and men alike; would a beast of the forest overcome someone like him, someone who knew the wilds, someone to whom open ranges and dark woods were no threat?

She was gazing out her window, in the darkness, in the rain. Was there someone out there? A dark shape, in the alley?

No, no there was not. She could scarcely see.

There was a knock on the bedroom door, and the first thought she had was Nocturne.

What a strange conclusion to come to.

When she opened it, Glenda was there, still dressed for the day, not having readied for bed. Ambrass wondered if elves and the half-elven did not need as much sleep as humans, or if Glenda was just superhuman of her own accord.

"Ambrass," she said. She was holding a candle in her hands. "A word with you, please?"

The rain picked up, the winds tossing this way and that, and as Ambrass sat on her bed Glenda stood there, talking in hushed tones.

"I would be negligent," said Glenda, "as your overseer, but more importantly as your friend, if I did not warn you."

"Warn me?" said Ambrass. "Of what?"

And then, before Glenda spoke, Ambrass knew what was coming.

"Many have fallen under Nocturne's influence," Glenda said. "Do not let it be you. Do not add yourself to the number."

"Shall I place garlic at my window?" Ambrass said.

"No," Glenda said. "He is no phantom or ghost. He is living and his blood is hot, like yours or mine.

"He is a creature of the night but that is by his own choice. It is by his own choice that he walks by moonlight. He is a vampire, not a specter. He is an heir to an ancient curse. And his influence is not by magic, but by honeyed words. By will.

"I saw the way his eyes looked upon you, Ambrass—"

"And who do you think I am?" Ambrass said. "Do you think so little of me that I would fall for Nocturne?"

"Be careful," Glenda said, and it was the words she did not say that hurt, not the words she did. "Keep yourself safe."

And with her candle, Glenda, innkeeper, the proprietor of the Dragonpaw Inn, left Ambrass's bedside and departed into the night.

Chapter Twenty-Four:
A Dangerous Man

Sleeping had been an insurmountable challenge for Reev since the night in the Library of Dendérion, since the night the book was opened and he had fallen into a dark dream, into what had felt like another world.

At odd hours he would get up, fearful of what he had seen. And he could still feel Lothan's fiery grip on his hand; he could still feel its lingering touch.

But Lothan was just a dream-being, something he or the book or some fell power had conjured up.

Still, though, he could not sleep, for worry about Wrinn, for worry about the dream, for the fiery feeling of a hand on his own.

He looked up to the mirror that was mounted on his wall. He lifted his hand and examined it, but there was no trace of redness, no trace of a burn. Yet when he touched his hand, it was tender and raw, as if it had been doused in flame.

"What happened?" Reev found himself muttering. "What happened to me?"

He peered into the glass of the mirror. For a moment he thought he saw tender white hairs growing on his hand, but when he inspected it closer, they were gone.

The door to the bedchamber opened.

Glenda was there in her night garments, with a candle in hand. "How are things, Mr. Reev?"

"I…" Reev began. "I am fine. Wrinn—"

"We are all worried," Glenda said. "I'm not saying you shouldn't be. But if anyone can survive in exile, it is him."

Her words did not comfort him.

"And before I leave you, I—what's that?"

Glenda was walking up to his window. "I thought I saw a face in the glass." She shut his curtains.

"We must be careful," Glenda said. "I've heard there are strange people in town. People who do not belong in Gallia. Men from the southlands."

"The southlands?" Reev said.

In the Northern World, in its provincial way, all of the south was lumped together. "Imperials are here often," he said.

"No, not Imperials," Glenda answered. "Men from far away, men who have never been seen in Gallia before. Men with strange names, women too."

All names were strange to the foreigner. It seemed only Reev Nax's name was strange to everyone.

His aunt was now in town. He wondered if she would know more, about his family name, about his father, about his place in the world.

~

The next morning he received a summons from Gastreel, in the way Gastreel most liked to summon him. A letter, sealed in wax with a G rune, was delivered on the doorstep of the Dragonpaw. Glenda knew better than to open it.

Unveiled, the letter was simple: "Come meet me. Rosetree Manor, first hour after noon."

On his way to the manor, he was mindful of the crowd and the faces in it, trying to take note of the strange people Glenda had referred to. There was a world beyond the Empire, south of it, a world that Reev knew nothing of. And there were likely worlds beyond that, all the lands the ocean surrounded.

But those faces he saw were only Gallians, dressed in the manner that Gallians dressed, speaking the Gallian tongue. He could see no sign of any intruders or foreigners, no people in strange dress or using a differing language.

At Rosetree Manor, he knocked on the door thrice, and he waited. He began to look about. He wondered if he had been sent here through deceptive means, if the wicked men that Glenda had spoken of had set up some sort of trap.

But who would dare set up a trap at the house of a wizard? Who would dare risk assaulting the pupil of Gastreel at his own home?

And he waited, and he wondered, and his legs began to grow stiff. He knocked a fourth time, and then a fifth.

And at last he gave up, deciding to depart, warily, with his hand ready to go to Doomblade's hilt. The daylight no longer offered comfort, nor did the rich people and town guards walking by.

Then the door swung open, and Gastreel was there in the doorway, mighty Gastreel, his body draped in a green robe, the white Staff of the Archwizard in his right hand.

"Reev," Gastreel said, "my dear boy. Come inside at once. Hurry!"

~

The halls of Gastreel's manor were dim. He had no servants—he considered it beneath him—but all was well swept and well cared for, everything prim and proper, completely clean.

"I had to wait," Gastreel said. "There are evil men about."

"That is what I heard," Reev answered as Gastreel led him through the dark halls. "Where do they come from?"

Gastreel led him outside, into the garden. High hedges surrounded the perimeter of the wall.

"Would it surprise you," Gastreel said, "that I do not know everything? That there are places on the map that I am not aware of?

"And yet I feel their purposes are for evil. They began arriving several weeks ago. They are staying in inns throughout Galiope.

"But where are they from?"

The birds were singing; the sun was shining. It was a perfect day, but the conversation had turned dark.

"Where are they from indeed? Not the Empire, it would appear. From further south, from some desert land or forgotten kingdom. They are garbed in red. The men are scarred, but the women are fair."

"Why are they here?" Reev said.

"I do not know," Gastreel said. "I suspect we will find out soon enough."

On a stone table, Reev could see a tattered book with a leather cover.

"What is that?" Reev said.

"I took it from the Library of Dendérion," Gastreel answered.

Reev gasped.

"Do not worry; I will return it. I am a dutiful patron of the library, or else the Sentinel would have forbidden my entry," Gastreel said.

"You are going back?" Reev said.

"Yes, I am wise to avoid the dangers," Gastreel said. "Do not worry about me, Reev. Worry about yourself."

He turned to the leather bound book and laid his hands upon it. When he opened the cover, Reev could see many of the pages were loose, yellowed, even disintegrated in places.

"What is it?" Reev said.

"I have not found the lost prophecies but the oldest version of the prophecies that are already known," Gastreel said. "This is in Old Elvish, a language even I find difficult to understand."

He began to flip through the pages and Reev winced as they crackled under Gastreel's thumb.

"It says here, 'He shall be *telantari*.' Do you know what that means?"

"No," Reev replied. Of course he didn't. His Elvish was

rudimentary, nothing compared to Gastreel's. If Gastreel did not know a word, Reev certainly wouldn't.

"This book, I do not know, but I think it was copied close to the time of the prophecy's writing," Gastreel said. "The prophecies record the properties of the Sage, the Hand of the Gods, and what he will do to vanquish the Enemy.

"What will he do? There are prophecies that are lost, that have been forgotten in the realm of men. And there are some that are inscrutable, some that not even the wisest elves understand.

"Like he shall be '*telantari*.' What is our next course of action, Reev? I do not know yet. I do not know how we shall proceed. But I fear we will be in danger the longer we dally here."

"Dally here?" Reev said.

"I spoke rashly," Gastreel said, and his face grew somber. "Galiope is safe. At least, it is safe for now. We will not leave anytime soon."

Reev couldn't bear the thought of leaving. Where would they go to? If Galiope was not safe, what part of the world was?

"He shall be '*telantari*,'" said Gastreel. "What is *telantari*? I cannot find it in any of the lexicons in my home. I wonder, if I go back to Dendérion, if I would be able to identify this word. It would take hours, perhaps days of searching."

"Do not go back," Reev said, and the harshness of his tone surprised him.

He supposed it was time to tell Gastreel everything he had seen, every last detail, every dark memory.

And when he had told Gastreel everything, about Lothan's gray eyes, about the two black beasts that were in the room, about the mountains of fire and about Lothan's forced handshake, Gastreel had turned some shade of white.

"Lothan," Gastreel said, "one of the Dark One's servants it seems.

"He makes no true offer to you. He is only trying to entrap you, to weaken you."

"There is something else," Reev said. "At an inn on the way back here, there was a man… I didn't want to alarm you. He tried to speak to me. He said he was working for Lothan, that Lothan was a rich patron of his but now I know it is so much worse.

"His name was Ivan Xandrast."

"Ivan Xandrast," Gastreel said, and all the air and lightness seemed to be sucked out of the garden. It was like speaking his name was a thing of ill omen. "I know that name.

"Come, let us go inside so no one can hear us."

~

Gastreel poked and prodded the embers of the hearth. The light shone in orange upon his bearded face.

"There is a land south of here, a land known as Kav," Gastreel said. "Ivan Xandrast was of Kav. He was a minor noble.

"But there was a war with Kav's neighbors, a great and terrible war, and Ivan Xandrast—it is said—descended into madness. He would burn entire towns. He would set the heads of the dead on pikes.

"He was a war criminal, so notorious that even the wizards council took notice of him. Then he disappeared from sight. Kav began to build a wall around its entire border, so that none could go in or out."

Reev gazed into the embers, bright red and orange, glowing with heat.

"I have not heard that name in years," Gastreel said. "Ivan Xandrast. It is a name I'd rather not have heard again, certainly not in the way you've told me of it.

"He has re-emerged, and it is a dark thing for the world, a dark thing for the world indeed.

"Perhaps you should not be staying in the Dragonpaw Inn. You should stay always under my guard, until this Ivan Xandrast is no more."

There was freedom in staying at the inn, freedom and mobility, the ability to set the course of his day and his life. But perhaps Gastreel was right. With Ivan Xandrast hunting him, with these men of the Far South wandering the streets, perhaps it was best not to be alone and unprotected.

"I guess you're right," Reev replied. "I will stay here, under guard. Ivan Xandrast is a dangerous man."

~

He dreamed that night of an agonized scream, a scream that echoed from the earth to the heavens, a man in chains, kept in a dungeon, bursting through his bonds and breaking free.

Chapter Twenty-Five: The Dhampir

From every corner of the Northern World and beyond, the Ranking Wizards had regathered. Assembled, now, at the top of the Tower of Pythor, the leaders of every order had taken their seats, Red, Blue, Gold, and more—with Gastreel of the Green Robes, the archwizard, sitting on a raised dais.

It had not been long ago that the wizard order had been perverted, that it had turned to madness. It was not long ago that the Archwizard Syrion had taken up a dark iron scepter, that the Baron Tuck had turned to forbidden magic. Still Gastreel was unsure of whether his rule would hold, that the wizards would not fall into lust for power again. But that was not the topic of discussion.

In the light of the starstones, Gastreel rose. "Wise men of the council," he said, "Ranking wizards all. What news do you have? What actions do you propose?"

Elothiel of the Starry Robes announced he had trapped and extinguished a group of Forbidden magic weavers. Lydia of the White Robes announced the sowing of *sindomas* seeds and the opening of a new hospital in Gallia.

But hanging over all was the trouble in the west, kingdoms crumbling, peril, the threat that the very throne of Zarubain might be no more. A new menace had appeared, a dark menace indeed, and fears lingered that the whole world might be swallowed up in it.

Then Cullen of the Brown Robes stood up, the oldest member of the wizards council. He had a long, unkempt beard and a cap that was as brown as his robes. In his hands was a knobby staff on which small blooms were growing.

"Councilmen." His voice was weak and barely carried through the room. "There is something like I'd never seen before. South of here in the great woods, the trees are dying in incredible number. There is death spreading at an alarming rate. Soon all Gallia will be in danger."

The looks on the faces of the other wizards were ones of mixed boredom and irritation. It seemed only Gastreel was interested in Cullen's report.

"Death like a desert," Cullen said, "in the green places of the world. We must do something to halt its spread!"

Each wizard spoke for as long as they wanted. It was custom for the archwizard to speak last.

Beyond Cullen, the other wizards spoke of minutiae, Anders of the Silver Robes that there was a shortage of wands at the university, Nemiel of the Red Robes that the Pan-Vardic Games were likely to be delayed, Sorriel of the Blue Robes that a new elven library had been discovered, Ghorghast of the Gray Robes that there was an increase in bandit activity in the Lune Valley.

Gastreel endured each wizard patiently, leaving them plenty of time to speak their mind and feel heard. And then, rising at the end of the council session, he struck.

"Men of the council," he said, "I have met here in this city a young boy whose talent is without compare, a dhampir, a child of a vampire and a human.

"When I took him to the Room of Determination, the crystals swirled about him like a storm."

"You took him to the Room of Determination without our consent?" said Nemiel of the Red Robes.

Gastreel had replaced each of the eleven seats of Ranking Wizards with partisans, but he supposed their loyalty only went so far.

"There is trouble, though," Gastreel said. "I have identified his *wyrd*. It is necromancy."

"Necromancy!" said Lydia of the White Robes. Her voice was filled with disgust. "We have agreed, ever since Jerek, that necromancy is forbidden, that those with that gift never be allowed into our order."

"We have agreed," Gastreel said, "but we may still allow it."

"And why would we?" thundered Elothiel of the Starry Robes.

"Because," Gastreel said, "as you remember… it was Jerek— curse his memory—that infused the masks of the Servants of Seymus with unlife. He brought the Servants of Seymus back before their time.

"Undeath allowed them to roam in their weakened state. Even in their weakened state they were terrible foes."

"What are you saying?" said Elothiel.

"Necromancy gave them false life," Gastreel said. "Only necromancy can undo Jerek's spell. You know this. We all know this. The masks are locked away in safekeeping, but even the mundane can see the tendrils of black smoke that waft up from them. Soon enough this false life will return."

"Enough," Lydia said. "Speak no more of the Servants of Seymus. I do not want to hear of them."

"Even if we allow him to be trained," said Nemiel of the Red Robes, "it will take years before he is skilled enough for such an operation."

"It would take years," Gastreel said, "for someone of lesser talent. But this Bala Rabaam is so gifted it may take only a matter of months."

"Necromancy shall never be accepted," Lydia snapped. "Not even the Black Robes will accept them. Odynomancers may cause aching and agony untold — we are wise to ban them — but necromancers are worse, blurring the distinction of what is most sacred… life and death. Necromancy will never receive my approval."

And at her words, Gastreel knew his gambit had failed, that

whatever happened with Bala, it would happen without the council's blessing.

No… I will not yet give up. I will not yet give up hope.

But the faces that greeted him were cold and unmoved, and Gastreel knew that at this time, this place, he would not get his way. The Convening of the Council of 1152 had failed him.

At least, it had failed him thus far.

Chapter Twenty-Six: Not Alone

"Every day the Perishing grows," said the Princess Nenré in the solitude of the camp. "Every day, the situation grows more dire. We cannot wait. We must act."

The trees overhead of Wrinn were without blemish; there were no brown spots to be seen, no sign of death.

Over the days he'd spent with Sinderion, Goni, and Nenré, he had learned that this was less a camp and more an outpost, a place where an oven had been constructed, where food was stored. He began to learn more about the elven spies who dwelled in the forest without human knowledge, reporting always to the king.

"What we are doing now is not working," Wrinn said. "We must go in… brace ourselves, endure it…"

"Foolishness," Sinderion said with a scowl on his face. "It will kill both plant and animal."

"How can we stop it," Fortunato said, "if we do not know its source?"

"We will uncover it," Sinderion said. "Somehow."

Nenré rose and gathered her dress. "Who of us here has powers of farsight? Who of us can look beyond this place? No one here."

"The wizards can," Fortunato said. "The wizards have an All-Seeing Eye, a looking-glass that can see anywhere in the world."

"Yes," Nenré said. "They do have the orb. It was stolen from elven safekeeping. It was stolen from my father's kingdom. So were the other two, the other two that were made."

"Why don't you go ask the wizards for aid?" Wrinn asked.

Nenré shook her head. "We will not enter an unclean place."

"Unclean?" Wrinn said, a bit shocked at the word. The elves, those born in the Elven World, were so high-minded, so disdainful of the other races, rejecting even those of their blood who were born abroad.

"You may go," Nenré said. "You may ask them."

"Have we not told you that we are exiles, miss?" Wrinn snapped.

"Enough of this," Sinderion bellowed. "Use a respectful address for the daughter of the king."

"Hush," said Nenré. "Let's all of us be quiet. Let's all of us have our time to think. We are all at the same task. We all have the same goal. We are on each others' side."

And as she stood up, her white robes and veil seemed to glow, to fluoresce in the sun's light.

She walked off into the woods. Sinderion followed her a moment later and Goni walked off in another direction.

Fortunato and Wrinn sat alone beside the cold remnants of last night's campfire.

"You should speak more respectfully to her, Wrinn," Fortunato said.

"And who is she to you?" Wrinn said. "Do you fancy her or something?"

For the first time in Wrinn's life, he saw anger in Fortunato's eyes. "Choose your words carefully," he said. "You may regret them."

She was the daughter of the elvenking, surely pampered from her earliest days. But maybe Fortunato was right. Maybe, for now at least, for the sake of survival and cohesion, he should keep quiet.

And Wrinn got up, grabbing his quarterstaff from the ground, and stalked into the woods.

~

In a forest hollow, Wrinn was caught up in his own thoughts.

Why are we here, he wondered, *and why is Fortunato so keen on healing the South Weald?*

Perhaps Fortunato thought the Gallian League would reverse his exile if he succeeded.

Wrinn knew the Blight threatened all of Gallia, and that included the people he loved. He supposed they did have to stop the Blight—but how?

They could not even enter the Blight without growing severely ill and dying. If they could not even venture there, how could they ever hope to cure it? How could they ever hope to heal this land?

"Son of the Forest." The whisper was so faint he could barely hear it over the sound of his own breathing. "Hide yourself."

He took it as a warning, and in a panic dived underneath a great bush. He tried to quiet his breathing, and as he lay there, he saw shapes emerging from the woods, the color crimson, a scarred face, a pale face.

There were two of them: a man, a woman. The man was in a bright crimson cloak, the woman in a cloak of faded brown. The woman was fair and raven-haired; the man had curly brown hair and a face that appeared ritually scarred. It appeared they were looking for something, or for someone.

The bad men… that was what the trees had called these people. It was a reminder that he, Goni, Sinderion, Nenré, and Fortunato were not alone in this forest. As he watched the strangers searching for something, he wondered whether their presence had something to do with the Blight.

No… How could people cause such an evil to come into existence?

They were talking amongst themselves in a yapping language, strange to the ears, not Gallian or Zarube or any language Wrinn knew.

They were drawing near, very near indeed, and eventually Wrinn shut his mouth, and dared not breathe at all.

Yet they began shouting. He had been seen. The woman drew from her side a great curved dagger and the man took a trumpet in his hand.

Wrinn shot to his feet, bursting through the bush heedless of the thorns. He struck the trumpet with his quarterstaff and sent it flying. He lunged at the woman with his quarterstaff, who blocked the blow with her dagger, but moving swiftly, he struck several times in swift succession. Eventually he sent her flying to the ground.

The man now was running, shouting wildly at the top of his lungs. Wrinn darted after him as fast as his legs would take him.

And soon Wrinn was upon him, knocking him to the ground with a harsh blow. He began to pummel him relentlessly, showing him no mercy, beating him with the butt-end of his staff. And as the man lay there, unconscious, racked with pain, Wrinn remembered—the woman.

She came flying out of the bushes, diving for him, catching him off-guard and sending him to the ground. Wrinn's quarterstaff fell from his hands. She pulled out her curved dagger, growling like a wild beast, eyes blazing with unreasoning wrath. She laid the edge of the dagger upon Wrinn's neck and prepared to slash.

"Praise Lothan," she said in the Gallian tongue, holding Wrinn down. "I consecrate this sacrifice to him."

A great black shadow passed them by and she was thrown off him. An immense beast had ripped at her neck and thrown her to the ground.

And in a daze, blinking, Wrinn looked up, and saw that it was not just a beast but a wolf, not a wolf but one of the mighty Black Wolves, with night-black fur and pinkish eyes, and not just a black wolf but Fortunato's pet, Tyra Jade.

"Tyra!" Wrinn said, joy rising up in him.

Yet there was motion ahead. A figure appeared, dressed in forest green, brown of hair…

Sinderion! Goni appeared behind him.

Sinderion had nocked an arrow to his bow. He was aiming the

weapon at Tyra Jade. "A black wolf! Rokahn must be near."

Nenré and Fortunato came stumbling out of the brush. "Stop this, Sinderion! Tyra Jade will not harm you."

The great black wolf was growling, but her ears perked up when Fortunato appeared in sight.

"She is mine," Fortunato said. "I raised her from puppy-hood."

The brown-garbed woman was bleeding on the ground.

"You are full of surprises, Fortunato," Nenré said.

"And look," she continued, pointing to the beaten form of the red-garbed man. "One of these folk is alive. We have a captive. Goni, bind him! We take him back to camp."

~

The captive, tied in silken rope, was still not conscious when they returned to camp.

Tyra Jade placed her enormous self by the campfire and sat dutifully down. Nenré winced as she looked at her.

It would take some time, getting accustomed to the sight of her. It had taken Wrinn some time, too. But Tyra Jade was a noble beast, loyal, and she despised rokahn and the dark things of the world more fiercely than anyone Wrinn knew.

Fortunato knelt beside her and petted her softly. "She was barely the size of my hand when I found her… there was a litter abandoned in a mountain pass. Of the little whelps only she had survived."

"Perhaps," said Sinderion, rounding the edge of the campfire, "she is not fit for the presence of a lady."

"No, you are wrong," Nenré said. "If she is well tamed—"

"No black wolf can be well tamed," Sinderion said.

"She is as tame as an eager dog," Fortunato said, "except when I set her loose on an enemy. Nevertheless, you are right, Sinderion. It is best if she guards the perimeter of camp."

And he clucked, and Tyra Jade hopped up, then turned and ran and vanished into the greenery.

Eventually, all members of their party turned to the form beside them, the man in the bright red cloak whose face appeared ritually scarred, now bruised and battered and beaten by Wrinn's quarterstaff. He was mumbling unintelligibly. Wrinn was sure he had broken something on that man's body.

"And who are these people?" said Sinderion. "Who are they that stalk these woods?"

"Our luck is ill if we are not alone," said Goni. "Especially if we are outnumbered. These people were looking for us. They are searching for us."

"How do you know this?" said Nenré.

"I—I—" Goni began, but their attention was diverted by the captive cursing in his foreign tongue. He opened his eyes, blinking slowly. Then his eyes widened, full of terror, and Sinderion and Goni hurried over to him to restrain him. Nenré walked up to him, Fortunato and Wrinn just behind her.

The man screamed.

"*Adada ié!*" snapped Nenré, and her white staff went flying from the corner of the campfire into her hand. Light burst forth from the tip of the staff, white light, blinding light. Wrinn could scarcely see. She was like a figure of light, as brilliant as the sun, impossible to look upon. And the face of the captive was one of terror.

"From where do you hail?" Nenré's voice echoed.

"Ur," came his answer, the voice of a mouse and not a man, barely audible against the sounds of the forest.

"And whom do you serve?" Nenré said.

And for once there was no answer, no attempt to respond.

"Whom do you serve?" Nenré said and her voice carried like the voice of some supernal being, some being that had come down from above.

But the man only winced, and he bit his tongue, and he

struggled furiously in his bonds.

"Whom do you serve?" Nenré said one last time, and crudely struck him with her staff.

He yelped and said, "The Master!"

And the light began to fade, and the sounds of the forest became evident, the chirping of the birds, the distant dull trill of the frogs. And the sun shone, and the clouds drifted overhead, and it seemed, for a moment, there was peace.

"He is too hardened," Nenré said. "But even by his own words we see that he is a servant of the Dark One. He will not tell us what we need to know. There is no place to keep him here, but he may yet be of use. Sinderion and Goni… you know what to do. You must take him to Mensiré Camp where there are cells for holding. Leave at once."

"They are going?" Wrinn said.

That would leave Wrinn, Fortunato, and Nenré alone. She was a powerful sorceress, but the two warriors offered another layer of protection, one that could not be discounted in a forest filled with enemies.

"They will be gone a few days," Nenré said. "We will be alone. We must keep careful watch. And now we see that we are lucky to have Fortunato's beast with us."

~

The camp was dark, and a light drizzle was falling, not enough rain to squelch Fortunato's fire. Sinderion and Goni had long since departed to Mensiré Camp, wherever that was and however long it would take.

The mission was again at risk, and every day the Blight grew, and death spread. It had never seemed so hopeless.

"You know," said Wrinn in the light of the fire. "I was right. Those strangers in the wood confirmed it. There *is* a man named

Lothan among them."

Nenré gasped. "Where did you hear that name?"

Chapter Twenty-Seven: The Watches of the Night

The way Wrinn told it, Lothan was a person, just one among the many oddly-garbed strangers in the forest. But Fortunato could tell the name meant something more.

"Lothan," Nenré said. "A forgotten legend. One of the Enemy's greatest lieutenants, or so it is said.

"But I do not know much of him. I know his reappearance is a sign of the end."

"The end?" Wrinn said.

"All things must pass away, even this earth, this wood," Nenré said. "All things die. All things that have a beginning will have an end."

Nenré had removed her veil, allowing the red locks of her hair to be visible. Her eyes were brilliant, brilliant like the sea, and there was a ghostly pallor to her face, a deep inner radiance.

She was a great sorceress, but Fortunato could not help but feel they were not safe here, that even with her powers of magic they had fallen far short of securing this place. The camp was hidden from view, so that even Fortunato with his skills at the wild could not easily find it. With diligent effort, however, it could be discovered.

Tyra Jade could take on one, two, a dozen men, but with overwhelming numbers they would surely fall and be struck down. Who knew how many were with the man in red…

"One of us should keep watch all night," Fortunato said. "I will take the first watch, you, Wrinn, the second, Nenré the third."

"Very well," Nenré said. "We must be careful without my two companions here."

~

The fire had died to coals and Fortunato was wide awake, without any trace of fatigue or exhaustion. The chirping sounds of the forest made a haunting music. Fortunato had his bow in hand. He knew Tyra Jade would let them know if anyone was coming, but still Fortunato was prepared to sink an arrow into any attacker.

It was late and the night was deep, and the full moon was rising above the trees. Twigs crunched ahead, a dark shape appeared in the trees, and Fortunato began to shout and raise the alarm.

Why had Tyra Jade not warned him?

The figure came bursting through the brush and Fortunato already had an arrow pulled back on its string.

The wan moonlight showed the figure of Sinderion, who was wielding his saber. His face was speckled with blood. "The captive escaped. Goni has fallen. Albendir Camp is compromised."

Albendir—that was their own camp.

And calmly and swiftly, guarding against panic, Fortunato moved with haste and caution. One by one Nenré and Wrinn were awoken, and with only the sparest of explanation Fortunato ordered their departure.

Under cover of night, they left the safety and provisions of camp; and under cover of night, a dark shadow joined them: Tyra Jade, Fortunato's best companion and friend.

Chapter Twenty-Eight: What's in a Name?

The sun was rising over Gallia, and in Reev's upper-story room in Rosetree Manor, he could see the light sparkle on the tile roofs of the mansions below. The city stretched into the distance, and ever-visible was the immense tower, the Tower of Pythor, where Gastreel had spent most of his days. The wizards were meeting and the meeting would last more than a week. Reev wondered what they would discuss, what adventures they would announce, what knowledge and news from the far corners of the world they would bring.

He began to dress for the day, donning a black tunic of fine wool and trousers that were brown in color. He did not know how he would busy himself today, but he knew Gastreel did not want him to leave Rosetree Manor unless it was absolutely necessary, for fear of the strange men in town and for fear of Ivan Xandrast, the man who had been hunting him.

And so, when he descended the stairs and there was a knock on the door, Reev thought twice about opening it.

The knock was persistent, however, and so, with Doomblade propped against the wall, in sight, he carefully opened the door a crack and saw—to mixed delight and surprise—that Aunt Ramona was there, a woman he had wanted to get to know but had not for fear of rejection.

Her hair was raven black, like Reev's, and her eyes were light, almost silvery. She was dressed in a black dress of satin that was simple but clearly made of the finest materials, a rich woman's dress if Reev had ever seen one.

"Is Gastreel in?" she asked.

"No," Reev answered. "He is with the wizards."

"I suppose that isn't surprising," she said. "They are in town, after all."

"Is there any way I may help you?" Reev said.

"No, not help me," she said. "But it would be good to get to know you, nephew. Do you have a spare moment to come to Sunstone Manor?"

"Yes. Yes, I suppose I do," Reev said, and though he remembered Gastreel's warning, this was his aunt; he had nothing to fear from her.

And quietly he left, and he shut the door, and Rosetree Manor was behind him.

~

It was a warm midsummer day. Here in Wodenscross Court, everyone was well dressed in satins, in brocades, and in other fine fabrics. It was a place where the rich and the well-connected lived, on Galiope's high, flat-topped hill. Every home, it seemed, was a mansion, and the shops here catered to the whims of the wealthy. On their way to Sunstone Manor, they passed a jeweler and a vintner, a goldsmith and a maker of trinkets. The roads were clean and well swept, made of cobblestone, and the mansions were great edifices built of basalt or even limestone, crowned with sparkling tiles.

A long walk and Sunstone Manor appeared, a vast space with three stories, built of reddish-gold stone. "This," Aunt Ramona said, "is my home."

Beyond the gate, gardeners were hard at work tending to the plants. It seemed Aunt Ramona had the staff of servants that Gastreel—for moral reasons or whatever they were—would not stoop to. She was now a woman without a husband. Reev wondered what his uncle the count would have been like.

"It is beautiful," Reev said, and he could see that many of the windows—like in Gastreel's manor—were of glass, not horn like so many in Galiope. They had a shade of almost blue, as if they were crystal.

~

A fountain was bubbling in the great yard. The servants were dutifully going about their business, one sweeping the walkway, another trimming the bushes, a few others watering the flowers.

Aunt Ramona seemed used to opulence. Her husband, after all, was a count from the west, from Zarubain. Yet that marriage, she said, had been annulled. What, Reev wondered, was "annulled"?

They sat down at a table outside that overlooked a row of roses and tulips. "Amée," Aunt Ramona said, and a red-haired servant who was trimming the hedges looked up. "Cakes and water."

And like a dutiful servant she left her place and hurried inside, and Reev would be lying if he said that the sight of it didn't make him uncomfortable.

"How old are you, Reev?" Aunt Ramona asked.

"Fifteen, now," Reev answered. His birthday had passed in quiet anonymity, with no celebration.

"Fifteen years ago…" said Aunt Ramona, and there was a dark tone on the edge of her words. "I was still in Galiope then. By that time, your father had disappeared."

"Disappeared?"

"Your mother was gone, I do not know to where. The city was in turmoil. It was the time of the Great Scare. Everyone had great conspiracies in their minds that the city was in the hands of demoniacs."

"Demoniacs?"

"Devotees of the Dark One," Ramona Nax said. "But things quieted down. By that time, I had not seen your mother in months. I was spending a lot of time in Sunstone Manor then… not going in, not going out."

"You lived here then?" Reev said.

"The manors of Wodenscross Court cannot be bought or sold.

"A young man left this manor to Simeon, to your father, in his will… and that young man died soon after. When Simeon disappeared, it went to me." A slight smile grew on her face. "But do not worry about the details. Just know that you are always welcome here."

Reev thought property rights went from father to son. But he did not care. He did not want Sunstone Manor, or any manor. He only wanted to know more from Aunt Ramona, more about his family, his past.

"And what of you?" Aunt Ramona said. "I knew Nimue was with child, that I would have a nephew or niece, but when I left for the west I never knew what became of you."

Nimue… And Reev realized, at the end of it all, how strange it was he had not known his mother's name. Sometimes he thought he'd dream of her at night, a warm and kind face, fair of hair, with dark brows against her eyes.

"What became of me?" Reev paused. "Well, I don't rightly know. Gastreel was there, with me, for most of my life, in Norwood. He hardly told me anything."

He hadn't—and now Reev began to resent it.

"Norwood," Aunt Ramona said. "A name I'd never heard of before—"

Amée the servant girl came walking up to them, a silver ewer of water in her right hand, a platter of pastries in the other. The pastries were of all colors, some covered in frosting, some drizzled with honey or dipped in toasted sugar. Amée laid the two items down before them and promptly left without a word from Ramona.

"I had a question," Reev said as Aunt Ramona poured him a glass of water and he took a pink pastry in his hand. "My name… What sort of name is Reev Nax?"

"What sort of name?" Aunt Ramona seemed amused by the question. But that amusement quickly vanished, and she grew somber. "What sort of name indeed. What sort of name is Simeon?

"I named your cousin Asher after his great-uncle, rest his soul. I was lucky not to have a family name. But if you want that question answered, you'd have to go to the High Country and talk to your pappy Kal. You'd have to go back up to Winter Ridge."

"Our family," Reev asked, "is from the mountains?"

"Father never forgave us for leaving the High Country," Aunt Ramona said.

Dark clouds were moving in from the west.

"Simeon wanted more than Winter Ridge. So did I. But your pappy Kal was always paranoid, always thinking someone was out to get us," Aunt Ramona said. "We left together, Simeon and I. Father was spitting mad. But it turned out well for us… at least until the Great Scare. At least until Simeon disappeared."

"How did he disappear?" Reev said.

Ramona looked up. "It looks ready to rain. Will you come inside?"

"No," Reev said, "I think I'd best hurry back to Rosetree Manor. Gastreel will be angry."

"So be it. A nice meeting, for certain. But don't let Gastreel hold you back, Reev. Don't let him control you like he did Simeon."

"Control me?" Reev began, but it was too late, the winds were picking up, the air had taken on a cold character.

He stood up, and Aunt Ramona grabbed the plate of pastries and the silver ewer.

"Oh," Aunt Ramona said, pausing despite the change in weather. "I forgot to mention.

"Someone came by Sunstone Manor last evening. Said he was looking for you. Said his name was Mr. Endicott. I told him you were with Gastreel, so you might expect a visit from him."

~

Mr. Endicott, Mr. Endicott…

It was a false name if Reev had ever heard of one, and as he hurried home through the whipping rain and the flashes of lightning, he realized he was not safe in Rosetree Manor anymore. No, he was not safe. Could Ivan Xandrast have followed him here? It was likely widespread knowledge that Aunt Ramona had returned, and that Reev was her relation.

He cursed his luck and hoped against hope he'd be protected, hoped against hope that he would be able to keep himself alive.

On his way back to Rosetree Manor, Reev caught sight for the first time one of the strangers that Glenda mentioned, a man whose face was ritually scarred, with a keen scimitar hanging from his belt.

Reev was not safe.

No, he was not safe.

Chapter Twenty-Nine:
4 Night Owl Way

One afternoon, a small, dark form stumbled into the Dragonpaw Inn's great hall, and Ambrass's heart sank.

It was Bala, and his oversized clothes looked dirty. The top hat that hung uneasily from his head was edged with grime.

"Bala Rabaam!" she said. "Where have you been?"

He did not look upset or rattled. Whatever had happened to him did not seem to bother him. He seemed to be in good spirits, even great spirits. He appeared almost chipper.

And in an instant, Glenda was there, and there was a look of shock on her face, then a look of worry.

"Ambrass," she said, "get a bath ready."

~

And at last, it was done, Ambrass first drawing a bath and heating the water bucketful by bucketful in the hearth, Glenda furiously washing Bala's clothing with soap and then hanging them to dry in the Dragonpaw's backyard garden.

And as they hurried to and fro with Bala watching, sometimes giggling with amusement, Glenda pulled Ambrass aside and said: "You know what this means. You must take him back to his father."

In the garden, away from Bala's ears, Ambrass gasped. "Why can't you do it? You are the proprietor of the inn.

"And why must we take him back? Nocturne is negligent… a poor father."

"He is," Glenda said, "but there are laws in place, and customs that must be followed. Bala is still under Nocturne's guardianship. You must take him back."

"And why me? Why can't you do the terrible deed?" Ambrass said.

"Because," Glenda said, then she seemed to clam up. "I… I… When he was on trial, I was a witness. I am forbidden to go near his house."

"Why hadn't you told me this?" Ambrass said. "And why will we take Bala back into danger? It isn't right. None of this is right."

Beyond the window, Ambrass thought she heard Bala giggling.

"The clothes are dry," Glenda said, curtly, matter-of-factly, with all the finality and command of a military officer. And she took the clothes off the line, and gathered them together, and shoved them into Ambrass's hands. "You are my friend. You are also my worker. You must do what the law requires and take him back."

~

Ambrass had been to Lonen Town only a few times before, in passing, and that section of Galiope—home to elves of the Lonen tribe—was not a safe place to be at night. There were still a few hours of light in the long summer day, and as she walked hurriedly she tried to take note of the time that elapsed, the number of minutes it would take to get back home.

She told Bala what was happening for his own sake, and Bala did not seem to be bothered. He seemed to have a cunning streak, and Ambrass wondered if his fear of his father was at least partially an act. She crossed the Bridge-O'er-Galios in the late afternoon light. Her feet had grown sore from walking. She was beginning to feel tired.

And then, like that, they were in the quarter of Galiope known as Lonen Town, and it was as if they were instantly in another world, another nation. The homes and tenements had white plaster facing, and their curved roofs were lined with shiny purple tile. The oval windows at the tops of the buildings were cross-hatched with iron bars, and throughout the immaculately clean streets were pallid elves with dark hair and eyes, who at worst scowled at Ambrass as she walked by and at best ignored her, as if she wasn't even there.

Glenda's instructions had been exact, but it was still difficult to make sense of them, to follow them perfectly. The street where Nocturne lived was little better than an alley, his home a narrow apartment, a subsection of a house.

"Turn," Glenda had said, "where you see the Bloodmoon Inn, and you will find yourself on Night Owl Way."

It was late afternoon. The rains of the day had ceased, and the air was warm when she saw the inn, a small thing of two stories faced with a wooden porch. She looked past it and saw an alley that the sun did not reach, a narrow street where carts could not fit, surrounded in its entirety by high homes and apartments. There, down the lane, were tenements, and as she looked upon the shady path, Ambrass could not help but feel a tingle of fear, a terrible touch of anticipation. Why was she here? For Bala? No. She was here because she had been sent; because Glenda had demanded she do this.

And so she bit her lip, and she braced herself. "Are you ready for this, Bala?"

"Yes, Miss Ambrass!" said Bala, and there wasn't even a hint of fear in his voice.

Bala, it seemed, was braver than his caretaker.

~

The apartment with a blue door, as Glenda had described it, was two stories high, thin but tall, and above there was a balcony with a wooden banister. In front of the door were several barrels and crates, and in front of that door a red rug, a rug whose color reminded her awfully of blood. And Ambrass took a few tentative steps, with fear suddenly filling her.

But Bala scrambled ahead and pounded on the door with his little fist.

Ambrass hurried over, trying to gather herself, trying to shake off the fear that was growing all over her body, causing her knees to weaken, causing her skin to break out in a cold sweat.

Bala was pounding so loud it echoed throughout all of Night Owl Way.

"Quiet, Bala!" Ambrass said. "I don't think he is home. We must go back."

And as if she had made some dark evocation, the door opened a crack, then wide, and a figure appeared, one whose eyes were red, one whose black hair was uncharacteristically tousled.

It was Nocturne Rabaam, Bala's father, perhaps the High Street Slasher.

And though Ambrass felt guilty about leaving Bala with him, she wanted to turn, to run away. And yet she didn't. She remained there, putting on an outward face of calm, trying to remain stone-faced and statue-like in Nocturne's presence.

Nocturne had been asleep, yes, asleep in the late afternoon. "Hello, there, Bala," Nocturne said. "Come inside."

Bala's chipper confidence evaporated. He stood still and looked at Ambrass and blinked slowly, as if he were waiting for her permission or something.

At that point Nocturne took note of her, looking at her in astonishment. "Hello there," he said. He opened the door wide then dabbed at his hair, he who had just awoken. "Ambrass, isn't it? From the Dragonpaw. Thank you for returning my child to me. Say, why don't you come inside for a bit? Have you ever tasted true elven wine, from *telanni* grapes? The Gallians call it Gerusivel."

"No, thank you," Ambrass began, starting to inch away.

"Please, Miss Ambrass, don't leave me," Bala said.

And Ambrass was aghast at how the little toddler was roping her in. She couldn't say no, now. It was as if they worked as a team.

But that, she knew, was not true. Bala was as innocent as they came, a product of an unfortunate union—human and vampire—one that likely never should have come to be.

It was a clean home with white plaster walls, a fine rug of animal fur, floors of tile—neat enough, beautiful even, but as Ambrass examined it, she could see it was without a woman's touch. A small table was near the door, with two chairs, and as Bala waddled in, Nocturne knelt down and said, "Why don't you go to your room?"

Glenda said he had made Bala sleep outside, that he had been totally negligent. But Bala dutifully did as his father had asked, disappearing down the hallway.

"Bala," Ambrass said, and she could feel her own cold breath, "is your son."

"He is," Nocturne said. "He has sure turned out well, considering who his mother is."

Bala seemed happy enough, but saying he had turned out well was more than Ambrass would grant.

She looked up. Nocturne had disappeared, vanishing through the door.

Ambrass was stuck in place. Should she leave without saying goodbye, just hurriedly run out the door and end this awkward charade?

But she found herself paralyzed, standing there alone, not moving, not walking away, immobilized from indecision.

And as soon as he was gone he was back, now carrying a bottle of wine, purple in color, and two glasses of sparkling crystal, which he promptly set down on the door-side table.

What a strange predicament she had found herself in, and she found herself questioning everything, the absurdity of the moment, the strained awkwardness of words unsaid. "I— I—"

"I must be going," she wanted to say but she did not say those words; instead she looked on helplessly as Nocturne poured two glasses of wine, and as he poured the liquid it fizzed and bubbled.

The wine, what he called elven wine, was colored pink.

By now the redness of his eyes was gone, his inky-black hair not quite so tousled.

She should have made a quick escape, while he was gone, said nothing and run for the hills. But no, she was sitting down. No, she was taking the crystal cup in her hands. No, she could not leave for fear of being rude, for fear of his wrath. And no, she was taking a sip of the elven wine, and it tasted good.

"It is delicious," Ambrass said.

"The grapes grow only on the coast of Lamdar," Nocturne said. "Even in other parts of the Elven World it is very expensive."

"How expensive?" Ambrass said.

"This bottle set me back two crowns," Nocturne said.

Ambrass spit some of the wine back into her cup. Two gold crowns was more than she would likely see in a month. "Two crowns?"

"Two crowns," Nocturne said. "So I'm glad you like it."

"I like it," Ambrass said again, this time quieter, this time more resistant. And she realized where she was, and who she was talking to. And she thought of going home. At the first opportunity, she would.

"You," Nocturne said, "are from Selwyn's Parish?"

"How did you know that?" Ambrass said, perhaps more harshly than was warranted.

"Most people like you are," Nocturne said.

People like her—gypsies.

"I'm glad to see some of you showing your faces in other parts of the city," Nocturne said.

The conversation wasn't going well but the elven wine truly was sublime, a mixture of sweet and savory, bubbling in her tongue as she sipped it. She looked at Nocturne, dark eyed, his hair black and slightly ruffled. She could see some of Bala's features in him; they looked similar save for Bala's white-blond hair.

She could see that he was strong, that through his tunic there were signs of a fine physique. But she knew he was dangerous, the High Street Slasher, Glenda's nemesis, and that she had better go.

"I had better go," she wanted to say, but no, she was staying put, staying still.

The wine cup was almost empty; soon she'd be able to break away, make a run for it.

And Nocturne—was he devious—began to pour a little more into her cup.

"That's enough," Ambrass said. "I think I've had my fill."

Was this how he plied Bala's mother? Was this how he wormed his way into her life? With her mind plied by alcohol, did he then attempt to corrupt her? Was that how the union came to be?

It would not be her; no, it would not be her.

The sunlight was shining in Nocturne's dark eyes. She took another sip. "And what of you, Nocturne? What do you, well… do?"

Nocturne smiled, and the smile frightened her. "I am a cook and a part owner of the Bloodmoon Inn."

She wondered how a cook could afford a two-crown bottle of wine, even if he were the part owner of the Bloodmoon.

"You and I are similar, Ambrass," Nocturne said. "We have a similar story. Our people are not from here."

"I should be going"—it was on the tip of Ambrass's tongue this time, and she was just a moment from saying it.

"You, one of the wandering folk; I, one of the druen."

Druen—what was that? Ambrass decided not to ask, but on further thought she guessed it was the proper term for vampire.

"I was born," Nocturne began, and Ambrass did not want to hear it, "far north of here, so far north you cannot get any farther, a place where the sun will not set for weeks on end in the summer and in the winter there is an entire month of night. Nardur is not for the faint hearted. I left there and eventually came to this place, where I was welcomed."

Her cup was almost finished, and then she could go.

"You… you and I are not so different."

"I was born here," Ambrass insisted. "I know nothing other than Galiope."

"Galiope," Nocturne said. "The Queen of the North. But do you know all of it?"

She took her last sip.

"Will you go on a walk with me?" Nocturne said.

What was she doing? Was she really not resisting? Was she really not saying, "No"? She was getting up, yes, she was getting up, but she was not refusing. She was going on a walk with him through the streets of Lonen Town.

What kind of person had she become?

~

Underneath the curved roofs of purple tile she walked, openly, with Nocturne at her side, and what few faces she saw now acknowledged her presence and scowled at her no more, at worst having expressions of barely-disguised amusement. *Yet another,* the faces said, *yet another falling into Nocturne's nets.*

But she had not fallen into any net. No, she hadn't, at least not now. She had been roped into this situation, unintentionally, by the little child she had so tirelessly cared for.

"Have you been to this part of town before?" said Nocturne.

"Only briefly," Ambrass answered. "Never for this length of time."

It was getting late; the sun was low in the horizon. It would set soon. She should think of getting back, but she had gotten herself into a dangerous situation, one she could not easily extricate herself from.

Eventually they came to a vista that overlooked the River

Galios below. And she found herself laughing lightly, though she did not know why.

"What is so funny?" Nocturne said. "Have I amused you?"

"What sort of name is Nocturne?" Ambrass asked. It was the first thing that came to mind.

"Nocturne," he said, "is a translation. *Dr'alynthi* is, 'night-song.' I call myself Nocturne to help you humans. My real name is Dr'alynthi Gangimmi Emorthi Drethuli Rabaam."

"That is a lot of names," Ambrass said, and she found herself giggling, though she did not want to.

Nocturne grabbed her hand, and his grip was strong, and fire seemed to course through her veins. "What sort of name is Ambrass?"

"An old name of the gypsy folk," she answered. "It means 'woman.' "

Or "lover," but she would not tell Nocturne that, not now.

They continued their walk, and Nocturne did not relinquish his grip, and Ambrass was disappointed at her own weakness, for she did not resist him or put up much of a fight, though she very much did not want Nocturne's hand on her own.

Was Nocturne so bad? Was he as terrible as Glenda insisted he was? Were there good attributes he had as well?

They did a lap around Nocturne's neighborhood, and Ambrass no longer cared about the curious looks of strangers. She felt a fire running through her, a fire she had not felt in months, and when they again reached Nocturne's blue door, she knew it was time to go home, and the thought she was disappointed confounded her.

"I must go," Ambrass said. "It's going to get dark…"

"I know," Nocturne said. "But before you go, take this."

From one of his pockets he took out a white flower, a chrysanthemum. "I took this from the forest. I thought you should have it."

"I… I…" Ambrass did not know what to do or what to say,

but again she helplessly watched herself take it, and grip it in her hands.

"Goodbye, Ambrass," Nocturne said, and she feared it was not the last she would see of him.

"Goodbye," she said, and headed off as the sun set in dazzling colors over the city buildings.

~

When she got back to the Dragonpaw, she deftly hid the chrysanthemum under one of her sleeves. Glenda appeared alarmed.

"You've been gone a long time," she said.

"I have," Ambrass said. "Bala wouldn't settle down. I had to be there with him, calm him down."

"Poor little child," Glenda said.

And as Ambrass left for her bedchamber, there seemed to be something on the tip of Glenda's tongue.

"I'm sorry for doing that to you, Ambrass," she said.

And Ambrass turned with a smile on her face. "Don't worry about it, Glenda," she said. "You did what you thought was best."

~

In her bed she laid the chrysanthemum, underneath her pillow, so that no one would find it.

"Dr'alynthi," she said aloud as she prepared to go to sleep.

What sort of name was Dr'alynthi Gangimmi Emorthi Drethuli Rabaam?

Chapter Thirty:
The Sundering

Dark was the night, and the clouds that wreathed the moon were like smoke.

Sinderion was trying to lead the party to another elven camp, one that had not been discovered, but Fortunato wondered if the gambit was unwise. He, Nenré, Sinderion, and Wrinn were alone, and the trek would be dangerous indeed, and now that an elven camp had been discovered, the strangers in the woods would be searching for others.

They were hiding in the bushes, all of them, together. Tyra Jade was following somewhere behind, keeping her distance but watching over them from afar, ready at any moment to go into a frenzy with punishing bites and scratches.

Sinderion said he heard one of the strangers nearby and it was easy to believe: the prior day had proven that they were crawling through the forest by the hundred, like a foreign army invading the South Weald.

In the dim light, far away, on a high hill crowned with birches, color appeared against the light of the moon, a shadowy figure riding by on a horse, her body covered in a hooded cloak. Behind her were more, several dozen of the strangers in a procession, men and women. Sinderion made a motion for everyone to keep quiet, and together, they watched the cavalcade ride by.

The woods were not safe, and Fortunato did not trust Sinderion's judgment. The woods were not safe, and Nenré and Wrinn were in danger.

"How far," Fortunato said at a whisper—a harsh whisper but a whisper, "to Danali Camp?"

Sinderion turned. "Hush," said Sinderion's murderous eyes.

A dark shape appeared just ahead, a tall figure just feet away Fortunato had not seen, and a trumpet blew, and then a chorus of trumpets.

Pandemonium broke free as if a seal had opened, Sinderion leaping forth and, after a few swipes, impaling the man with his saber. There was the sound of galloping hooves, then a deafening whinny, and Fortunato drew back, farther into the bushes.

Sinderion was now engaged in a melee with a rider on a horse.

Nenré staggered forward with her staff and Fortunato drew even farther back. He nocked an arrow to his bowstring, pulled back, prepared to shoot.

And the rider on the horse struck a dolorous blow, and Sinderion's severed head went flying from his body. The body collapsed to the ground, and Nenré wailed in agony, broken-hearted, overcome with despair.

Nenré was now in the clearing, clearly seen, and the wicked men were coming in from all corners. Fortunato remained silent and still in the bushes. He could not overcome so many foes.

Nenré had dropped her staff. She rose, placing her hands above her head, and the wicked men by the dozen were filtering in from the clearing, on this most black and terrible night. They were shouting in their foreign tongue, their words indistinguishable, indiscernible to others.

The moon was a pale mistress overhead, the clouds veiling it and unveiling it in quick succession, and a swift, cool wind was gusting through the forest.

"You, woman," said a man's cruel voice, crudely speaking the Gallian tongue. "Are you and your friend alone?"

"Yes," said Nenré, "it was Sinderion and I and no others. No one else came with me."

She was convincing, and Fortunato would have believed her if he had been one of the wicked men.

"Bind her!" said the cruel voice.

One figure took her staff. Others, Gallian traitors judging by their unscarred faces and their tunics and trousers, crudely cinched her hands with rope.

"We take her to Milik for questioning!" the voice said once more.

There was the sound of hooves like a storm; Fortunato was now crouching. It was up to him and Wrinn to save her.

Wrinn… Where was Wrinn? He was gone. Had he slipped away?

Thunderous were the hooves, terrible was the sound of shouting. Seconds turned to minutes, minutes to hours. Fortunato remained still, fading in and out of sleep.

Dawn was spreading its light over the forest. He was alone.

Nenré was gone, and so was Wrinn.

Chapter Thirty-One:
Son of the Forest

At a river, Wrinn stopped his flight. The sky was gold and red.

He stooped down, cupped his hands in the cold water and took a drink. He had run, and the gods smiled on him, for he was alive, he was safe, and he was breathing free.

The water refreshed him, the cool stream that babbled by the stones. The memory of last night's horror was still all about him, lingering over him like a hungry ghost.

"Son of the Forest," a tree whispered, but he was tired and he didn't want to hear it. All he could think about was his own survival, evading the wicked men who had defeated them.

"Son of the Forest," the tree said, "look to your right."

And he did so, and saw there, growing by the banks of the river, a great bounty of mushrooms, dense brown mushrooms that he recognized as good to eat.

At the sight of them he realized how hungry he was, how famished, how empty his stomach was. And he hurried over to them, the brown caps just barely visible in the morning light.

He helped himself to them one by one, and as his hunger began to ease, other things rose to the fore of his mind. The horror of the night began to reverberate in his mind. Fortunato was in danger. Nenré was in danger. Sinderion had fallen and so had Goni.

And as his body gathered strength, as his hunger faded, he began to despair at the lost cause. Like a coward, he had run, darting away at the first sight of danger. And now he was alone, helpless by himself in the woods, completely lost, not knowing where he was or where he would go now.

He had betrayed his friend.

Or had he? As long as he was alive, he would try to find him.

As long as he was alive he would try to rescue Fortunato, and also Nenré. He yet had his quarterstaff; there was some strength left in him.

He put his hand on one of the birch trees. In his mind he asked, *Where is he? Where is Fortunato?*

"Focus—" the whisper was deafening— "on the true problem. Worry not for your friend. The Blight grows every day. Every day millions of us die."

They would be of no use, these trees. All they cared about was themselves, their roots, their lives. They did not care that Wrinn's friend Fortunato was in danger, that the mission was at a loss, that it would be in their best interest for Wrinn to find him.

"I cannot do it alone," Wrinn said, aloud this time, as if the trees had ears, as if they understood the sound of his voice.

"You are not alone," the chorus of trees echoed in his mind, a thousand, a hundred thousand speaking at once. "You are not alone… we are with you."

"And the Blight will kill me if I enter it!" Wrinn said. "Just like it is killing you."

His voice echoed through the riverine valley. He wondered if the wicked men were nearby.

"It will kill me," Wrinn said. "I cannot help you. I wish I could, but I cannot. I can do no such thing…"

"You must," the trees were a haunting chorus, a chorus millions strong, speaking in one voice, their roots connected, their minds as one. "We will die if you do not help us, Son of the Forest."

"It will kill me!" Wrinn was shouting now, and if any of the wicked men were nearby, they would hear. "It will kill me! I am an elf! I am mortal!"

"The flower which blooms at night," the millions of trees said. "The flower which blooms in autumn. The flower which blooms when we begin to fade."

"*Sindomas,*" Wrinn said. "*Sindomas.* Is that the key?"

"The flower which purges poison from moving things," said the countless millions, all as one. Their voice in his head was like twisting wood, the shutting of a door, the rubbing of sticks together. "You must go. You must go now. We will lead you to the flowers which shall infuse your blood."

"Lead me to my friend," Wrinn said aloud, again, not at a shout this time. "Lead me to my friend, and I promise to you, I will do as you ask…"

"Let us confer," the trees said, a million as one, ten million as one voice. "Let us confer amongst ourselves."

Chapter Thirty-Two: Mr. Endicott

By day, Gastreel was gone.

By night, he was in Rosetree Manor.

But most of the time, Reev was by himself, alone, remembering the night at the inn, the night on the road, the night he had first met Ivan Xandrast.

Now that he had rejected his offer, Ivan Xandrast would want to harm him.

Upstairs, Reev was looking down upon the street, remembering what Aunt Ramona had said, that someone claiming to be "Mr. Endicott" had asked for him. And though there was no way to know for certain, with things going as they had, he was sure beyond surety that Ivan Xandrast had found his way to Galiope, that he had come into contact with Aunt Ramona, that now—with Reev locked inside the house of a powerful wizard—he was waiting for the perfect moment to strike.

Reev had some skill with Doomblade, but he was no master swordsman. Fortunato had taught him a little and he had fought in the Battle of Galiope. But against a skilled warrior he would be no match. Against Ivan Xandrast's saber, he'd scarcely be a challenge.

The streets below were largely empty, but every once in a while, someone would appear. He was in the richest part of Galiope, and it was also the safest part. Not everyone was allowed into Wodenscross Court, but Ivan Xandrast was no doubt a master of deception, a cunning person that could easily slither his way past the guards.

Reev knew it was the last day of the wizards' meetings. After today, Gastreel would be home during the day, and they could confront Ivan Xandrast together. After today, Reev would be protected, and Ivan Xandrast's efforts would become all the more difficult to accomplish. Tonight, when Gastreel arrived home, there would be a new order of things, and Reev would be able to breathe easy again.

But for now, he was not able to breathe easy; for now, he was watching the street, not taking his eyes off it, from the upper story window. The days had not been kind to his fears. He seemed to be growing more and more anxious as this "Mr. Endicott," that is, Ivan Xandrast, refused to show himself.

Slumped against the window he sat, watching, waiting. He had slept hardly at all last night. The aristocrats of Wodenscross Court walked by, the men in their doublets and fine breeches, the women in their billowing gowns and cauls or chaplets. Every once in a while a guard would pass by on the street, or several of them at one time, giving Reev a bit of well needed comfort. Doomblade was slumped against his chest, and he was leaning against the window. The blinking of his eyes turning to winking, the winking to long periods shut.

~

He woke to a loud noise, a great cracking sound. Outside, the late afternoon sun was shining in gold colors over the empty street.

He took up Doomblade, his hand quivering, his breath shallow with fear. The sound had been thunderous, like the cracking of wood, the breaking of a door. Was he no longer alone?

He stepped outside the upper-story room, going to the very threshold of the stairs. And he stayed put, and he remained silent, and he listened.

He heard nothing. All was silent… and then, a footstep.

Reev put aside his fears, running down the stairs to confront Ivan Xandrast, Mr. Endicott, or whatever name he chose to use today. He tried to cloak himself in the same bravery he'd used in the Battle of Galiope, but his hand was trembling as it held Doomblade, and he feared whatever occurred next would be unlike it, more terrible, more grave.

Carefully and quietly, like some masterful warrior, he went through Rosetree Manor room by room. He peered into the great hall where the hearth was and saw that its ashes and embers had turned cold. He peered into the study, into the two rooms that had been set aside as libraries. He peered into Gastreel's bedchamber and then the unused servants' quarters.

Then he headed toward the kitchen, which led into the garden.

The door had been broken, and standing there amid the tiles of the floor and the implements of cooking was Ivan Xandrast.

He seemed changed, wounded yet more terrible for being wounded. There were marks on his face and great gouges on his arms, as if he had been tortured. There were marks on his wrists where manacles had been tightened.

And he clutched in his hand some sort of polearm, a metal rod in its center, and on either side of the rod his sabers had been fixed. It was one of the double-bladed swords Reev had read about, the ancient butterfly blade. Using it well was something only a master swordsman could do.

"Mr. Endicott," Reev said.

Ivan Xandrast's deceptions had not worked, and Reev wanted him to know it.

"You came to the house of my aunt," Reev said, "badgered her for information. Tried to lay a trap for me…"

"Lay a trap?" There was a madness in Ivan Xandrast's eyes, a deep unsettlement. Reev had seen that look in the insane, in people who could not take care of themselves. "I laid no trap. I followed you here. I challenged you like a brave champion, like a great knight, according to the rules of honor.

"You call yourself the Hand of the Gods, well, I am a Hand as well, the Hand of Master Lothan, his fighter in the mortal realm.

And by his might, I sentence you to die, Reev Nax, for refusing his most generous offer."

It was as if the mouth that spoke was not his own, that the words that came out sprang from another source. It was as if Ivan Xandrast had been taken charge of by a spirit, as if there was a deep darkness that dwelt in him, one that would not be easily purged.

"The gods will protect me," said Reev.

"No, no," Ivan Xandrast said. "The Master laid his hand upon your own; now the gods despise you. They will not aid you. They will consider you unclean, beyond help."

"No," Reev said, "no, they won't." And despair was mixed with fear as the sensation returned, the fiery feeling on his hand, the imprint of a grip.

And Ivan Xandrast jerked forward, and Reev jerked back. A flurry of blows met Reev, in such swift succession that he almost dropped Doomblade. Several slashes had come within a hair of his throat. Ivan Xandrast was a master indeed, a master of the sword, a master of the butterfly blade.

The fiery grip, the imprint flared. Such pain filled Reev's hand he began to lose his grasp on Doomblade. He cried out in agony; he called on the gods but there was no answer.

"Who are you, Ivan Xandrast?" Reev said. "Why do you wish to harm me?"

"Accept Master Lothan's offer," said Ivan Xandrast. "Accept the offer and I shall not harm you. This is your last chance.

"Help him unseat Seymus and then, then you shall reign in darkness, Reev."

And with a wild cry, one that came from deep within, Reev took Doomblade in his throbbing hand and struck at Ivan Xandrast in furious succession, flinging all his strength and all his energy at him, and drove him from the hallway back into the kitchen, through the broken door, into the garden.

But Ivan Xandrast deftly struck, and Doomblade went flying,

and clattered to the ground.

Ivan Xandrast dropped the butterfly blade and drew from his pockets a black metal shard. He tackled Reev to the ground and plunged the metal shard into Reev's forearm, where Lothan's grip still lingered. The pain was infernal, and it burned at his skin. The pain was beyond words; it was beyond belief.

And Reev found himself curling into a ball, his eyes watering in pain, overcome with agony. He winced as he sat up, full of unspeakable torment. Ivan Xandrast was gone, had disappeared through the hedges.

Chapter Thirty-Three: Necromancy

It was the final day of the meeting of the council. Much had been discussed, countless hours of poring over the news of the world and making decisions on this or that bit of minutiae.

And for the last time in the year 1152, the wizards had assembled in the top story of the Tower of Pythor. Gastreel still had Bala on his mind.

He had begun to realize that, though he had tried to pick loyalists, there were certain attitudes that were endemic among the wizards, and certain topics where he would not be able to push his will on them.

All wizards had spoken their final words, the White Wizard, the Blue Wizard, the Gold Wizard and everyone… everyone except the Green Wizard, the archwizard himself.

"Wise men of the council," Gastreel said, "we have at last one more decision to make.

"I will not go against your collective instruction. This body is built upon consensus. But I bring up again the matter of the iron masks the Servants of Seymus wore.

"The wizard order has been purged of necromancers, ever since Jerek the Black became a renegade. No petitioners have been accepted. Those necromancers already at work have lost their rank.

"But only necromancy can halt what necromancy began. This Bala—"

"Have we not told you what we thought?" said Lydia of the White Robes. "With repetition you will only anger us and further drive us away, Archwizard."

In the end, an archwizard was only as powerful as his allies on the council. Gastreel had come to learn this. Where Syrion, the last archwizard, had been able to cajole and gain control of his eleven associates, Gastreel, it seemed, was not capable of such presence and speechcraft.

"And yet," said Elothiel of the Starry Robes, and the stars on his blue robe seemed to fluoresce. He stood up. He was tall, a giant of a man, and his long white beard was interspersed with black. "And yet perhaps, Gastreel's words are not those of a fool. Indeed, who of us here knows how to destroy Jerek's spell? How by fire or ice can we end the magic of death? The Servants of Seymus must never be allowed to reconstitute. We must never again allow them false life."

"And this young boy," Lydia the White Wizard said, "how will he learn? Who will teach him? There are no necromancers anymore, none that are left."

"There is one," Gastreel said, and the council hushed.

The name was one all knew, but one that had largely been purged from memory. One necromancer did remain, a wizard who lived among the hills and crags of the land of Palaskov, a wizard of the Black Robes.

"Aleksander," Lydia said. "Surely not…"

"If we do allow this," Elothiel said, "if we do agree… who else is there left to teach him?"

Hearts were being softened; minds were being opened. Would a necromancer again be allowed into the wizard order? Would Bala become the first in many decades?

Chapter Thirty-Four: Wounded

Reev was trembling, shaking, in a cold sweat, lying upon the floor, when the door to Rosetree Manor opened.

Gastreel was there, but it was too late; he had not protected his ward. He had not protected Reev.

He had failed.

"Reev Nax!" Gastreel's voice carried with magic as he ran desperately over to Reev's shaking form. "What is this? What has happened to you?"

But Reev, chattering, as cold as winter on this warm summer evening, could not speak even if he wanted to, so violent were these tremors, these pains.

Gastreel's eyes looked beyond, down the hallway, into the kitchen, at the broken door.

"Curses," he said. "I have failed you. I have failed you! I presided over the council and neglected what is most important. I failed you! I have failed you!"

But the fever and the violent shivering prevented thought, and Reev lay there in a pile, unable to do anything but suffer. The wound had done him in. The wound had done him in! He began to drift asleep.

~

Gastreel shook awake his young ward, overcome with guilt, overcome with fury. It had been madness to leave him unattended, madness and foolishness.

He looked about Reev's body, searching for the wound. And on Reev's left forearm he found it, a dark black mark, a mark edged with deep purple. What devilry was this? What fell weapon had made this mark?

He only knew, or greatly suspected, the one who had made it: Ivan Xandrast, the man lost to the pages of history but who had reemerged. And who was this Ivan Xandrast? How had he done this to Reev? How had he made this wound, and was it in Gastreel's power to heal it?

"A curse on your house, Ivan Xandrast," said Gastreel, though Ivan Xandrast was now long gone and night was beginning to set in over the city of Galiope.

Gastreel scooped Reev's slight form into his own hands. He was quivering and he had lost consciousness.

"Wake up," he said softly.

"Wake up," he said again, and infused his words with magic.

And Reev's eyes opened. He was trembling, and it was clear he was having a difficult time breathing.

"Stay awake," Gastreel said. "Try to remain conscious. You may never wake again if you go to sleep."

And carrying him, Gastreel wondered just what he should do next. How could Reev be healed? What medicine would reverse this fell wound? And what indeed had caused it?

What had caused it? He looked again at the black mark, edged in purple, and saw that it was growing, not shrinking. He touched it gently and in his mind's eye saw fire and blood.

Chapter Thirty-Five: Pursuit

For two days and two nights, Fortunato had followed the tracks of the wicked men. For two days and two nights, he had followed their, and hopefully Nenré's trail. What had happened to Wrinn? He suspected he had run away. But for now, at this very moment, he could only afford to think of Nenré.

He crouched down on the forest floor. The morning light was filtering green through the trees. He bent over some grass and saw that it had been trodden upon, and the tracks had been left merely hours ago, at worst. He was gaining on them. Soon he would be upon them, the party that had stolen away Nenré. And then what? Could he overcome them then? He would try… at an opportune moment, an arrow through the neck, a sword thrust through the chest in the dark.

He had followed the forest's contours through valleys and ridges, under sunlit hollows and past trackless swamps. He had eaten the last of the road-bread, but he could not afford to think of hunger now. The bits of food he'd stashed away from Albendir Camp were gone now.

And Sinderion had fallen, Sinderion and Goni, two warriors, the king's best. And Wrinn… Wrinn.

How would Fortunato find him now? If, supposing the impossible, he managed to rescue Nenré, he would not depart these woods without his friend.

He looked up. By his own instinct, he rolled under some great ferns. He remained still; he held his breath.

There was talking up ahead, two shadowy figures, speaking to each other. Their strange tongue he could not understand, but quietly he remained still, not moving, his hand ready to draw

Amenhir in a moment's span. He would not suffer the same fate as Sinderion and Goni. These wicked men would learn to fear him.

From the shadows another joined them, and as Fortunato waited, his eyes began to adjust to the light, and things came into focus.

The one who had joined them was not of them. He was a Gallian, wearing a tunic and trousers, brown-haired, blue-eyed, and Fortunato, for some reason, thought he had seen that face before, that it was one he knew, one that was even familiar. But he could not place it. He did not know where or even if he truly had seen that face before.

A word distinguished itself from the forest sounds, a word from their far-off conversation: "Milik."

"—killing us—" he heard another.

"—killed ten men—"

"The wild thing."

"Careful… be careful."

The leaves hid Fortunato, the green leaves of the ferns. He tried to listen as best he could, but even remaining still, they were far-off, and he could not hear everything.

As to this Gallian cavorting with the wicked men, he was not the judge and jury, but he took note of the face, tried to imprint it in his mind. If there were Gallians in league with these invaders, justice needed to be served, and he had every confidence it would be.

Still his hand was an inch from Amenhir. But he stayed his wrath and let them talk. Nenré was counting on him. Nenré was captured, and only he could rescue her.

"—Eventide—

"—The council—"

"—Milik—"

"—Reev Nax—"

At the sound of Reev's name, Fortunato perked up. Why would

the name of Simeon's son be a topic of conversation? What did these wicked men and this Gallian traitor have to do with him?

"—aldermen—"

"—Empire—"

"—the west—"

One by one, they began to walk away, disappearing into the greenery. They vanished into the shadows and Fortunato waited silently. He waited until his knees throbbed, until his legs ached, and when he was sure he had waited long enough, he waited another several minutes.

He was alone in the forest, under the ferns. He was alone. And he resumed his tracking.

~

He followed the tracks up and down a hilly country, where ashes and birches crowded out the sky and the open spaces were overgrown with thorns and brambles. The wicked men had covered a vast distance since that dark and terrible night, since the capture of Nenré. Fortunato had followed them as swiftly as he was able, but even a master tracker could not move as swiftly as they could; even a master tracker had to occasionally pause and find the trail.

As the day wore on, he began to wonder if they had killed Nenré, if all he was doing was for naught. But he pressed on, hurrying through fields, past fen and marsh, past ponds and springs that were forgotten by man, through clearings and thick brush and beside lakes that had no name. The vastness of the South Weald was hard to comprehend, and if one ventured just a few short miles from Galiope it was likely to swallow you whole.

It was dusk and the long shadows were growing, the light fading, and after the lengthy summer day, night was almost here. Soon, the moon would arise, but the ashes and the birches, the maples and the hickories, would allow in precious little of its light.

Here, the night was deep and dark, but this time of year, it was thankfully short.

In the Empire, every household had its household gods. In his household, the gods of his ancestors had been invoked in times of peril and in times of want. Under his breath, he prayed to the household gods of Petro of Ríva and his son Fortunato. "Give me speed," he said under his breath, "give me speed and give me Nenré, unharmed and well."

The shadows were gone, now. The gloaming twilight was here. And Fortunato was desperately hungry.

Yet even in the dimness, he could see little dark shapes, mushrooms, a small bounty that might not fill him up but would provide him with a little sustenance.

Quietly and quickly, he hurried over to them. He could see that they were browncaps, not poisonous, and there were barely a fistful's worth. But they would do for now. He would not light a fire for fear of alerting the wicked men; he could not let them know he was on their trail.

The browncaps, uncooked, were tasteless, but they would have to do.

And as they entered his stomach, he became aware of just how hungry he was, how weak, how starved his body was for nourishment. Focus had replaced his hunger, keen eyes and attention on this or that trail.

But it was dark now, and he could follow the trail no more.

For a while, he crouched there, listening to the chirping of the crickets, the far-off trilling of the frogs. He felt like something had changed in the woods or in the air, something inexplicable, something he couldn't put his finger on.

He hadn't really thought his effort through. He did not know how he would rescue Nenré. He doubted he could do it by his own strength, his own effort. What was one man against the force of a hundred?

Thought and planning had its place. Like so many other times in his life, he was merely acting in the heat of the moment, and he would take full charge of the consequences later.

Again he prayed to the household gods, "Give me speed and give me Nenré, unharmed and well."

There was movement up ahead; one of the great bulky, twisting yews began to move. Legs distinguished themselves, blinking eyes that were yellow, hair of moss—no, it was hair, but it was green.

"A Forest Giant." Fortunato gasped at the sight of it, something he had not seen in all his travels, something he had never encountered before and thank the gods he hadn't.

It was half as tall as the trees, blending in with the scenery, but as it moved, its bulky humanoid form became clear, its nose overgrown with fungus and the beginnings of blooms, and birds nesting in its hair.

He had heard of these creatures, and he knew that some tried to hunt them, for their hearts were said to heal illnesses. But few could ever overpower a Forest Giant, even with a force of a hundred or two hundred. They were the guardians of the woodland places, the deadliest foe one could encounter in Gallia's ancient forests.

He watched its lumbering, bulky form, more than ten feet tall, sway as it walked away. It had not harmed Fortunato, though it had certainly smelled him. Forest Giants were not meat-eaters, but anger and surprise them and you would face their wrath.

Its shadowy form left the area, and as Fortunato waited, he heard a loud yawning yawp. He had been spared from danger.

He mightn't be so lucky next time.

~

The beginnings of dawn awoke him, and he renewed his pursuit. Up and down hills and rugged terrain, through low valleys and beside stagnant springs he walked and sometimes ran, trying desperately to catch up with the party, hoping desperately that Nenré was in one piece. And as he ran, he began to smell death in the wind, and he knew the Blight was nearby, that it was getting closer. The Blight, the elves had said, was spreading at an alarming rate, and if nothing was done it would cover all Gallia—what they called "Alonar."

Crouching on a hill, he saw bent grass. He half walked, half skidded down into the valley below, seeing the imprints of boots in the dirt and signs of a massive party everywhere. He was gaining on them; he could see these imprints were recent, almost fresh. They were merely a few hours ahead of him now, and if he continued his dogged pursuit they were liable to stop for too long or at an early hour, and then he could catch up with them.

Up and down hills and rugged terrain he walked; through low valleys and beside pools and lakes that had no name he ran. He continued to run, and as he ran he could not help but feel his household gods were with him, watching him, leading him to the woman he wished to save, the king's daughter, Nenré.

Chapter Thirty-Six: A Weapon of Shadow

At night, Reev's mouth would foam, and by day, his tremors would continue.

Gastreel had brought his young ward secretly to the Tower of Pythor, telling no one, not even Ramona Nax, for fear Ivan Xandrast would learn his location. Beneath the Tower of Pythor was a room that served as a hospital of sorts, a place of healing, to take the critically wounded.

On a bed he placed Reev, examining him carefully. He was stripped down to his loins, and though his eyes were open, he would not respond to words. He was conscious but unable to speak, and at intervals, his trembling would increase.

The wound on his forearm had further blackened, and area of purple bruising had spread to most of his arm.

Lydia the White Wizard, the most skilled healer in the wizard order, was touching him gently. "What is this, you say?" she repeated Gastreel's question. "This is devilry. Diabolism. The weapon that created this I do not know. "It is possible he will need elven healing."

"And how would we acquire that?" Gastreel said.

He recalled the Lady of the Wood, the one who had been found dead and skeletonized, her orchard rotted away and her deceased lover beside her. The Lady of the Wood, the one who had been believed to be a myth, could have healed him, perhaps, but she was gone now.

"I do not know," Lydia said. "If it is of utmost importance, you may use Tedron's Gate… go to Danarion."

"And would the elves let him in? Would they allow him to be healed there?" Gastreel said. "They do not take kindly to foreigners, especially humans. And Tedron's Gate may not work anymore. It has not been used in some hundred years."

"You are right," Lydia said. She touched the dark black wound and jerked back. "I sense… I sense…

"I felt I saw fire. Blood. Death. A dark weapon caused this, a weapon of Shadow. This boy will not survive, Gastreel. He will not… I am sure of it."

"He must survive," Gastreel said, "or there is no hope for the world."

Lydia pursed her lips. She was due to leave Galiope tomorrow morning, and Gastreel doubted she would linger here on Reev's account.

Gastreel knew that Reev was strong, that he had faced grave challenges before. But he had been dealt a baleful wound, which even Lydia—an expert at healing and in the histories of the ancient world—could not mend.

"It is not dark iron," Lydia said. "I know that. He does not show the symptoms.

"And the wound is jagged. It was not made by an even blade, but by some sort of metal shard. Yet the foaming at the mouth, the distant stare… this is a weapon of the Enemy, but we know the Servants of Seymus are gone. They could not have done it."

"Ivan Xandrast," Gastreel said. "Ivan Xandrast did this."

A look of bafflement fell over Lydia. "Whatever do you mean?"

"He has returned," Gastreel said. "I do not understand the manner of the return. But he has been hunting Reev. He has been attempting to harm him."

Gastreel still had not told the partisans on the council that Reev was the Hand of the Gods. There was a limit to their belief, and it was prudent not to let them know, for he still did not trust them.

Lydia appeared annoyed. "Ivan the Impaler… And what evidence do you have of this?"

Evidence. Proof. The wizards demanded it in all cases,

whenever a claim was made. But Gastreel had only Reev's word, and his own suspicions.

"How shall we heal him?" Gastreel asked.

"I cannot heal him, Gastreel," Lydia answered. "I cannot. I am sorry. Now, I must depart."

She left, and now Gastreel was alone in the hospital chamber with the staff physicians.

"I will not give up," Gastreel said to Reev's trembling form. "I will not give up on you."

Chapter Thirty-Seven: On the Trail

The day waxed late, and as Fortunato crouched on a hill for what seemed like the thousandth time, he realized his sense of hope was beginning to fade. A wind was blowing and death was on it, but so too was a chill he recognized, a chill felt late in the summer, the herald of autumn.

It was warm yet and many weeks remained, but if the South Weald was dangerous in the summer, it would be deadly in the winter, when snows would pile up in drifts higher than one's head, where food was nowhere to be found. Add starvation to the threats you faced and even an experienced man of the wild was likely to be overcome.

His searches for food throughout the day had begun to slow him down, and he had begun to fall behind the wicked men's trail. If Nenré was still alive, and that was doubtful, he was beginning to lose her, and Fortunato feared he had lost Wrinn irrevocably. How would he find his old friend now?

Wrinn, he had learned, had a gift, a gift common to the elves of the Forest Realm, but could that gift actually allow him to survive? How long would he last in a place where wolf packs prowled, where bears brown and black would grow hungry, where giants half as tall as the trees lay in wait, camouflaged by their very bodies, liable to be surprised or angered?

All was at a loss, and Fortunato of Ríva was failing. If there ever was any hope, it was dwindling fast.

Late in the day it was, and on the edge of the wind was death and the threat of winter. The Blight grew every day, but Fortunato again invoked his household gods—who had not listened—and with resolve anew, continued down the trail.

~

The sun was shining through the birches and the maples. It was almost twilight. Fortunato, haggard and exhausted, hungry and thirsty, knew it was almost time to stop his journey for the day. He began to wonder if he should give up, but he had come this far.

He rounded a high hill and at the bottom was a vast ravine, a deep valley, a great crevasse.

There, in the waning light, there was death.

Was this the death he had smelled?

Bodies lay mangled there, dozens and dozens of bodies. They were the bodies of the wicked men. They were the bodies of the ones he had been tracking. In number, he guessed there were twenty corpses, and they were fresh.

The sight of death erased all thought of hunger and thirst, and he had become alert. What had killed them?

They were dead perhaps an hour. Fortunato was almost upon the surviving party… but what had happened?

Cautiously, he made his way down the great valley, sometimes sliding, sometimes descending.

Death was not easy to see. Even now, such carnage was difficult to witness, though Fortunato was hardened, though he had seen war, though he had killed before.

For fear, he drew his bow and nocked an arrow to it. He scanned the bodies, looking for any sign of Nenré.

The men had been beaten almost to a pulp. Some had their heads caved in, others their chests. And yet none of the bodies were Nenré's.

Crumbs were scattered on the forest floor, bread crumbs on the carpet of fallen leaves. There were bits of road-bread that these wicked men carried lying unattended. They had left the food in their great panic.

"What killed you?" he asked of the bodies.

There was a great yawp, which echoed through the valley. Fortunato looked up and saw, on a high hill, a Forest Giant, its skin the color of birch-bark, its hair green and matted with leaves. In its hand was the tree trunk it had used as a bludgeon. But it was staggering aimlessly, and whenever it moved it would stumble back a few steps.

It was blind.

Only Nenré could have blinded it, though why she had saved this party of wicked men, which had captured her, Fortunato could only guess.

Hope anew rose within Fortunato, and with it, the thrill of the hunt, a quarry just at the edge of his fingertips. He would go as long as the daylight would allow. He would find Nenré. He would rescue her. He was sure of it now.

Yet as he gathered the road-bread, doubts began to drip in again. The incident with the Forest Giant had reduced them by twenty-one men, but how many were left? Any rescue of Nenré would be a challenge indeed.

Chapter Thirty-Eight: Lord Calion

For the first time since Reev was wounded, his eyes opened, and there was life in them.

It was the twenty-third day of the month of Sextil, the 1152nd year of the Empire, and Reev Nax was in Gastreel's house, in his care.

Yet for the life in him, the wound had worsened. The blackened mark had gotten blacker, the purple a deeper shade of purple. And Gastreel had tried everything, everything that was in his power, even scouring for days on end and at last finding a tea of *sindomas*, which proved of no avail.

"Reev," he said, "can you hear me? Can you understand me?"

Reev's eyes widened, his labored breathing turning into great sucking gasps, as of someone emerging from the ocean, almost having drowned. "I saw," he said, "the Lady of the Wood... I saw... an elven face... I saw a great stone, three stones piled on top of each other. A great cherry tree, and in its branches was a house."

The three stones piled on top of each other, the Chimney Stones, were a landmark of Estenmere, the marker of a great wood.

"Come to me," Reev said, and his voice was changed, it was not his own, "the lord of this house, or else you shall die, and the world will fall."

The life and light in his eyes was now fading. He was slipping back into shadow and darkness. Had he received a true sending from an elf-lord, a message delivered by dream?

There were no elf-lords now, none in Gallia. The elves had long retreated.

But the Lady of the Wood had been thought to be a myth, a story of legend and nothing more. Then she had been seen, her bones and rotted orchard discovered, and it was known that she had been there, hiding in secrecy, keeping away from prying eyes.

What was there to gain? There was everything to lose, for hope rested in this young boy.

But going to the Chimney Stones in the vague promise of finding help would test Reev's health. His fragile state could be easily upended. Rosetree Manor was a familiar place to him, and he was always under Gastreel's watchful eye, always under his careful monitoring.

No, he could not go on such a journey, could he? His body was racked with chills, his fever was worsening. How could he afford to be transported there?

And even if this was a true sending, a true message, how then could they find where to go?

No. No, they would remain, and Gastreel would watch over him, try new remedies, attempt to bring him back to health through whatever methods were available. His wound was not of dark iron; he could therefore recover, if watched over carefully. Gastreel knew a little healing. He was capable.

Gastreel pressed his fingers against Reev's chest, even drew his fingers near the wound. Fire he saw, and blood, and death, a barren land, a pile of skulls. And he fell backward and a vision assailed him.

~

An elf-lord sat there before him on a chair of red wood. A crown was on his head, a crown sparkling with diamonds, and his hair was almost white. Green were his eyes, and dark were his lips. On his fingers were rings of all sizes and colors, some with rubies, others with emeralds or sapphires.

"The boy will die," he said, "and all hope will be lost if you do not bring him to me before dawn."

It was a sending, a dream-message sent by a powerful elf-lord, a phenomenon Gastreel had read about but never experienced.

"I will post thirteen of my warriors at what you call the Chimney Stones and what we call *Ruendir*. They will take you here.

"You must bring him to me before dawn, or he will die, and all hope will be lost, for you and I, for elves and man alike. The world indeed will fall."

"It is two days' journey," Gastreel said. "Two days' journey! It is impossible to get there before dawn!"

"I did not tell you how to get here," said the elf-lord. "I only told you what will happen if you fail."

~

And Gastreel was back, back in Rosetree Manor, now lathed in a cold sweat, now struggling to breathe. As he looked upon Reev's form, dressed only in a loincloth, he was convinced what the elf-lord said was true, that his young ward was at the very threshold of death. Wait a little longer and there would be no hope, for him or for anyone else, for man or for elf. The world would fall.

Gastreel dressed him quickly, wrapping him in a shawl.

Then Gastreel tied him to Ivy's saddle and they set out for the Tower of Pythor, where they would avail themselves of all the tools to be had there.

As they departed Godsgate, the night was falling and the dark was setting in.

With a crystal wand of accromancy, he would give speed to Ivy's hooves. The wand exploded and white flame seemed to burst forth, and through the bounds of time and space Ivy was given speed beyond what she had been capable of. Down the road he raced, hugging the edge of the vast forest known as the South Weald, going from the Royal Road to the Strathbrad Road, and finally to the road that went to Estenmere.

And when he turned, he expended his second wand, and white

flame greater than the first exploded in his hand, and Ivy ran faster than before, given speed untold, and haste unheard of.

Down the road she ran, sometimes at a gallop, sometimes at a canter, and time itself bent to Gastreel's will. The air blew against Gastreel's face like a torrential gale though the night sky was still, and at each bend in the road he feared he would crash and fall to his ruin. But his hand guided Ivy, as the wind borne of speed blew, as mile after mile passed him by, distance crossed in minutes in what should have been hours.

He expended his third and final wand late into the night, well after dark, and Ivy galloped on, but her strength was waning, and as she ran as fast as she was able, Gastreel feared she might die.

They were not yet to Estenmere, not yet to that land, let alone the Chimney Stones, and the moon was veiled by clouds, and the darkness was inky black. Gastreel was growing so tired as he rode, he was trying desperately to stay awake, to remain alert. So much depended on him. The weight of the world was on him, the fate of elves and of mankind.

Ivy was losing strength. She was barely moving now and Gastreel's eyes were winking shut. Over the trees, a little light was shining in over the horizon. They had crossed the border into Estenmere, but the Chimney Stones were still far off.

Dawn was at hand. All hope was lost. Gastreel had failed not just himself, but everyone, everything he loved.

And light appeared, glorious light, a white figure riding on a bay horse. Behind him, perhaps a dozen other figures rode. They were all elves, and the bay horse was an Elvish horse, with a horn of gold emerging from its forehead.

"Gastreel Osiris!" said the rider on the bay horse. "Lord Calion sent us to make the rest of the journey. You are not far off. I will take the boy. You may ride with my companions to the Chimney Stones. I will go with haste."

Reev was hauled onto the bay horse as the light of dawn slowly grew, and the sun's light struck terror into Gastreel's heart.

"An!" the rider on the bay horse said and took off at a gallop, at a speed no wand of accromancy could replicate.

With the twelve other riders, Gastreel continued down the road at a speed the exhausted and wearied Ivy could manage. All was in the rider on the bay horse's hands, now, and in the hands of Lord Calion, whoever he was.

Chapter Thirty-Nine: Serpentax

Lord Calion's house was in a cherry tree, one you had to use a ladder to ascend, and one that was hidden perfectly in the forest, so perfectly no human would ever think to look.

The house itself, built in the great tree, blended in as well, but now, at night, lanterns were glowing, lanterns lit by starstones, and starstones dangled by strings from the eaves of the house, shedding light all about.

Gastreel stamped his boots on the rug. He waited, as was protocol.

"Come in, *quilenthi*," a pure voice rang out, and Gastreel did just that, entering the house of Lord Calion, the caretaker of Alonar.

Lord Calion was more glorious than in Gastreel's dream, his body bright and full of health. Soon he had laid down Reev upon a wooden table, and his hands were deftly touching the wound, which he had opened with a knife.

Beside Lord Calion was a pair of bloody tweezers, and on the surface of the table, infinitesimal fragments covered in blood.

The sun was beginning to shine over the forest. The light was growing but it was not yet here.

"You did well, *quilenthi*, getting here," Lord Calion said. "Another hour and he would have died."

"And what is it?" he said. "What ails him, Your Lordship?"

Calion looked up, and his green eyes contrasted starkly with his whitish hair. "This," he said, "is something I thought I'd not see.

"A little while ago, one afternoon, I was stirred into a panic by a vision, a conviction that an act of incalculable evil had been done. And I meditated and I prayed, and then an answer came to me. A dark weapon had been used against the Sage, though how dark I did not know until now."

"And what is it?" Gastreel said. "What weapon was used?"

He lifted up one of the tiny, bloodied metal fragments, barely perceptible to Gastreel's eye. "A crude shard of Serpentax, the Dark One's own sword."

"How can the Dark One wield a sword?" Gastreel said. "He is immaterial."

"Immaterial to mortals," Lord Calion corrected him, "but nonetheless his sword was in the mortal realm. The Nibollen crafted it for him, so great was their greed for gold and jewels.

"The First Shadow War ended and the Dark One never became material according to our reckoning. The sword Serpentax was destroyed by the first Sage Antheleon.

"And the sword was lost to history, at least until now. It is poisonous beyond words. Only the Sage could survive it. And only a master of evil could wield it, only one consumed with darkness. A warlock did this, a powerful warlock."

Warlocks were things of legend, people who served the Dark One and his servants, who, in exchange for power, gave up all the light that was in them. That was what Ivan Xandrast had become, if Lord Calion were to be believed.

"And will Reev survive?" Gastreel asked.

"He will," Lord Calion answered, "but it will take days for him to recover, weeks and months, perhaps years, for him to become as he was.

"Hope yet endures, Gastreel. By your haste he has been rescued. When all bits of Serpentax have been removed from the wound, then I will seal it. Then we will keep him under our guard.

"Things are not all well in Alonar. The Enemy is at work in the forest you call the South Weald."

Chapter Forty:
The Hunter

Death was in the air, and death was on the wind.

The Blight drew near, and it grew in size every day, and Fortunato was on the trail, less than an hour behind the party of wicked men, now. Through forgotten valleys he had run, through hollows and over hills and past nameless ponds he had traveled. The air was sweltering and a heat wave had come to the South Weald, making the smell of death all that more potent and sickening, a million or ten million trees and animals dying. And since his focus had been on Nenré, the crisis that was the Blight had been in the back of his mind, not something he could act upon.

He could not act upon it in any case. Perhaps the best thing was to evacuate Gallia, but how could you evacuate an entire land, and would the Blight spread beyond it?

With strenuous effort, Fortunato began to ascend a high hill crowned with trees, and from the vantage point he saw the vast woodland below. But due south of him, uncomfortably close, he could see brown death, and a sickly air rising upward, a sickly air that obscured the sun and all it shone upon. He could not see much farther than the edge of the Blight, the part where the trees had begun to die and fall and all vegetation wither and wilt away.

"Wrinn," he said to his household gods, "wherever he may be... keep him safe. Lead him home."

The remains of Albendir Camp likely had been swallowed up in the Blight by now, or would be soon. Had the rate of death changed? Would it spread, now, by more than a quarter-mile a day? Was the rate of death increasing? Fortunato could only hope not. Hope was all that was left for him now, hope that was fading away and growing fainter by the moment, hope that was dwindling quickly to nothing.

He drew Amenhir from his side and kissed the flat of its blade. The enemy would fall into his hands tonight. Perhaps if he envisioned it, then it would happen. Perhaps, if he hoped and he prayed, Amenhir would slake its bloodthirst, Nenré would break free from her captivity, and Wrinn would find his way home.

"To the death," Fortunato said aloud, "to the death of the wicked men, I go."

And he took off at a sprint, following the trail, following the contours of the trodden grass with all due speed.

He was a hunter and the wicked men were his prey.

Chapter Forty-One:
The Blue Door

"Why," Glenda said, "don't you take the evening off? You've been working so hard all summer. You need a little rest, to keep up your energy."

Ambrass, covered in flour in the kitchen, looked at her overseer a bit sidelong. "Are you certain?" she asked. "Are you certain you don't need me?"

"I always need you," Glenda said, "but you need to be well. A bit of time off this evening, all of tomorrow if you want it. I need my second-in-command to be well rested and fully capable."

"Well, thank you," Ambrass said. "I suppose I can't turn such an offer down."

So she bathed and dressed, and put on her finest attire: a gown of red cloth and leather. She looked full and true, like the gypsy she was, the gypsy she always would be. There was sunlight yet. She thought, perhaps, she'd go for a walk.

Outside, the streets of Gallia were resplendent with afternoon light, and men and women of all classes were outside in the warm weather. Ambrass began to walk through Middletown, through the Town Square where merchants were hawking their wares from their stalls, where commerce was still underway on this late summer evening.

But Ambrass knew the summer was waning, that each hour, each day, each passing week she would grow older. Autumn would be here soon, the trees turn to brilliant colors, and fog would come to the low valleys, and frost would crown the grass. Each hour, each day, each week and month Ambrass, the daughter of Gaida and Kunakil, grew older, one step closer to death's inevitable approach.

"Fortunato," she said under her breath.

Was he yet alive? Was it possible for him still to love her?

And another name came to mind, one she dared not speak again, one that evoked the moonlight and the darkness beneath the stars.

That name, the one she did not speak aloud, belonged to someone she had not seen in many days. He had feigned interest in her and then abandoned her, never coming by, never stopping in at the Dragonpaw Inn. He had shown interest in her and desire, and then that interest, it seemed, had vanished. If she presented herself now, at that house with the little blue door in Lonen Town, would his interest in her begin anew?

The thought of doing it was preposterous, preposterous indeed. But tonight was supposed to be a full moon, and not just a full moon but an especially bright one, the brightest Galiope would see in years. Under the full moon, people were bound to do crazy things. What did they call it? Lunacy.

She found herself walking on the Bridge-O'er-Galios in the late afternoon light. She laid her hands on the edge of the bridge, breathless. She felt tired, exhausted almost, out of breath. And she felt she was being tempted, tempted to do something no reasonable young woman would do, tempted to do something that no one in their right mind, with any wits left, would even conceive of doing.

She could see the curved roofs of Lonen Town from where she stood, rising above the river and the river-walk.

What was she thinking? Was she really conceiving of this?

And there was the matter of Fortunato. But Fortunato, it was claimed, was dead. And if he were alive, her impulsive words had ended any hope of their love.

She looked again at the curved roofs of Lonen Town. What madness afflicted her? What strange state of mind had come over her that she had thought of going to Nocturne's house, to the blue door? Why was she tempted to do such a bizarre and dangerous thing, and why was the temptation growing stronger by the moment, by the second, by the minute?

There were dangers, great dangers, such as the character of the man himself, which she was not sure of. There were dangers, such as how he would interpret the manner of her arrival. There were dangers, of herself, for her ability to withstand his spell.

The idea was ludicrous, and on the night of the full moon, it fit the definition of lunacy.

She thought of Nocturne himself, his dark hair, his pale white skin, and a shiver passed through her. The moon would soon arise, and as soon as it appeared, the lunacy would take over, the irrational state of mind that fell on people on nights when the full moon shone.

"Dr'alynthi," she said aloud, and immediately regretted saying the word, for as she did the temptation grew stronger, unbearable even, and she looked upon the curved tile roofs of Lonen Town, far away, and desire overcame her fear, desire she did not want or fully understand.

~

At the threshold of Lonen Town, where the road began to ascend the great hill, reason again returned. It was brief. She had stopped in the middle of the road, and the sun was casting its long shadows over the buildings and the city trees.

I have come this far. She took her first step into the wild dark night.

Some of the Lonen women were staring at her curiously, the Lonen women in their purple *sarés* that covered their hair, but most ignored her. It was as if she was the invisible woman, not really there, not even present, and she couldn't help but resent it.

When the Bloodmoon Inn appeared in the light of the setting sun, reason once again tried to assail her, and she froze in place, realizing just where she was and what she was doing. Truly, what *was* she doing? Why did she ever come back?

But Night Owl Way was right there, the house with the blue door.

She could turn back now; it was her last chance. She could go back to the Dragonpaw Inn, pretend none of this happened, and no one would know she had ever gone on this crazy journey, this journey she had made on a late summer evening.

And yet she had come this far. Would she go back now, though her fingers were trembling, though underneath her dress she was shaking? She would knock on the door, say, "Hello, again," and how would she explain the reasons for her return? She would think of an excuse. She would tell him Glenda had sent her, to check on Bala. Yes, to check on Bala.

Oh, dear, what have I done? What have I gotten myself into?

A cart rattled by, almost running her over, and she was sent running, or hurtling, into Night Owl Way, a run that ended at the little house with the balcony, the little house with the bright blue door.

At the blue door she hesitated. There was yet time. There was yet time to turn back. Still she could leave, head back to the Dragonpaw, end this craziness, this lunacy.

But she knocked on the door and waited, and at that moment she was the closest to running of all prior moments, but she quickly tried to gather herself, to gather her confidence, her poise, and the door opened, and there he was.

His hair was inky black, recently combed. He had recently awoken, Nocturne Rabaam, the druen—or the vampire, or whatever term someone would use. A wry smile grew on his face. "Why, Ambrass, it is good to see you. Shall you come in?"

No questions about why she had come, or what she was doing here. It was as if he knew and she did not.

Bala was there, sitting at the door-side table with a pile of pastel chalks and a slip of parchment.

"Bala," Nocturne said, "why don't you go to your room and

take your coloring with you?"

Without a word, little Bala got up and did just that, and doubt was growing in Ambrass, doubt and fear, wonderment at what had come over her, wonderment at what she had done. She was in the lion's den, now. How could she escape?

And Nocturne was staring at her, and his eyes were as fire. He did not ask her why she had come, for he knew, though she told herself she did not.

How many had fallen into his nets? She was like a bird trapped in a snare, a fish caught by a hook. And though she could run, she did not.

"Shall we go for another walk?" Nocturne said.

Chapter Forty-Two: Get The Girl

The moon was rising over the birches and the maples, and the last bits of light were leaving the forests of the South Weald when a cry rang out and reached Fortunato's ears, a cry he recognized instantly.

"Nenré!" Fortunato gasped and stormed over the hill, holding Amenhir in both hands.

At the top of the hill was a great bowl-shaped depression, where some two hundred of the wicked men had gathered. Through the leaves, vines, and bushes Fortunato peered, and he could see, far away, Nenré tied to a wooden stake, her white clothes torn and sullied by dirt.

Facing her was a man black of hair, with a wild dark beard and crazed eyes, on whose back was tied a double-sided sword—the ancient butterfly blade. This, Fortunato presumed, was Milik.

"Tell me," hissed Milik, and his voice carried through the trees.

Baleful was the moon. Low to the ground, it was colored yellow, and the stars were just beginning to appear.

"Where is your master, Lord Calion?"

"I do not know!" said Nenré.

"You lie," he hissed. He was madness embodied, a person with no scruples, no moral fiber. And he was drawing from his pockets a serrated shard, a jagged piece of dark metal that sparkled in the moonlight. "You know what this is. And I will cut you with it if you do not tell me."

"Enough!" Nenré said.

And shapes were moving, drifting in the eaves of the trees, shapes Fortunato could just barely detect out of the corner of his eyes.

"Adada ié!" Nenré said and light flashed forth, a moment, a stunning blow.

And Fortunato, giving no heed to danger, barreled down into the crevasse, outnumbered by hundreds to one, careless of the danger, careless of death.

~

Ambrass was holding Nocturne's hand again, and they were on the river-walk below Lonen Town. The moon had arisen and it was as bright and magnificent as the astronomers had promised. Its light reflected in glittering white in the waters of the River Galios below.

What am I doing? she asked herself for perhaps the tenth time.

Their eyes met in the dark of night, and the fire was still in Nocturne's eyes, fire burning bright.

"How old are you?" she asked him, and, leaving his side, stepped up to the edge of the river-walk.

"Would it surprise you to know," Nocturne said, "that I was born in the 1063rd year of the Empire?"

"That would make you…"

Ambrass had always been terrible with arithmetic.

"Eighty-nine years old," Nocturne said.

"So you're older than my nan," Ambrass said, and for a moment doubt bubbled over again, a bubble that quickly burst. But what had she expected? He did not look old at all, forty at the oldest, but elves aged slowly—even, she supposed, elves cursed by the vampire's thirst.

The vampire's thirst. What had she gotten herself into? In what manner did the druen drink blood? Was that what Nocturne was after? No, no, it couldn't be.

He had drawn near her; but there were voices echoing, and with Nocturne right behind her she looked back, and saw the forms of two people descending the stairs to the river-walk.

'Dr'alynthi!' a woman's voice called out, and the way she pronounced his name was like that of a native.

For a moment, jealousy stabbed Ambrass's heart, but then the two forms became visible, one, a lanky woman with salt-and-pepper hair and the other, a short and stocky man with a bald head. They were as pallid as Nocturne, and if Ambrass had to guess, she would say they were both druen.

"Ambrass," Nocturne said, touching her shoulder, "meet my friends... Drassané and Omagon, the other owners of the Bloodmoon."

And for a moment there was fear in the pit of Ambrass's stomach, visions of a blood-feast conducted publicly in the night air, on the sanctity of Galiope's river-walk.

"Hello," Ambrass said.

"This," Nocturne said, "is the girl from St. Selwyn's."

Had he spoken of her to them?

Doubts resurfaced, the last doubts she'd have of the night.

She drew again near Nocturne, and he took both her hands in his.

"I will dance for you," Ambrass said, gazing into Nocturne's eyes.

There was a touch of amusement, then confusion.

"Remember," said Ambrass, "when you came into the Dragonpaw, and you asked me to dance, and I said no?"

"How could I forget that rejection?" Nocturne answered.

Drassané and Omagon were looking at them with amused grins, but Ambrass did not consider their presence welcome.

"Drassané, a tune. Omagon, a beat," Nocturne said.

The female druen procured an ocarina from her shirt pocket, and Omagon began to slap his knee as if it were a drum.

And underneath the moon, beside the glittering waters, Ambrass twirled and leapt, then spun around. She dropped to her feet and rose and skipped this way and that. She jumped and hopped and did a pirouette and her dance ended in Nocturne's steely grip, with her lips just a few inches from his own.

hopped and did a pirouette and her dance ended in Nocturne's steely grip, with her lips just a few inches from his own.

Chapter Forty-Three:
For Nenré

The moon was shining bright, and underneath the bright and shining moon, the sound of iron striking iron echoed. The crazed man, the one called Milik, had parried Fortunato's strike with Amenhir on his butterfly blade.

Chaos had consumed the camp of wicked men. Throughout the forest, glowing shapes had appeared, beings of light with swords in their hands, and as they encircled the men, the men had begun to flee.

A flurry of blows with the butterfly blade followed, in quick succession, and Fortunato just barely parried them with Amenhir. The man was a master swordsman; the very fact he used a butterfly blade proved it.

And underneath the bright and shining moon, Fortunato was driven back, up to the edge of the ridge, and thank the gods for the beings in white, whatever they were.

Nenré was still bound, and at an opportune moment, Fortunato drew from his side his adamant knife Glyrnslayer, and he hurled it at her feet.

The crazed man Milik responded with a flurry of blows greater than the first, a whirlwind of steel, and Fortunato parried just barely. He almost lost his grip on his sword.

The man was a master, and with the butterfly blade he was like two men, two swordsmen at once, both with equal skill.

Far off, Nenré had the adamant knife in her teeth, and as she was standing there, she was trying desperately to reach the bonds on her hands.

The white figures of light were beginning to fade; the wicked men who'd remained were shouting, taking note of the illusion—

the illusion no doubt cast by Nenré herself.

The blows of Milik's blades were like a storm, a storm where the rain was steel, the lightning Milik's curses, the dark clouds his terrible eyes.

Milik had driven Fortunato to the edge of the crevasse but had not overcome him. Fortunato looked afar and saw the wicked men were coming at Nenré, wicked men with scimitars and cruel knives. Nenré was still bound, still desperately trying to break herself free.

And over the high hill, Tyra Jade came leaping, Tyra Jade, the black wolf, the animal that was like his daughter. She tore a wicked man by the neck and hurled him to the ground, and those wicked men approaching Nenré dared no go farther.

Some turned and ran.

And over the edge of the crevasse, just feet from Fortunato, a dark shape came hurtling through the air.

Wrinn it was, Wrinn with his quarterstaff, and, flanking Milik, he began to strike.

Wrinn had changed. His hair was matted and filthy, with leaves in it, his tunic and trousers torn and in places showing his skin. He was like the wild boys of legend, the wild boys who were raised by wolves and lived in the desolate places.

The wild moon arose on this most wild of nights.

Hope was rekindling in Fortunato's heart.

Then horns began to blow. The wicked men had called for reinforcements. They would soon get them.

Fortunato had very little time.

~

Nocturne had swept Ambrass into his arms, and under the cover of moonlight he was carrying her through the river-walk.

Fire was coursing through her veins, hot-blooded fire, fire such as she had never felt. And under the moon they were talking, and she was giggling.

"Have you been to the catacombs?" Nocturne asked. "To where the ancients would bury their dead?"

"No, I haven't," Ambrass said, and the fit of giggling started again. "Why ever would I?"

"For education," Nocturne said. "Or exercise.

"The entrance is in Greenwater."

As Nocturne carried her up the steps toward the openness of the streets, Ambrass no longer cared what people would think of her, the things they would whisper under cover of dark, the gossip they would repeat in the solitude of their homes. Ambrass and Nocturne passed by night stragglers openly, and Ambrass was in Nocturne's grip, reveling in each moment. She did not care what they thought, or what the town guards thought. For now, there was only this instant, only this night.

The full moon was immense in the sky as Nocturne carried her to wherever he would go. Under cover of night, they crossed the Bridge-O'er-Galios into Middletown. Under cover of night, Nocturne turned, and following the river bend, took her to a place she did not know.

She envisioned herself as the Dark Queen of the Night, She of the Tombs, with Nocturne enthroned as king. She envisioned that—and she did not need to envision any longer—he was carrying her in his arms.

Chapter Forty-Four: Company

With a cry of exertion, Nenré broke free of her bonds.

Wrinn and Fortunato had Milik cornered. There was fear in his eyes and it seemed he thought he would fall.

With a mighty blow, Wrinn sent his butterfly blade flying.

Milik fell backward, eyes black with hate. He ran forth and grabbed a knife from his boot.

There was a great flash of white light and he fell to the ground.

Nenré approached, her staff of oak now in her hand. Milik was on all fours, feeling around, clearly blinded. Yet for his weaker position, he was murderous all the more, calling out curses, reaching for his knife.

Fortunato prepared a killing blow.

"Do not kill him," Nenré said, and her word was his command. "Look at him now, the piteous creature."

And yet there were more pressing challenges ahead. "We have company, Nenré," Fortunato said, and, running over to her, took her by the hand. "Come on, Wrinn… Tyra… haven't you heard the horns?"

The wicked men had scattered. In the dark of night, another horn blew, then a dozen more. Soon, they would be in danger anew. Soon, they would be at an end.

~

In the dark of night, Nocturne carried her, and the lights of the hill of Wodenscross Court were high above her. The houses were growing dilapidated, the streets becoming filled with potholes, but Ambrass cared not. Nocturne was carrying her through the wan moonlight, and fire was coursing through her veins, fire as she had never felt before. At the lust in Nocturne's eyes Ambrass winced, but she let him carry her through the streets, though they were not alone, though people in the shanty slums of Greenwater were staring at her.

She was limp in his arms as they passed by the dark buildings, and the moon, white and full, was their ever present companion— Ambrass, She of the Tombs, and Nocturne, the one who carried her.

It was late, very late at night, and Nocturne had taken her to a forgotten side street, to the pitch black entrance of a tunnel. In his arms, Ambrass watched, and she waited, and she trusted Nocturne, for there was no one else to trust. When they descended into the inky darkness, the smell of must was all about her.

Then fires were lighting in a burial chamber, green fires.

"What are they?" Ambrass was going to say but Nocturne answered before she spoke, "Ghost fires, the ever-burning flames."

In the center of the room was a sarcophagus, a sarcophagus etched with words: "Lord Merryweather." And the walls of the catacombs were lined with skulls, each skull like a brick in a brick wall.

And Nocturne laid Ambrass upon the cold of the stone floor and began to undress. What resistance she had was gone by his spell.

And when he was undressed he began to undress her.

The first time was pain, the second pleasure, the third sublime.

And underneath the catacombs they would remain until dawn.

Chapter Forty-Five:
A Time for Choosing

As Fortunato took Nenré by the hand, he felt in his heart a great sadness, a betrayal, though he did not know how or of what. Was it that Nenré had decided to leave Milik alive?

Behind him, Milik was growling, as if he were a beast, fumbling for the knife he would never find, which Fortunato had hurled into the woods.

The horns blasted louder than ever, just feet away. Fortunato took Nenré and forced her forward, darting for the woods. But in a moment's span they were surrounded and the sound of pounding hooves were all around them. In a moment's span, all had changed. In a moment's span, the hollow crevasse in the center of the hill was filled with people.

But as Fortunato stood there, gripping Nenré's hand, he could see these were not the wicked men, not the men from afar.

They were elves, riding reindeer, having been sent to rescue Nenré.

"Stop this!" Nenré shouted in the Elvish tongue as the riders circled around Fortunato and then Wrinn and Tyra Jade. "These men rescued me! They are responsible for saving me! You were late… I would have died if not for Fortunato of Ríva, if not for Wrinn and this wolf."

The elves on the reindeer were pointing lances at Fortunato; Nenré was now behind them.

"And where is the warlock?" said one of the elves, clearly the captain, dressed in a suit of mail and a shining helm. "Where has he gone?"

"I do not know, Yamenvi. Why don't you go look for him?" Nenré answered.

Fortunato sheathed Amenhir. Before the massive size of the reindeer, Fortunato felt small.

Yamenvi, the captain, barked orders, indistinguishable orders in a dialect of Elvish Fortunato did not know. "Bind these captives," he said to another.

"Do not." Nenré's voice echoed over the hills, over the night. So powerful was her voice it sounded like a message from the gods. "Do not bind them, or I shall blind you all. They are the ones who rescued me. And we have a mission yet to accomplish. The Blight—"

"The Blight will spread," said Yamenvi, the captain, and his reindeer snorted as it stirred uncomfortably. "Your father has given orders to abandon the mission. Moreover, he has ordered that all elves leave Alonar."

"That may be my father's command," Nenré said, "and it may be his desire. But I am the daughter of the king, and I order you that you leave us at once. I will not abandon Alonar. I will not abandon these woods.

"And I will not abandon my friends. *Parda!* Leave us, now, Yamenvi, or else I will deal you a wound you will not recover from; you will never see again."

Yamenvi's reindeer reared up slightly on its hind legs. "Very well, my lady," Yamenvi said in Elvish. "*Ananda,* men! We find the warlock and bring him back to Lord Calion.

"The king's daughter has chosen death."

~

The thunderous hooves of the reindeer were long gone. In the crevasse, the four companions—Wrinn, Tyra Jade, Nenré, and Fortunato—stood alone.

Fortunato took Nenré's right hand in his own. "You have been through much grief, Nenré. And yet I fear you may have chosen ill.

"We cannot stop the Blight. We cannot heal this land."

"We can," Wrinn answered, and his words stunned Fortunato. "We can find its source. We can enter the Blight.

"*Sindomas* is the key… *Sindomas.*"

Chapter Forty-Six: Safe Haven

When Reev awoke, something like a terrible nightmare lingered, something far worse than a nightmare. He did not remember the dream, only memories of sharp pains, of fiery mountains and yellow lakes, of a throne built out of skulls, and of eyes made from bale fire.

His eyes were adjusting to the morning light, and he could see that he was on a sick-bed, that Gastreel was in a far corner of the room.

They were in a treehouse.

"Gastreel," Reev said, "where am I?"

"My boy!" Gastreel shouted and ran over to him. "You are conscious again… thank the gods."

"Where am I?" Reev repeated himself.

"You are in the house of Calion, an elf-lord… and it is the twenty-fifth day of the month of Sextil, the year 1152."

"And where is this Calion?" Reev said. He was still shocked, still in a state of trauma, still wondering just what had happened to him and why.

He looked at his forearm and saw a wound that had recently sealed, and at that moment he remembered the afternoon in Rosetree Manor, the afternoon Ivan Xandrast had found him, the afternoon Ivan Xandrast had stabbed him with the metal shard and caused pain beyond human endurance.

"Calion is not here," Gastreel said. "He and the elves are preparing to leave Gallia."

"What…? Why…? Wrinn…?"

"Not the elves born here, but the elves who have lived here in secrecy, keeping watch over what they call Alonar," Gastreel said.

"And why would they leave? Would they have us be alone?" Reev asked.

Gastreel walked over with a cup of something—water. Reev took it in his hands and drank it.

"Lord Calion said that as soon as you awake, we should go to meet him."

"And where is he?"

~

When Reev whistled in his special way, now standing underneath the trees, he was surprised when Cobalt answered the call a little while later. His Elvish horse had followed him here, the horse that had belonged to his father and now belonged to him. As he saw his ruddy coat, his gold mane, the amber-colored horn that extended outward from his forehead, he wondered at the precious gift he had been inexplicably given.

And then he remembered the manner that Gastreel had found him. The wizard had been walking home; out of nowhere Cobalt, Reev's father's horse, had shown himself.

His father, Aunt Ramona said, had disappeared. Was there a connection, somehow?

"Come on," Gastreel said, "mount up. We ride for the Ford of Arddor."

~

The roads wound through dark forests, and the deeper they got, the farther away civilization seemed, the more wild their surroundings, the more deadly. The birches, oaks, and maples seemed to swallow them whole, and there were ponds and little lakes in increasing number.

At last they came to the ford, the Ford of Arddor, which

crossed the River Fessen, and there Gastreel stopped, and waited.

"Were we meant to be met here?" Reev asked.

"No, not necessarily," Gastreel said. "Just wait. Keep totally quiet. Keep your mouth shut. Don't even breathe."

And Reev did just that. And as the wind blew, the sound of music became apparent, the sound of the harp and of the timbrel.

And Reev, at the sound of the music, trotted off in the sound's direction, into the thick of the woods.

Suddenly, they were in the camp of the elves, the camp that was so well hidden. And just past the road, disguised perfectly from unfocused eyes, hundreds and hundreds of elves had gathered.

There were so many, in fact, Reev began to feel boxed in.

They were dressed in robes of green or gold or azure. Their eyes were bright, and despite the gravity of the moment, they seemed cheery, even joyous.

Up ahead, underneath an oak, nearby the harpist and the timbrel-player, was a man on a wooden throne, a man with hair so fair it was almost white, wearing a crown of diamonds on his head. Reev felt he had seen him before.

"*Quilenthi,*" the man, surely the Lord Calion, said. "And you have brought him. The Sage."

Yet for his cheer, there seemed to be a hard edge underneath it, and there were worry-creases on his forehead, and he appeared disturbed.

"What might have taken weeks has taken days," Lord Calion said. "The Sage can walk again.

"Come here. Come close. Here in our camp, you will find peace and rest."

~

Throughout the day, dozens and dozens more elves arrived to camp, dozens and dozens of elves, all preparing to leave. And late in the afternoon, Reev took note of a great masonry box, a container that was carved from stone. "What is that?" he said quietly under the sound of the wind.

"There in that box," said Lord Calion, "are the bones of the Lady Amané and her lover Lamadon."

The Lady of the Wood...

"They will be buried. They will rest with their fathers until the end."

"I met her," Reev said. "I met her not long ago."

"She was the oldest living elf," Lord Calion said. "She came to Alonar seeking the garden of the gods, and she found it. She was promised to see the Sage before she died, at least that was what she told her father. Was it the gold apples that kept her alive or the promise? I do not know."

How could a promise keep someone alive?

She had been wise and powerful, beautiful and terrible, a force of power to be reckoned with. Reev owed his life to her, and so did Gastreel. Without her aid, he would have died.

It was a great loss to see her dead. Against her great power who could possibly stand? Now that power was gone, and other powers were growing—dark powers, the powers of Lothan.

There was the sound of thunderous hooves. More elves were arriving. Three came through the brush and greenery, two girt in mail and with swords, riding on horses. The third, in the center, was on a white-colored Elvish horse, in an azure tabard. He was handsome, radiant, with hair the color of driftwood. His eyes were blue. Sheathed to his side was a sword of *estirion*.

"Prince Vélerion!" Lord Calion shouted. He got up from his throne then knelt down.

Reev and Gastreel followed a moment later, as did the rest of camp.

"Rise, Lord Calion," said Vélerion, and Lord Calion did just that. "Have you seen my sister? I cannot leave without her."

"Your sister was captured," said Lord Calion. "A rescue party was sent to retrieve her.

"If she were dead, I would feel it in my heart. She yet breathes. She yet lives."

"Alas for her," said Prince Vélerion. "A warlock leads these wicked men..."

~

Bonfires were lit, but in a company of so many hundreds, Reev felt safe. They were well protected, and beside warriors, there were also archers and spies, scouts keeping watch.

Lord Calion had brought a chair up to his own and Reev was sitting in it. Gastreel was far off, on the perimeter of camp.

Harpists were playing, the elves were laughing and speaking amongst themselves, and despite the joy Reev witnessed, his wound had begun to flare up. It was as fire.

"What will happen to Gallia when all of you leave?" Reev said to Lord Calion. He wondered if he should have used an address, like "Your Lordship" or "Your Majesty" or the Imperial "Your Excellency."

"Death is spreading all over Gallia," said Lord Calion, "a great death. A perishing of plants and animals. A death we cannot heal, for we cannot enter this Blight, this Perishing.

"That is why you must come with us. You must come with us into the courts of Danthemari. We must prepare for war."

"I can't leave," Reev said. "I can't abandon my friends. I can't abandon Gastreel."

"The wizard will come with you," Lord Calion said. "But other than him, you must be alone. We cannot risk detection, or trust anyone who is not worthy of trust."

"I can't," Reev said again.

"If you do not," said Lord Calion, "you will be in danger. The mission will at risk—"

"—and what is the mission?" Reev said.

"That," said Lord Calion, "requires much thought."

The summer night was growing thick, the air intolerably warm. Reev was well fed, and with their cakes and venison pies they had also brought wine, elven wine such as Reev had never tasted before.

He could not believe these elves had been in Gallia, that so many had hidden under the noses of the Lord Eventide and his government. For how long had they been here? For how long had there been spies, hiding away in what the elves called Alonar? How could they have avoided detection if the occupation were for centuries, as Gastreel had indicated?

The elves were dancing in the light of the bonfire.

There was a gust of wind, a gust with a hint of autumn on its edge. Reev thought of Fortunato, of Tyra Jade and of Wrinn.

Chapter Forty-Seven: Sindomas

"Nenré!" shouted Wrinn. "You all right?"

He had a bundle of *sindomas* in his hands, so many tender unopened blossoms they threatened at any point to fall.

"I am fine!" Nenré shouted back, a good distance away from him, in another clearing.

Wrinn could not let her be captured again, though since that night on the hill, he had not seen any of the wicked men. It appeared they'd been scared away. But Wrinn could not take any chances, and he would guard her with his life now. It was his duty.

Tyra Jade was not growling or barking. Up ahead, she was a solitary figure, on the edge of the clearing.

There was a noise, a noise Wrinn couldn't place, and—on alert as always—he followed that noise, and he was in another clearing, and he could see Nenré laughing, and Fortunato right beside her.

What would Ambrass think at the sight of this?

But Wrinn knew that love between true elves and humans was unheard of, especially not with a princess like Nenré.

"Are you going to help?" Wrinn said.

"Of course," said Nenré.

But Fortunato and Nenré were empty-handed. Under the light of the moon they had found not a single sprig of *sindomas*. If they were to enter the Blight, they would need a lot of it, more *sindomas* than Wrinn could really fathom.

"Get to work!" Wrinn said, and then left them, pushing his way through some ivy and tangled growth.

~

By the time their night ended, they'd all found *sindomas*, Nenré a single sprig, Fortunato three sprigs, Wrinn so many he could not hold them all.

And as Fortunato lit the night's fire, doubt began to creep into Wrinn's mind, a sick fear in the pit of his stomach. He wondered if what they were about to do was reckless. He wondered if the trees were wrong, or worse, guileful, that *sindomas* really couldn't protect them from the growing brown death.

But Wrinn had made a promise, a favor for a favor. He would honor it if he was able, and Fortunato and Nenré had agreed to go with him. They were trusting his word, and Wrinn hoped to the gods that his word was true, that he was right, that the *sindomas* really would keep them alive. There was only one way to find out, a way filled with risk, with danger.

Tomorrow at dawn, he would learn the truth, at the risk of his life. Tomorrow at dawn they would enter the Blight.

Chapter Forty-Eight:
The Prince

It was still dark when Reev awoke in the elven camp. Figures were moving, scattered throughout the perimeter, but the sky was dark and most of the hundreds of elves were asleep in their bedrolls.

Reev, wide awake, felt the stabbing pain in his forearm anew.

Getting up, he stepped over the sleeping bodies.

The air was wonderfully cool, and the heat of the day had not yet arrived. He thought he'd get a drink of water from the river; he was horribly thirsty and his stomach growled.

Against rocks, the river babbled. The moon was still visible, low in the sky. Reev guessed they were still in the region of Estenmere, not far from the town of Estenberry and the famed Berrypool. He wondered if he'd ever go back to Galiope, if he'd be able to resist the combined pressure of Lord Calion and Gastreel. He did not want to go to the Elf Lands. He did not want to leave his friends behind.

He stooped down, took some of the moonlit water in his hands, and drank. It was refreshing, ice cold. The River Fessen had its source high in the peaks of the Dragonteeth Mountains, and even now, in the summertime, it was chill to the taste.

"Are you who they say you are?" a voice echoed from above, and when Reev looked back, he saw the prince, Vélerion, standing there. He was in his blue tabard, and his *estirion* sword was clipped to his side. His hair was long, dark in the dim night, but his eyes gleamed with moonlight. "Are you the Sage, the one who will defeat Seymus?"

"I am Reev Nax," he replied, and as he looked up, he found he was uncomfortable, that he did not want to be alone here with Vélerion.

"I fought with your father, Simeon," said Vélerion. "Many rokahn did we hew down together."

Who had his father not fought with, and where had his father not been?

"Some humans thought your father was *velati sonoren*, the Prince of the Dawn," said Vélerion. "But we elves knew he was not. So how do we know you are the Sage?"

"Lord Calion says you are."

He was climbing down, and soon he was at the river, just inches from Reev.

"Let me see your wound," said Vélerion.

"I would rather you not," Reev answered.

"Very well," said Vélerion. "Did the wizard tell you that you were cut with the Dark One's own sword?"

"No," Reev said. "He did not."

"He does not tell you much, it appears," Vélerion said. "But if you can survive such a wound, perhaps Lord Calion is right. Perhaps they are all right. And if it is so, you must come with us when we leave Alonar."

"I am not going with you," Reev wanted to say, but he remained silent.

"Lord Calion is a wise man," said Vélerion. "He was a good caretaker. He watched over Alonar for many decades. But now he will return with the rest of us. We will go. Battle and blood and a red morning awaits. Queer things have reached my father's ears. Alonar soon shall fall. The elves would be in danger, and so will you be if you remain."

For a while there was only a gentle rustling of wind. The morning air was cold, but light was beginning to appear, the faintest and vaguest hint of illumination.

"Is there something you want from me, Prince Vélerion?" asked Reev.

And again there was a pause, longer than the first. The birds suddenly began to sing, hundreds at once, the sign of imminent dawn.

"Nothing I want from you," Prince Vélerion said. "Nothing that you can give me.

"How strange is it," he went on, "that a human should be the one to defeat Seymus, when we elves are the Light's firstborn."

Signs of morning were growing. Reev wondered what the morning meal would be.

Prince Vélerion turned and left. As he walked up the ridge, Reev heard him saying, "My sister, my sister."

Chapter Forty-Nine: Fortunato of Ríva

A cliff overlooked the trees below. Nenré was on its edge and Fortunato was right behind her.

"Yanenré," he said softly in her ear, "will this be the last sunrise we see?"

"Why use my full name?" she answered.

"Shall we be formal, truthful, on the day we enter the Blight?" said Fortunato. "Shall we speak our full names and tell all our truths on the day we die?"

Nenré spun around, and her beautiful blue eyes seemed to sparkle as the light began to appear on the horizon.

"What truth?" said Nenré. "What truth would you have me know?"

A slight smile was on her lips, and the truth Fortunato wanted to speak was hovering just on the edge of his tongue.

"The truth," said Fortunato, "that I may love you."

The smile vanished. "No," said Nenré. "No, you do not love me. You do not speak the truth.

"You do not love me, Fortunato of Ríva. There is another one you love."

What had Wrinn told her?

"She is gone from me," answered Fortunato. "She does not love me."

"You and I, we cannot ever be more than fellow fighters," Nenré said. "You are a human, and I am the king's daughter. It cannot be. It will not be."

"It can," Fortunato said.

And for a while she was silent, for a while her resistance seemed to crumble.

But off in the distance there was the sound of shouting. Wrinn had stirred awake. The moment of doom had arrived, the day of what seemed like certain death, and death it would be without love, doom it would be without Yanenré Iradahir speaking the truth.

~

Besides the tea of *sindomas* they would drink, besides the petals and stems they would chew like a gum, Nenré had woven necklaces of *sindomas* they would wear around their necks. They would stuff their pockets with *sindomas* as well.

In the still of the morning, Fortunato kissed the flat of Amenhir and asked the gods for their luck. What they were about to do, some might call the height of foolishness. But whatever it was, their path had been decided; there was no going back now.

"Wrinn, Nenré," Fortunato said, "we either succeed together or we perish together. Let us go forth boldly."

And they took off at a quick pace through the undergrowth of the South Weald, going southward, southward toward the brown death.

~

Even before they reached the Blight, the plants were growing stunted, and when the first of the death appeared, it appeared suddenly. The air was choking. Beyond a sea of dead grass were withered and dead trees whose leaves had long fallen and some of which had collapsed entirely, falling to the ground on the sick dead earth.

Overhead, the sky was like a haze, almost a reddish color, and the sun wavered in the thick poison air. Fortunato felt as though his body was being assaulted, that it was being laid waste, that something vile and even unnatural was at work here. Yet he could breathe clear, and though the Blight extinguished all life in its path, *sindomas* was in his blood, and at each moment, he chewed *sindomas* like a cud.

He drew Amenhir and looked about the great brown death, the forests of dead trees whose leaves had withered and fallen, and up ahead, a lake whose water was black and whose reeds and bulrushes had shriveled to dead yellow stalks.

"What horror," said Nenré. "I had not imagined seeing such horror in my time.

"It is all dead… all withered."

"And we must go on," Fortunato said.

~

The skies were growing redder as they pressed deeper in, the air drier and tasting more and more of smoke and sulfur. Entire forests were laid waste, and the trees that stubbornly stood tall threatened to collapse at any moment. The lakes and ponds were blackened and murky, and Fortunato—though he was growing thirsty—knew he could not drink any water in this poison land. Everything was dead, everything was dying, everything—it seemed—was at an end.

He looked back at Wrinn and saw that he looked as well as could be expected, that he was not retching like he had when he first entered the Blight. *Sindomas* was coursing through all of their veins, but how long would the effect last, and just how would they find the source of the Blight? How would they locate it when the Blight was so vast, when it stretched for untold miles?

The skies were red, almost scarlet. The sun was beating hot on them and the air was poison.

And Wrinn… Wrinn began to speak. "I hear something faint," he said, "like… like a hammering."

"A hammering?" Nenré repeated his curious words.

"Show us the way, Wrinn," Fortunato said, and as they took off at a brisk jog, he wished Tyra Jade were here, but he knew she and her kind were not amenable to eating *sindomas*, that the Blight would be too dangerous for her.

~

The air seemed to grow thick, and the dead trees were becoming desiccated sand-colored columns, or otherwise had crumbled to dust entirely. The ground was growing dry, and no grass was left to be seen; it had been withered and blown away. The ground was dry dust and increasingly taking the properties of sand.

Wrinn stopped for a moment, clearly exhausted. It appeared exerting oneself in the Blight was far more difficult than exerting oneself elsewhere. Fortunato was growing fatigued, but they could not afford to delay. "We cannot afford to delay," he said aloud, and Wrinn brusquely nodded.

"You are right," Wrinn said, panting. "You are right. I can already feel the *sindomas* leaving me."

"Chew some more," said Nenré, and Wrinn nodded, plucking one of the flowers from his makeshift necklace.

Leaning on his quarterstaff, Wrinn breathed a little while longer, though the air was poison, though the air was not sustaining for life.

And fear began to grow in Fortunato, fear that they had not done the right thing, fear that they soon would die. How much longer would the *sindomas* protect them? How much longer would the *sindomas* keep them alive?

Without a word, Wrinn began to jog again, but it was a labored jog. They were all growing sick.

And Fortunato prayed he had not led Yanenré Iradahir, the daughter of the king, to her death.

~

Dust turned to sand, trees disappeared, and soon they were traversing up and down great dunes.

It was like the deserts in the southern parts of the Empire, the waterless places where travel was impossible. It was like a desert, but Fortunato had to remind himself he was in Gallia.

He had removed his shirt, tying it around his head to keep the sun from glaring in his eyes. And he was exhausted, and it seemed a sense of doom was falling over them all.

"Do you still hear it?" Fortunato asked.

"Yes," Wrinn answered. "It's getting louder."

But what if that hammering sound were irrelevant? What if it meant nothing? What if Wrinn, having pushed them here, was now pushing them in an unrelated direction, a forced march that would sap them of their strength and eventually lead to their deaths on these hills of sand?

"Come on," Fortunato said, "let us make haste."

And Wrinn agreed, though his steps were growing lumbering and labored, though it was clear the energy was beginning to leave him—the energy and all hope. They had come to a place of dry death, a place where life could not survive, a place that, if left untouched, would cover perhaps all Gallia.

Up and down the dunes they climbed, following Wrinn's direction, and all the *sindomas* in the world could not mend their strength or give energy to their steps. At times, Fortunato felt his eyes begin to shut of their own accord, but he knew if he fell down and slept, he'd die like those trees, and his body would join these dunes of sand.

Yet up ahead, on one of the dunes, there was a dark shape, and Fortunato shouted for Wrinn and Nenré to stop. Against the wind, through the blowing sand particles that stung his eyes, he strained to focus, to look.

The beast moved about on four thick legs. Its head was like that of a deer, with two great antlers. But its brown coat had coarse fur like that of a bear.

"What is that?" Wrinn cried, and the creature took note of him and began to charge.

Nenré flung out her staff, but her movements did not have their normal lightness or their usual quickness; she was dazed and fatigued as well.

Fortunato rushed forward.

Wrinn ducked out of the way of the creature's charge.

And Amenhir came hammering down on the creature's neck. About half of it was severed.

The beast gave a great cry and turned to gore Fortunato.

There was a blinding flash and the beast lost its vision. As it stumbled about in confusion, Fortunato dealt it a killing blow.

"What was that?" Wrinn said.

Nenré's expression darkened. "I fear," she said, "I fear… I think I know."

Its head was rolling through the sand. Its blood was blackish-blue, like that of one dead.

And Wrinn, staggering, dazed and delirious, walked on, up and down the contours of the hills of sand, through this scorching poison desert that had inexplicably appeared in Gallia. He was following his ears, the sound he had claimed was a hammer. But was he just imagining it? Was it just a trick of the wind, or a delusion sent by the Blight itself?

~

Up and down they walked, and Fortunato's strength was drained, and he despaired at what had happened to him, and where he was. He had chewed every last *sindomas* flower from his necklace and put the last *sindomas* flower from his pockets in his mouth. The sun was glaring, the heat nigh unbearable. And it began to dawn on Fortunato that they were stranded, that they soon would die, that he should not have listened to Wrinn, that they should have abandoned Gallia to the Blight because it was impossible to reverse.

No, he told himself in the glaring sun, as sweat stained the tunic he'd turned into a headwrap and drenched the trousers that he still wore, as the *sindomas* began to leave his blood and the poison air began to fill him. *No, no, I will not give up. I will never give up.*

And then he heard it, a metal ring, followed by a rush of fire, so faint he could scarcely hear it over the wind.

"I can hear it," Fortunato told Wrinn but Wrinn by now was delirious and did not respond.

And he drew Amenhir from its sheath. "Come on, Wrinn," he said. "Come on! Walk!"

Wrinn had fallen still, and Fortunato grabbed him, pulling him to his feet.

"There is only a little while left… only a little while," Fortunato said.

And Wrinn, shocked out of his delirium, began to lumber on, up and down the hills again, through the desert that had come to Gallia.

"A little while more," said Fortunato and gave Wrinn a light push.

They rounded what seemed like the highest dune of all, and then, breathless, stopped and looked at the valley below.

There, in that valley of drifting sand, was a sight Fortunato had not expected, a sight he would not have expected in a thousand years.

It was a great foundry, big as a cathedral, and from where they stood it was still perhaps a hundred yards off.

The windows on its black walls glowed with flame, and the sound of the hammer was deafening now.

From its front entrance, something was staggering out, an

immense creature, a thing with the head of a bear and a great bulbous body, a foul mixture of two un-mixable creatures, a joining of two things that should not be joined.

"As I feared," said Nenré, "this is Lothan's Forge, where he outfits the Enemy's armies.

"A Fell Smith is here, one who oversees its operations. He cannot be killed but by the power of the gods."

Wrinn had stooped over and was retching, and vile vomitous liquid was escaping his lips. The poison was beginning to reach him, and it was do or die now. It was now or never.

"Then by the gods' help we will slay him," Fortunato said, "because we must."

"How did I not see it?" said Nenré. "How did I not know? The Forge kills all life. Its workings are recorded in history. How did I not know the influence of Lothan had come to Gallia?"

"That does not much matter now," said Fortunato. "We have a monster to defeat."

"We cannot defeat him!" cried Nenré.

"We will," said Fortunato, "because we must."

And staggering on, weakened, the poison beginning to strike him too, he walked down, descending the slope of the hill of sand and began to make his way to the Forge where the battle would be fought, perhaps the last battle of his life.

Behind him Wrinn staggered, and following a moment later, Nenré. They approached the Forge with as much bravery as was in them. Fortunato, bearing Amenhir in his hands, forced himself onward as the blade glimmered in the light of the sun.

And before the great foundry, he found himself stopping, breathless, and there was the sound of grinding wheels, wheels grating against one another. The fires in the windows flared and smoke poured out of the Forge's roof.

The great doors of Lothan's Forge began to open. A shadow half as tall as a tree appeared, a creature humanoid in shape, a hooded cloak draped around it and where a face would be. Eyes glinted in the sun.

In its hand was a mallet, the sort of mallet smiths used to beat and shape metal. When it spoke, winds seemed to blow and the skies and all their surroundings seemed to grow darker.

"Fortunato of Ríva."

Its voice sent a deathly chill through Fortunato, and though it was blazing hot outside, he felt he were in the depths of winter.

It dropped the mallet from its hand, drew up its hands, and a sword appeared in them, a mighty sword of black-colored steel.

"You cannot slay me," the Fell Smith said, and its voice was like a winter wind in a snow-covered gulch, a freezing hand grasping hold of Fortunato's heart.

It struck and Fortunato dived out of the way.

It slashed and Fortunato ducked under the whistling blade.

It stabbed and Fortunato parried.

And there was the sound of shattering, and Amenhir had been riven in two.

It slashed and with a mighty swoop, nearly severed Fortunato's head, but with just an inch to spare, Fortunato dived underneath of it, falling to the ground.

And the Fell Smith laughed, seeing that the warrior that would be his prey was defenseless.

Wrinn came charging in. Quarterstaff met fell sword and the quarterstaff broke into a thousand pieces, sending its wielder far to the ground.

And again the Fell Smith laughed, and its laughter was like an icy wind.

Doom was all about Fortunato, terrible doom, and in desperation, he grasped what was left of Amenhir, and summoning all his courage, fought harder all the more.

With the shard of his sword he slashed, cutting the edge of the Fell Smith's robe. He slashed harder, all the more, and the raw metal edge split open some of the Fell Smith's ghostly white skin. Black gel seemed to ooze from the wound, then dissipate into smoke.

And Fortunato fought with more ferocity than ever, knowing if he relented for even a moment, the Fell Smith would strike again and cut him down.

There was a blinding flash, sent from Nenré, but that flash did not so much as stun the Fell Smith.

And Fortunato leapt into the air, as high as his legs would carry him, and the desert wind seemed to aid him as he did.

With the shard of Amenhir, the broken blade that was left, he pierced the face of the Fell Smith, and its hood came undone, and its ghostly white body was bared to the sun.

In agony, it cried.

The windows of the Forge blew out, shards of glass everywhere, and the entire building seemed to quiver and quake.

"Who are you, Fortunato of Ríva?" said Nenré. "How were you able to do this?"

The body of the Fell Smith seemed to be burning. Its ghostly white flesh was turning to red, then ochre, then burnt black. Then it began to drift apart, carried away by the wind, fading away into sand.

"Who are you, Fortunato of Ríva?" said Nenré.

"Who are you?"—the question echoed in his mind as the winds blew, as his body slowly began to succumb to the poison of the Blight.

As Lothan's Forge began to collapse of its own accord, catching fire and sending up a towering column of smoke, sickness was taking over Fortunato of Ríva, a deep sickness such as he had never felt before.

"Who are you?" Nenré's voice echoed in his mind as his face hit the sand of the Blight. The last thing he heard was the whistling of the wind and the burning of Lothan's Forge.

The last thing he saw was Wrinn and Nenré collapsed beside

him.

And the last thing he thought of was Nenré's question: "Who are you, Fortunato of Ríva?"

~

A man was appearing before him, an elf whose hair was so fair it looked almost white. On his head was a crown of diamonds, and his body was clothed in a white silken robe. He was in a forest well-watered and lush, and the light of the sun was shining on him.

"You have done what is impossible," said this man, this elf. "Now awake! Awake, and take with you the king's daughter, Yanenré, and your friend. Come with her to *Thas Pardanden*… she will know what it is I speak of."

~

When Fortunato awoke from his stupor, some of the poison had cleared from the air, and the winds had stopped their blowing, and the sky was more blue than red. The sun was low in the horizon. It was evening, almost night.

Some of the poison seemed to clear from him, shrinking in his blood, not growing. And he could breathe, but just barely.

He could breathe.

The Blight was fading.

Ahead of him, Lothan's Forge was a blackened shell. The winds were not stirring, and the sunlight was casting eerie shadows over the sand dunes.

Nenré was breathing, and so was Wrinn. And so Fortunato hurried over to them and grabbed a hold of them, and shook them until they began to stir awake as well.

Nenré's eyes opened, for a moment with terror, but then she realized where she was, and who it was she was with.

"*Thas Pardanden*," Fortunato told her, "do you know where that is?"

Chapter Fifty:
The Rescue

It was the evening, and in this gathering-place of elves, called *Thas Pardanden*, Reev was sitting beside Lord Calion in the place of honor. Earlier in the day he had heard a wretched cry, a cry such as he had never heard before, but no one else had heard it. It had been the cry of desperation, the cry of one who had lost, the cry of one defeated. And for hours, it had disturbed him, but he alone had heard it.

Gastreel was off in the corner of the camp. Prince Vélerion was in the distance, in sight. And as Reev sat there, there came the sound of horns blowing, dozens in unison. And Lord Calion stirred in his seat.

From the edges of the trees came riders on reindeer, elven riders whose bodies were covered in suits of mail. Riding at their fore was a man in a shining helm, and in that man's hands, strapped in front of him, was Ivan Xandrast.

"Lord Calion," said the man in the helm.

And Calion rose and put a hand to his heart. "Yamenvi. You have brought us something, or someone."

Ivan Xandrast's mouth was bound in rope. His eyes still had that blank, empty look, but he was unable to move. And at the sight of him, Reev had a thought… a thought that Ivan Xandrast had not been totally responsible for his actions, that he had been driven by an inescapable force.

"We found the warlock," said Yamenvi, and he lowered his visor, baring his green eyes. "We found him wandering the forest in the shape of a black dog. Today, this afternoon, we captured him. And then we rode with all haste to you."

"Thank you, Par Yamenvi," said Lord Calion. "You have done

what is required of you."

Prince Vélerion was approaching them. "My sister! Where is my sister?" he said.

"Your sister made a poor choice," said Yamenvi. "She was with a human man and a *dra'datsi*. Nonetheless, she is safe."

"A human man," said Prince Vélerion, and his voice was filled with disgust.

"She is coming back," said Lord Calion. "Soon, she shall be here. I have sensed this."

Prince Vélerion turned and walked away, uttering curses under his breath. And Yamenvi, with his great thews of arms, lifted up the warlock and cast him before Lord Calion's feet.

Gastreel was approaching, leaning on his white staff.

"A warlock's end must be swift," Lord Calion said. "Disarmed, he is powerless here. Look not into his eyes, lest he bewitch you.

"Par Yamenvi… shall you do the honors? A swift slicing of the knife, a cutting of the throat?"

"No," Reev said, and his own speaking surprised himself. "No, do not kill him."

And he was rising out his chair of his own accord, and he felt fire growing inside him, a familiar feeling. One he had felt before.

~

"Come out of him, Lothan!"

Gastreel watched as Reev approached the warlock, and the warlock did not react, just stared at Reev in anger and in bafflement.

"Come out of him, Lothan!" Reev said again, and this time Ivan Xandrast twitched, and under his mouth there was a low growl.

"Come out of him!" Sundering was the tone of Reev's voice, final and definite, and the air seemed to shimmer around him.

Ivan Xandrast gave a desperate cry and lunged at Reev, reaching for him with his hands.

There was a glimmer of sunlight. Reev's palm struck Ivan Xandrast's forehead.

And Ivan Xandrast went limp, still like the dead.

~

"Has the Sage killed him?" said Par Yamenvi.

"No," said Lord Calion, "no. Look upon him. He yet breathes. There is life in him."

Reev had tried to drive out Lothan. He did not know if he had succeeded, but looking at Ivan Xandrast's limp form, he did not know if he had done the right thing, if Ivan Xandrast deserved death. There was total silence in *Thas Pardanden*, and in the stillness only the singing of the birds was heard.

And then Ivan Xandrast sat up, and there were gasps among the elves gathered there. No longer were Ivan Xandrast's eyes black, but instead they were a shade of chestnut brown. It was as if a different person inhabited his body.

"Where am I?" said Ivan Xandrast. "Who… Who am I?"

"Ivan Xandrast," Reev said, "you are Ivan Xandrast."

"Yes, that is who I am. But I suppose… I suppose I wish I were not."

~

In the light of the bonfires, Ivan Xandrast, still bound, began to tell Reev, Lord Calion, and Gastreel a story—a story they had not heard before.

"As a young man," he said, "I had watched the land of Almania impose themselves on my country… I had seen their *landswehr* and their military officers raid and burn down villages, and hang my people from nooses. I had seen their warriors ravish our women.

"And a deep hatred was born in me, a deep hatred that became my reason for being.

"And when we lost that war to them, and lost the fertile land of Rodnerov, I was in despair. But then a man in a black robe and an iron mask came to me, and at first, I thought he was a phantom. But he told me he could give me indescribable power, power that I could use against the Almanians, and I believed him. I believed him! Yet he told me I would have to journey far, to the land of Naron Da, to where the shadow is.

"And I left and I followed him, this phantom, this apparition. I followed him south, and at desperate times, in the deserts and the waterless places, I'm convinced it was my hatred for Almania and only my hatred that drove me on and allowed me to go.

"And through jungles and forests we went, through deserts and mountains, until at last I was there, a place of black rock, and a great and terrible dark tower before me. There were sights there I do not understand, beings of nightmare, creatures untold.

"And there the phantom led me. I was tied to a rack… tortured. And I realized my journey was for naught.

"Then… darkness. What happened next, I do not remember. I opened my eyes, and I was here."

"You did an evil thing," said Lord Calion, "and I am sure you knew it then. Hatred is a poisonous thing; it destroys you and eats away at the fiber of your bones."

"Will you kill me?" said Ivan Xandrast.

"That is not for me to decide," said Lord Calion. He looked to Reev.

Reev shook his head. "We will not kill you. We will not kill you, Ivan Xandrast."

"Please," he answered, "call me Xan. That is what my friends and those I love call me."

Reev stirred uncomfortably in his seat.

"Will you remove these bonds?" said Xan.

"No," Reev answered, "not yet. But sometime soon, we will."

The sound of harp and timbrel, the strain of the fiddle rose into the night. Reev had been at *Thas Pardanden* for many days now, and he wondered how many days he would remain. He supposed, when all the elves in Gallia arrived, this large group would depart in unison. And there was the matter of him leaving with them. Gastreel had said nothing about it.

~

It was days later and the weather was positively autumnal. Though the leaves were green, a cold wind was blowing, and Reev was by himself, alone. Xan's bonds had been cut, and he had even been given his two-sided sword, his butterfly blade.

There was a pool the elves liked to walk to, a pool they called the Wishing Pool, and Reev was alone there. The crickets were chirping, but winter was on its way and soon all bugs and creeping things would die. Would he soon go as well, in a different way? Would he be leaving Gallia and the human realm, going away to the city of Danarion with these elves?

From the darkness of the pines, a dark shadow was emerging, a silhouette, and for a breathless second Reev reached for the hilt of Doomblade.

"My boy," said a voice, and Gastreel appeared, Gastreel with his long gray beard. "Here you are. I was trying to find you."

"And you found me," Reev said.

"Yes, yes," Gastreel said, "I suppose I did."

He came up to the edge of the pool, and now both their reflections were in the waters.

"Are we going to the Elf Lands?" said Reev. "Are we going to Danarion?"

"Well," Gastreel said, and his voice grew softer, fainter. "I think we ought to. I think that it is what is wise. You will be safe there, and so will I be. The Enemy cannot see that far; his spies are not there.

"I would have to resign as archwizard…"

"I do not want to go," Reev said. "I do not want to leave my friends… I don't want to leave Aunt Ramona."

"Aunt Ramona, yes," Gastreel said, and there was amusement on his features, and light in his eyes. Then his expression darkened. "If you do not wish to leave, then I will not force you to. We will remain… We will remain in Galiope."

Was there something on the edge of his tongue?

"Come with me," said Gastreel. "You should not be alone. Tonight they are serving lamb shanks on a bed of vegetables. And wine, a lot of wine."

~

Days passed, and summer rolled back in. A heat wave stretched over *Thas Pardanden* and even the trees seemed to be withering. Fall came in fits and starts, but sometime soon it would arrive, and on its heels there would be winter.

Reev, sitting in the place of honor on that day, knew that the journey for these elves to their homeland would be long, and that traveling in the winter would be difficult and dire indeed. Lord Calion had said they were waiting for one more person, one more elf, and that if she did not show up today, then they would depart without her in the morning.

At noon, there were shouts in the camp, some cheers and some jeers, and up ahead, on the eaves of the trees, three figures appeared.

One of them was a woman in white, a woman with red curly hair, beautiful, blue-eyed, radiant, with a long smooth staff in her fair hands. And the other two… the other two!

"Wrinn! Fortunato!" Reev cried.

He ran up to them, meeting them each in a long embrace.

"Milik!" Fortunato cried on the sight of Xan, and drew his adamant knife.

But the elves rushed up to him, and told him, "We are not to harm him, on the orders of the Sage."

~

That night Fortunato, Wrinn, and the Princess Nenré joined in the feast, and the feast was greater than all others, for they used up the remaining food that they would not carry with them. There was the light of fires, and there was dancing. Wine was poured—all of it that remained. Wrinn sat next to Reev and regaled him of a great story, of he and Fortunato entering what he called the Blight, of wicked men who wandered amongst the trees.

And the night faded, and their rest was total, sublime. Reev dreamed of a green land where it was always summer, where snowcapped peaks loomed high above him and where one always breathed free.

Chapter Fifty-One:
The Gift

It was dawn and Fortunato and Wrinn were with Nenré.

Fortunato was looking at her, and there was desperation in his heart, because he knew she was leaving.

What the elves called the Wishing Pool was in front of them, and in Nenré's hands was a thick red staff of lacquered wood.

"Gifts I bring to you both," said Nenré. "And this first gift is for you, Wrinn, a quarterstaff made from red yew from the forests of Doncalion. A quarterstaff fit for my father's bodyguard will certainly be suitable for you."

Wrinn's eyes lit up. "Thank you… I—thank you… I will wield it well, I promise."

"I am certain that you will," Nenré said. She handed it over to him, and when he touched it, his delight seemed to grow. "And now, will you give Fortunato and I a moment alone?"

"Of course," Wrinn said, looking at Fortunato mischievously.

He walked off and disappeared into the greenery.

And Nenré was there, and he and she were alone. Her eyes were watering. "Fortunato, I have thought on what you have said, and I… and I…"

From one of her robe pockets she drew out a length of white cord.

"This… This is my gift to you. A gift of remembrance."

She took Fortunato's left wrist in her hand and fastened the length of cord around it.

"By this, remember me, Fortunato of Ríva, as I will always remember you."

And she peered into Fortunato's eyes, and a single tear fell down her cheek.

"Do not let my brother see what I have given you."

~

The elves were preparing to depart, and the carts were loaded with goods and foodstuffs. Fortunato was by himself, alone, thinking on Nenré's words.

Lord Calion was approaching him, Lord Calion in his fair robes and gold belt. "Fortunato," he said, "the human who slew the infernal Smith.

"The story of the elves of Alonar is ending. We are departing, at last, after many thousands of years, and we will never return. War is nigh and the world is coming undone. But you… your sword."

"It is broken," Fortunato said. "The Smith smote it in two."

"We elves are leaving, but we can linger a little while longer," Lord Calion said. "There is a forge here at *Thas Pardanden*, and a smith who will not strike you, and who can forge it better than it was.

"Where are the pieces?"

~

The elf-smith beat the pieces back together in the molten hot fires of the forge.

When he presented the sword to Fortunato and Lord Calion, the metal gleamed and it was lustrous, and letters had been written upon it in gold.

"It was called Amenhir," said Lord Calion. "Now Danenhir it will be called, because you slew the infernal Smith and delayed the time of Alonar's trouble.

"It still seems impossible that you have done this. But you did, and the Enemy has not foreseen you thwarting his plans.

"No human is better deserving of the title *quilenthi*. And if the world's troubles ever take you to Danarion, know you are always welcome in the house of Calion."

Fortunato took Danenhir in his grip and gave it a swing. It was light and splendid in his hands. "I thank you, Calion, and I thank you, smith."

And as Calion and the elf smith departed, he caught them looking at the white cord that had been fastened around his wrist.

~

Fortunato, Reev, Gastreel, and Wrinn, the four companions, stood by in *Thas Pardanden* and watched the elves depart. Nenré could not look at them, so great was her sorrow. In robes of gold, of green, and of azure they were walking in their thousands, heading north along the ancient road. Like supernal beings they were in the sun's light, and the sun's light glittered on their hair. For thousands of years, they had lived in the forests of Alonar, but now that story was over. For thousands of years, they hid among the trees and kept watch for the sake of their king, but now, the elves of Alonar were gone.

Chapter Fifty-Two: The Departure

"You aren't coming with us?" Reev repeated Wrinn's words. "Why not?"

"We are exiles," Wrinn said. "Didn't you hear?"

Without the company of the elves, the forest did not seem so peaceful, and it did not seem so safe. Ahead of them, underneath some trees, Fortunato and Gastreel were talking. Somewhere in the woods was Tyra Jade and somewhere out there, who knew where, was Xan, against the wishes of Fortunato.

"You will come back into the city's good graces," Reev said, "or else I'll come out here and we'll be outlaws together."

"No," Wrinn said. "Living in the woods is only for experts. Leave that sort of thing for me and Fortunato."

"Well, anyway," Reev said softly. "I'm glad you're all right. I'm glad you're alive."

"I can take care of myself," Wrinn said, and out of the corner of his eye, Reev could see Xan approaching, a dark shadow in the trees, with his butterfly blade strapped to his back.

"Step back, warlock!" Fortunato shouted from afar, and Xan stopped his approach.

He seemed hurt by the words. Fortunato had drawn his sword, and his sword seemed to shine more than it had before, as if a coat of luster had been applied upon it.

A sad expression fell over Xan, and he seemed shrunken, a defeated man. "I will not intrude on your company any longer," he said glumly. "I will go to the city of Galiope, if they will take me. Thank you, Reev Nax, for saving my life.

"And to the rest of you, goodbye."

And like the elves of Alonar before him, he walked off and

disappeared from sight.

~

They spent the night together in what was left of *Thas Pardanden*, and though the elves had taken their food with them, Gastreel had with him road-bread.

The night was gloomy without the presence of the elves, but they had each other, and for that, Reev was thankful. And more remained to be done, more in the city and elsewhere, for Reev knew that a great council had been declared in Galiope, that the representatives of towns and the priests of the great churches and the wise from all over Gallia were meeting as one. What dolorous event had caused it, Reev could only guess. And there were other things Reev was thinking of as well, and other people. He was thinking of Glenda Half-Elven, the proprietor of the Dragonpaw Inn, of Bala Rabaam, and of Ambrass the serving girl.

Chapter Fifty-Three:
In the Daylight

The days since the night in the catacombs had not been easy. What had come over Ambrass that night she did not know, but she knew she could not help herself, that she had met Nocturne three times since then, and that now her overseer Glenda and most everyone in Galiope, everyone who cared to know, knew.

She was in the inn, sweeping absently with her broom, and she could see that her craft had suffered since the lunacy of the full moon overtook her. The floor was clean, but she would not happily eat off it.

"Ambrass," Glenda said from afar, and over the days, Ambrass could tell her overseer was disappointed in her. She had been disappointed in her ever since that incident, that incident underneath the light of the full moon.

"Will you go fetch some water? We must cook the night's supper soon."

"Of course," Ambrass said. "Right away."

And she set her broom against the wall, and headed into the kitchen to grab the pail.

~

The day was cool, and on the edge of one of the city trees' leaves, she saw a speck of red, a speck of red as if it had been painted by a brush. Autumn was coming; it was coming soon.

The city streets were filled with people. There was news, strange news about a great death in the South Weald, a blight of plants and animals that had stopped as suddenly as it began. And she thought, not for the last time, about Fortunato, now dead.

"There she is!" a man howled at her on her way to the well. He was fat, and there was a wart on his nose. He was dressed in an old-fashioned style, with a buttoned-up tunic. "There she is, the vamp's bride!

"Do you know, my lass, that Nocturne is a bugger? A bugger! I thought that was illegal according to our laws, punishable by hanging."

"And what is it to you?" Ambrass said, passing him by.

She had dealt with dark looks and dirty stares before, glares and things said under the breath, but she had never been openly accosted and harassed before. She supposed there was a first time for everything.

Of Nocturne she was not ashamed. She was ashamed that she was not wed. Yet she could not seem to break free of his spell.

~

Braised beef haunches they would serve, and a cornucopia of boiled apples and pears to celebrate the coming autumn. The Dragonpaw Inn cellars were well stocked with beer, and amply supplied with wine. Though Ambrass's reputation had suffered greatly, still the Dragonpaw was the busiest inn, and still—for those with an open mind, who were not bothered by the open fraternizing of different races—it was the place to be.

And so she served with a gloomy feeling in her heart, and the words, and the vile looks, seemed to catch up with her. It was easy to put on a bold face, but being the town pariah was not easy at all. At least once, she had been anonymous, just a serving girl of no note, but now, now everyone talked about her. She was the cause of gossip and rumor, a source of entertainment for the fair ladies of Wodenscross Court.

"Glenda." She had walked up to her overseer. "Do you mind… Do you mind if I have the night off?"

"As you wish," said Glenda, and at her words Ambrass walked off, but she could feel Glenda's eyes on her.

~

Late in the night, as Ambrass expected, Glenda walked in to check on her.

"Are you all right?" she asked.

"No," Ambrass answered, and it was the most truthful answer she had given in days.

She was sitting on the bed, still dressed for the day, and Glenda joined her.

"Well," Glenda said, "I told you, didn't I?"

"I don't need to hear 'I told you so,'" Ambrass said. "A man approached me today, openly, on the street, and began shouting all sorts of curses. I thought it didn't bother me at first, but sometime tonight, it hit me… Sometime tonight, it hurt."

"Well," Glenda said, putting a hand on Ambrass's shoulder, "this is the path you have chosen.

"To walk in the night. And you did not resist the full moon, did you? No, you did not.

"Don't allow what others say to bother you. They don't know you or your life. I tried to stop you, Ambrass, but I failed. And now I will do my best to help you."

"Thank you," Ambrass said, and her eyes began to water and her lips had started to tremble.

Glenda thought so little of Nocturne, but it seemed only Ambrass could see the good in him. Or was it true, the rumors, the vampire's spell, the power of honeyed words, the art of suggestion?

And then a memory came to Ambrass, a memory from the edges of this sudden love affair.

"You said," she began, still trying not to sob, "that you were a witness at his trial."

"I was," Glenda said, "but I had best not talk about that now."

"Why don't you?" Ambrass said. "Please tell me. Aren't you my friend?"

"I am," said Glenda, "and I don't want to hurt my friend."

"Please," Ambrass said. "Please tell me… You were a witness."

"It was the twenties, the late twenties. Things in the city were starting to come undone. There was crime in the streets, more than usual, and the Dragonpaw had been robbed twice.

"And I… And I… Are you sure you want me to tell you?"

"Please," said Ambrass.

"The murders on High Street were just beginning. And one night, I was walking home and I saw someone breaking through a window, and, well, if you gave me one hundred pence I would have bet seventy that it was Nocturne.

"The next morning, that person was dead, a man known as Baron Ackley. He was a rich man, a noble, and he owned several great estates in Gallia.

"And I was announced as a witness at Nocturne's trial. And when my turn to speak came, I found I could not say anything. I… I still wasn't sure, and I had at one time considered Nocturne to be a friend."

"So you caused him to go free?" said Ambrass.

"No," Glenda said, "even without me, the evidence was weak. And the jury was not convinced.

"They did not convict him… they also did not exonerate him."

"So," Ambrass said, "you think I am in danger."

"No," Glenda said. "In my heart, I do not. I do not think Nocturne was the High Street Slasher. And I believe he truly does love you in a way, but I… I…"

"What?" Ambrass said.

"As soon as Bala was born, a little while afterwards, Nocturne discarded his mother," Glenda said. "Didn't want anything to do with her. Her name was Lucy Cotter. She still lives, as far as I know, in Greenwater.

"Sometimes I think all he really cares about is pleasure."

"Well," Ambrass said. "I think I ought to get to bed. It is late."

And yet she had been going to bed later and rising later. She had been behaving differently ever since that night in the catacombs. It seemed, though she did not want to admit it, that she had changed.

~

Glenda had left, and the candle was burning in Ambrass's room. Ambrass had not seen Nocturne or really anyone besides Glenda and the Dragonpaw patrons since yesterday. It was late, probably almost midnight, though she had not heard the church bells ring. And the moon was out, and it was glimmering in her window.

She thought she saw a dark shadow cross the moon. She peered through the window, into her alley, and saw the wet ground, the rain that had not dried. And her body felt sore and distended, and she found she could not get comfortable.

Tomorrow, in the moonlight, she would meet Nocturne again, and Omagon and Drassané would be with him as well.

And when her eyes looked upon the window sill, she caught sight of the torn off piece of cloth, the green fabric that had been part of Fortunato's cloak. And she wept and she wept.

She wept for herself, and for what she had lost.

Chapter Fifty-Four: Masks

It was announced, the day before the Council of Galiope, that there would be a night of festivities, and as soon as Gastreel and Reev returned to Rosetree Manor they found a letter on their doorstep.

"A masquerade," said Gastreel, reading the letter, "at the house of your Aunt Ramona.

"It does not seem appropriate in the circumstances. But the Gallian nobility will use any excuse for a party, I suppose, even a serious council of war."

"War?" Reev said. "Who is Gallia fighting with?"

"No one, yet," Gastreel said.

In the great yard of Rosetree Manor, in the light of the sun, he took Reev's left forearm in his hand. He examined the wound, what was left of it, a small upraised line of flesh, a healed scar.

"It has healed well," said Gastreel. "Lord Calion was a master."

Reev missed the elves already, though to humans they had been unseen, though their presence had not been known.

"It still hurts sometimes," Reev said, looking at the healed scar, "when I think on dark things."

"Then do not think of dark things," Gastreel said.

In the great yard, in the cool of the day, they were lingering.

"What is going to happen to Fortunato and Wrinn?" Reev said.

"Fortunato is a master survivalist," Gastreel said, "and your friend Wrinn has discovered a gift of his own. And you will see them again sometime, perhaps very soon. Even if the Gallians don't restore them, then… then…"

"Then what?" Reev said.

"I—" Gastreel looked at Reev, and his gaze became tender,

warm. "We will see them soon. They will be your friends, Reev, for a long while. Perhaps until the end."

"The end?"

"Time to prepare for the masquerade," said Gastreel. "The party begins tonight at sundown."

~

To Reev's surprise, Gastreel already had masks ready, as if he had been to a masquerade before. Gastreel's mask was white with green ribbons, and Reev's mask was gold-colored with a great green streamer running down from it.

"Must I go?" said Reev, gazing at the ridiculous mask in the kitchen.

"I think it would be wise," said Gastreel. "There is no place I'd less rather be, either, but we must listen and eavesdrop and learn before the great council takes place.

"It is a council of war."

War, but Reev would not be told against whom. Was Prince Vélerion right, that Gastreel did not tell Reev everything? He resented that Gastreel did not trust him. But to Aunt Ramona's great masquerade he would go.

~

When Reev and Gastreel arrived, holding their masks over their faces, the crowds had already swelled to enormous proportions, stretching into the yard of Sunstone Manor. At the sight of so many people, Reev wanted nothing more than to run back to Gastreel's house and never think of this again.

"Your aunt," said Gastreel, "said she will be in a purple gown and a mask with yellow ribbons. Your cousin will be in all black and have an impish mask with ribbons of blue."

Gods help me, Reev thought. But for the sake of Gastreel and Galiope and the council of war, he would endure this. For a higher cause and a higher purpose, he would go and participate and immerse himself in Aunt Ramona's masquerade.

The sound of laughter greeted him, bodies packed against one another, people talking, servants ferrying plates this way and that. There were wine glasses in every hand, and servants were coming by with silver ewers, making certain that no glass was ever close to empty. Reev began to push his way through, and he hoped to blend in to Sunstone Manor's dark corners, to talk, hopefully, to no one at all.

The party was in full swing inside, and the great hall was one of splendid magnificence, the walls so white they could not get any whiter, a chandelier of crystal glass dangling from the impossibly high ceiling, a great staircase lined with red carpet that stretched far up into the second floor. There were pipers playing songs and the strain of a singer rising above the dull chatter of the crowd. The platters the servants carried had all manner of food, sweet and savory, pastries and river fish, meat puddings and all manner of cakes and breads. And Reev felt exhausted at the sight of so many people, the great dames in their billowing feathered gowns, the rich men in their finely pressed black breeches. And he was tired, and growing hot, when he saw one of the great dames with a billowing purple gown the color of a peacock. It was Aunt Ramona in her mask, a mask with the great yawning smile of a comic actor.

Reev could hear her talking with someone, even from where he stood.

"Your marriage to the count wasn't so good, I take it," said a man in an orange-edged white mask.

"No," said Aunt Ramona, playing the part of a great dame. "No, it wasn't.

"His first wife, Síanne, threw herself off a belfry. As the years went on, I began to see why."

There was scattered, uncomfortable laughter.

"Some said she was one of the gray folk, you know, the child of a ghost and a human, and that she would linger in cemeteries and the places of the dead."

Reev, still holding up his mask, wanted nothing more than to get out of this place, and as he stood there, desire was quickly turning into desperation.

A voice stirred him out of his thoughts, a young voice, a voice he had never heard before. "Reev?" And he turned, and saw a boy there, one about his size, dressed in jet black clothing and wearing an impish mask. "You are Reev. My cousin." The Zarube accent was faint but present, the accent of a western aristocrat.

They were connected by the bonds of blood but their upbringings could not have been any more different. Reev had grown up in a small house in Norwood, in the Empire's hinterlands, and then at an inn run by ratlings. Asher... well, Asher Nax Bensange had grown up in the house and estate of a great lord, of a count no less. What would he think of his poor relation?

"I... yes... Asher..." He felt intimidated by his cousin, intimidated even to be here at all, in any capacity.

There was a long pause, and nothing was said, and the uncomfortable feeling was so thick Reev could likely slice it with a knife. What could he say? What words could he use? He was glad to have a cousin but what connection did they have, what bonds did they really share?

"My mother said you were raised by rats," Asher said.

His cruel words about Skreek and Neek, and by extension himself, were like a jagged knife, twisting in his stomach.

"Ratlings," Reev said, and he found himself falling backward, shrunken, through time, through the space of the great hall.

He had to get out of here. He did, for himself, for his own sake.

~

As he hurried down the street, he thought he heard the voice of Gastreel crying out to him, "Where are you going?"

But he did not care. He did not want to be here, nor did he want to be in Wodenscross Court or near Aunt Ramona or his cousin. He would go back to his room in the Dragonpaw, and there, he would be alone.

He had long left the gates of Wodenscross Court, and he was walking in the shadow of the Tower of Pythor, through Middletown. The darkness of the night was deep, and the light of the streetlamps was flickering.

And a face appeared before him, a face with scars the shape of letters, a terrible face that drew all his breath away from him. He recalled the stories Wrinn had told, and the warnings Glenda had given him of the strangers, the foreigners in Gallia who did not belong. A hand grabbed his; he struck the scarred man in the face. He wheeled around, drew Doomblade, his sword, and peered at them, seeing there were about a dozen of them there. A dozen strangers. More than he could handle.

"Who are you?" Reev said. "Who are you people?"

One of them, a woman, had drawn a bow.

"Who are you?" Reev said.

"Praise Lothan," the woman answered.

Chapter Fifty-Five: Searching

The masquerade was in full swing, even late into the night, and despite his better judgment, Gastreel had imbibed more than a glass of wine. He needed to have his wits about him in this nest of silver-tongued vipers and as he walked, he was growing more alarmed, making passes room by room, looking for Reev and the mask that had been made for him, but there was no sight of him, nothing and no trace. Where was Reev? Where was Reev? He had promised to stick close by.

Yet a voice was calling out to him. "Mr. Gastreel," Ramona's voice was cooing. "Or as we say in the west, *seigneur.*"

There she was in her great purple gown, and flame yellow ribbons lined her comic actor's mask. Beside her was her son, in an impish mask, and surrounding her were the great dames and the city masters, the ones who would decide the matter of war tomorrow.

"Hello," said Gastreel, and he looked about in that instant for Reev but he could not find him, he could see no sign of him.

"Hello," he said again, and he sounded like a bumbling fool, but that was quite all right.

"This is Mr. Gastreel," said Ramona, "or should I say, *seigneur.*" She had had a bit to drink. "When I knew him last, he was only the Ranking Wizard but he now he is the leader of them all."

"Yes, we know Gastreel," said someone in a blue mask, a man.

Gastreel felt he still did not belong in Gallian high society, and he knew some people did not believe he was the rightful archwizard, that he had forced himself as head of the council. In a way, he had. He had brought about the end of Syrion and the other great wizards. He had replaced the wizards council with partisans.

And where was Reev? Where was Reev? He looked about once more and could not see him, could not find him. Where was his young ward, the one he was sworn to protect? He could not let him slip through his fingers again.

Ramona was babbling on. She and her brother could not have been more different. She was a tireless social climber, while Simeon had been a selfless man at heart, and his fame had not been something he sought.

Ramona had already changed the subject. "You know, I lived in that castle more than ten years with Count Elfraine and did you know he had eight children by Síanne? He had plentiful servants, but still it was a terrible lot of work…

"And Ash is my only child."

Where was Ash? He had slipped away, disappearing off somewhere.

"Say, Gastreel," Ramona said, and the wine was clearly flowing through her blood. "Will you not put on a show for us? A show of magic? Of lightning?"

"No," Gastreel said, and she knew better than to ask. "That is against the laws of wizardry."

"Oh, laws, laws," Ramona demurred, and behind her mask, Gastreel was sure she was rolling her eyes.

"By the way, Ramona," Gastreel said, and at last he could hold his peace no longer. "Have you seen Reev?"

"It is hard to know," said Ramona. "Everyone here is wearing masks."

And there was giggling among the coterie surrounding Ramona, but Gastreel was not amused. He had failed Reev once, to great cost. He could not and would not fail him again.

And so he departed the giggling nobles who surrounded Ramona, and began doing another pass of Sunstone Manor, room by room, wherever the party was taking place. He wondered if Reev could have run off somewhere to play with his cousin Ash, but wasn't he too old for "playing" and childish games?

The night wore on. The wine glasses emptied, and soon there was no more wine in the ewers the servants were ferrying around. It was late at night, and still, though Gastreel searched for Reev, he could not find him, had no idea where he was.

Could he have gone home to Rosetree Manor? Gastreel supposed it was a possibility.

"I," a woman in a red-ribboned mask was saying to him, "am the Master of Ceremonies for the city of Galiope. Heather Blackmarsh, at your service."

Who was it? Gastreel did not care, he did not care to know her. Her breath reeked of wine, as did most people in this party, and though Gastreel wanted to leave, he would not without Reev.

The church bells began to sound, the tenth hour after noon. It was late, a late night indeed, and though Gastreel was tired and his legs were sore from standing, he could not and he would not leave without Reev.

And he stood there, as tired as he had ever been, and the party was over. Another round of inane talk and self-serving compliments to the hostess would be under way, one final hurdle to get through and Ramona's masquerade would be over.

Heather Blackmarsh left Gastreel's side and he was by himself again, hoping against hope that he would find Reev, hoping against hope that his young ward would appear in his sight and his muscles would relax with sweet relief.

One by one, the great dames, the city masters, the parish priests and the minor barons began to filter out the great doors of Sunstone Manor. One by one, they left, and the church bells began to ring again, eleven hours after noon, and then it was Gastreel there, Gastreel with Aunt Ramona, her son Ash and their bevy of servants. "Where is he?" Gastreel said. "Where has he gone?"

"I saw him earlier," answered Ash.

And Gastreel felt anxiety beginning to grip him. He should

never have left Reev out of his sight.

"I am sure he is quite all right," Ramona said. "I can have my servants search the house if you wish."

By now, she had removed her mask, revealing her long black hair, her pale lips and grayish-brown eyes.

"No," Gastreel said, "no, that is quite all right. He would not have gone upstairs. He must have gone back to Rosetree Manor."

"A masquerade can be a frightening thing," Ramona said. "You never know just who you are talking to."

"That," Gastreel said, "is what I'm afraid of."

And saying no more, he turned and pushed open the great double doors, and the grandeur of Sunstone Manor was behind him.

~

The streets were dark and lonely, but there were people out and about, and that struck Gastreel as strange. Under his breath he found himself praying compulsively, uttering desperate pleas for Reev's safety, begging for him to be all right, healthy, in one piece.

And he knew that whatever had happened, whatever had occurred, he could not react. The Council of Galiope was set for tomorrow at dawn. He could not skip the Council of Galiope. No, he could not. The matters they would discuss were grave, far graver than Ramona's silly masquerade would indicate.

Whatever had happened, he knew his hands were tied. He reminded himself that Reev was resourceful.

He would check first the rooms of Rosetree Manor, and then he'd walk all the way to the Dragonpaw if he had to. Under his breath he was praying, begging the higher powers. He had a bad feeling, a very bad feeling.

Chapter Fifty-Six: The Plot

The wicked men had tied Reev's hands with rope and taken Doomblade from his side. They had stowed him in a covered cart and in that manner they were leaving the city, and every time the cart bumped along the road, he could feel his heart up in his throat.

He had thought surrendering was the best option available to him. He could not stop them, not all at once.

And what would they do with him? They surely meant him harm, that was beyond doubt. But who were they? Their tongue was foreign and he did not recognize any of the words. It was not Imperial, nor was it Zarube, or any variety of Elvish. The insignias the men scarred themselves with were no insignias Reev recognized.

And so where did they come from? Reev knew only that they did not belong, that they were not from Gallia, that they were not from this place.

He'd had a chance to avoid all this pain. He could have been with the elves now, bathing in the light of the Lord Calion and in the radiance of the Princess Nenré. He could have been on his way to Danarion, the City of Light, but he was not.

And the darkness of the night was deep, and perhaps a guard would search the cart before it left.

Yet he would not give up hope.

~

Late in the night, the cart ground to a sudden halt. There was scattered talking, distant to Reev's ears, but he heard a name uttered, "Alden."

And there was more scattered murmuring, and after a long delay, the cart began to move once more, and he could tell by the diminishing foul smell and the increasing freshness of the air that they were out of the city entirely. The wicked men had succeeded.

The chirping of the birds began, a sudden melody, a melody that gave life to Reev's heart, and he realized he had fallen asleep, that it was almost dawn. His first thought was that he was in his room in the Dragonpaw, but his eyes adjusted and the memory of the prior night returned to him, and he realized the grave danger he was in.

Yet through the trees, he could still see the walls of the city; he was not far.

One of the wicked men appeared before him and began shouting indistinguishable orders in his tongue.

A group of men and women grabbed him by his heels and arms and hauled him out of the cart.

Reev could see above him a watchtower of eroded stone, whose roof was missing and whose crenellations and battlements were long gone.

He remembered seeing that watchtower on his way through the Royal Road, but it seemed these wicked men, wherever they were from, were using it as a base of operations.

"What do you want from me?" Reev asked.

There was indistinguishable barking, more yapping in the foreign tongue, but one word he recognized: Serpentax. Vélerion had told him what that word meant. And anew, he was afraid. Anew, he began to wonder and to plot, to think of what he might do, if he might risk running away.

But he could not risk it now, not when his arms and feet were bound tight with rope, not when he was surrounded by perhaps twenty wicked men.

Where were these people from? Perhaps Reev would never know.

The sky around him had a little trace of light in it, and the air was fresh. It was almost dawn, and Reev knew that the Council of Galiope was about to begin.

Gastreel had said it was a matter of war.

He would, by now, be worried beyond belief, beyond words. Would he still attend the council, or would he refuse to attend out of concern for Reev? Reev did not know.

He thought of Fortunato, of Wrinn. He thought, even, of Ivan Xandrast. He wondered if he would see them—or anyone—again.

The words of his cousin Ash had spurred him away, caused him to make a foolish choice, to walk home openly in the streets, at night, when strange men were wandering among the buildings of Galiope. He felt his eyes water. He had not thought the end would be like this. No, he had not imagined his life ending this way. But all lives had to end. All of them did.

The sun was beginning to rise; he could see it slowly emerging through the trees, and the sky was turning brilliant colors of pink and red, of gold and blue. A chill autumn wind was blowing, and he looked south toward the farmers' fields. The harvest would begin soon. How good it would be to be one of those farmers. How good it would be to be anyone else but him.

Chapter Fifty-Seven: The Council of Galiope

The faces in the Galiope Town Hall were no longer wearing garish masks. In the chamber of grim basalt, there was a great space between each seat, and on the floor was the symbol of a hawk, the city's patron animal. Torches flared in each corner of the great room, and the faces that greeted Gastreel were no longer wearing garish masks, no, they were not—grim they were, serious, and the party of the prior night was only a silly memory.

For them it was, but Gastreel was exhausted, having spent most of the night looking for Reev, collapsing at some unearthly hour at a rented bed in the Dragonpaw Inn. And now, as matters of war would be decided, his mind would not be at rest, and his decisions could well be flawed.

At the greatest seat of all was the Lord Eventide, Chancellor of the Gallian League, and by his side his wife Fiona.

And as dawn appeared in the high windows, through the door came the ambassador who had made this request, an ambassador sent by the king of Zarubain himself. He was in a scarlet doublet with tight black breeches and a dark hat with a wide brim. His name was Armande.

"Gentlemen of the Council." His Zarube accent was thick, so thick it was like a mockery of Zarube accents. "I bring to you grave tidings from the west.

"The Empire is rising, and even now it is preparing its invasion. The heartlands of the west may fall to the Empire—indeed, they will, without help.

"We of the Northern World, we the Zarubes, and you the Gallians, we are brothers, and though we have fought before we are of one blood, of one cause."

Passion was in his voice, passion for his country, a genuine love of Zarubain, and genuine good feelings toward Gallia.

"If we fall, the king will not be able to aid you," said Armande. "If we fall, you will be alone and you will face this monstrous Empire for yourself. And if we fall, the whole of the north will fall, and then… then what is left?

"Slavery. Destruction. The burning of towns and villages, the slaughter of cities."

And yet Gastreel knew the Empire would leave them in relative peace if they surrendered—under their dominion, but at peace.

"I ask you, free peoples of Gallia, for your aid, a contingent to aid us in the west, to preserve the liberty of the Northern World for posterity." The king had chosen well in picking Armande; his passion was evident and it seemed there was no guile in him. "I ask you, free peoples of Gallia, for your aid, to preserve our liberty, for the futures of the children of Zarubain and of Almania and of Gallia."

There was a pause; the request had been made. The Lord Eventide, Chancellor of the Gallian League, sitting next to his wife the Lady Fiona, spoke first.

"A good cause," he said. "But many have tried to halt the Empire's advance. All have failed. What say you, Lord Gastreel?"

"I…" Even now Gastreel felt distracted, absent and not paying attention to these most grave of matters. He focused, regained his composure, and spoke as strongly as he was able. "If Gallia sends its young men to fight, then we will be declaring war against the greatest power of our time, the greatest power the world has ever seen.

"Whatever we decide, we must realize this. We must keep that on our minds."

"Are you well?" the Lord Eventide said. "You speak sooth, but your face is pale."

"It is Reev… I cannot find him," Gastreel said, and it was the most inappropriate time to complain, the most inappropriate place as well. The faces in the Council of Galiope looked angered.

Then the Lady Fiona spoke. "Reev Nax," she said. "The hero of the Battle of Galiope."

And then one other spoke, a city master, the Lord Alden. "A town watchman said he was with the men of Ur."

And the faces in the council grew grave, the Lord Eventide and the Lady Fiona above all. Gastreel had thought perhaps they did care about Simeon's son.

And they did care, after all.

Chapter Fifty-Eight: The Summons

Tears were in Reev's eyes. The skies were cloudy. He had been under guard for many hours now.

What a moment to die, what a way to go. And in the worst manner it would be, the worst manner imaginable.

Through the trees there was a commotion, the sound of shouting voices.

One of the strange men, the tallest one Reev had seen, was walking toward him. There was a coterie behind him, men and women alike in dark cloaks, and Reev would guess the group at the watchtower now numbered fifty.

The tall man spoke, and again the only word Reev understood was "Serpentax."

And a woman handed the tall man a cloth-covered object, and he uncovered it, and it was the greenish-black shard of metal from before. But when he touched it, there was steam and smoke, and his hand began to burn, and he screamed and flung it to the ground.

It was the shard of the Dark One's own sword, the shard Ivan Xandrast had carried, which these men—not warlocks—apparently could not touch.

The tall man cursed angrily, and out of the side of his mouth said, "Milik…" And he pointed to the city walls, and in strained Gallian, said, "Go get him…"

~

"You will find no love of the Empire here," said the Lord Eventide, "but our history with Zarubain is fraught, and when have you ever given *us* aid? When have you ever come to *our* assistance?"

"We have aided you," said Armande the diplomat. "When the Grand Duke of Almania wished to go to war with you and bring you into his dominion we stopped him. We threatened him with our own soldiers, with the Knights of Lorh.

"And for centuries we have been at peace, and for centuries we have been allies. And now the Northern World is in danger, not just the west. If we do not band together at this moment, our peoples will all become slaves."

"Just as you enslaved the elves," said the Lady Llewyn, an alderwoman from the town of Leyshaw.

And Gastreel could tell her words stung Armande, and stung him more deeply than he would ever admit. He seemed to almost shrink before them.

"Zarubain's history is not without its flaws," said Armande. "The king has agreed to free any elven slave who will fight, and I myself have freed my own slaves, the ones who served me all my life."

"A last stand," said the Lord Eventide. "A last stand is what this is. And we know, and I suspect you know, Armande, that the odds are not in our favor. The odds of success are not good. They are not good at all.

"And I suppose we all agree some things are worth fighting for, against even impossible odds. But we cannot send young men to die for pure idealism."

"Idealism." When Bartholem, the Rector of St. Sigmund's Cathedral, spoke it seemed all were hushed, all listened, and all revered him. "Righteous causes often seem impossible. They stretch the bounds of what we think can be done. And this day, I can think of no better cause than the cause of our liberty, that we in Gallia will not lose our freedoms, that we will remain standing. Idealism? No. It is not idealism, Your Lordship. It is a righteous cause."

And the faces Gastreel witnessed, encircled around the room, seemed to give no disagreement. As always, the words of the rector were considered truth, though Gastreel twitched inside, believing this Council of Galiope of 1152 might commit itself to an act of absolute foolishness.

"I went to the west," Gastreel began, and he felt Armande's eyes upon him. "I went to the west and saw that it was crumbling. I am not sure that sending thousands to their death—"

"Why give up so easily?" said Armande. "Why allow doubt and misery into that mind of yours, Mr. Wizard?"

And at that moment, Gastreel knew he was outnumbered, that folly might win the day, that this act of reckless foolishness that could cost Gallia its freedom might be agreed to.

Then the Lady Fiona spoke. "Archwizard Gastreel is a wise man, one whose wisdom has served the city well. We should all listen to his advice."

And for a while their minds seemed to open up, and Gastreel had hope this course of madness could be averted.

~

It was now about high noon, and Reev was stirring uncomfortably in his bonds. In these woods, in the shadow of the ruined watchtower, he was looking at the city. In the distance he saw a dark figure approaching, alone.

Time went by, an hour it seemed, and then the figure was there, a figure with shaggy dark hair and a black beard, muscular and brown-eyed, with a butterfly blade strapped to his back. This was the one they called Milik, whom everyone else knew as Ivan Xandrast.

The tall man, the one who had tried to touch the shard of Serpentax, approached Xan and began talking, first in his language, then, after a moment of confusion, in the Gallian tongue.

"Serpentax," the tall man said. "I cannot touch it. You must cut him, Milik."

"I am not your *milik* anymore," said Xan. And he drew his butterfly blade, and the wrath in his eyes was incalculable, beyond anything Reev had ever seen.

~

"How many soldiers do you need?" The Lord Eventide's voice echoed through the great spaces of the Galiope Town Hall.

"Ten thousand is my hope," said Armande.

There were scattered mumblings, a hiss or two, but Gastreel heard no spoken objection.

"Ten thousand young men," the Lord Eventide said, "sent to fight for this cause, for the cause of the Northern World. Where would they go?"

"We have need to fortify County Belidere, and block the way to our capital," said Armande.

"And if they counterattack?" said the Lord Eventide.

"The Grand Duke of Almania has agreed to protect your flank," said Armande. "If this proposal is agreed to."

And there was silence, and Gastreel observed the faces in the room. And it seemed besides him and perhaps the Lady Fiona, no one else thought this was a reckless action, an action that could lead to Gallia's doom. Armande's tongue was too polished, his genuineness too perfected. The king of Zarubain had known just who to send, and he had known the right manner of his sending.

Madness, folly… Gastreel could call it any number of things. But he would not convince these faces, these people, these proud northerners whose egos and heartstrings had been tickled by the silver-tongued diplomat from the west.

"And what is the consensus of the people gathered here today? What do you all believe we should do?" asked the Lord Eventide.

Bartholem, the rector, spoke first. "I say we aid our brothers. I say we join with them, that we defend the Northern World."

Without objection, the motion would be carried; it would be agreed to, and it would become law.

And Gastreel knew his objecting would make enemies. He knew it would cause them to question his loyalty and his love of Gallia. But even knowing this, he spoke. "I think it is rash," Gastreel said. "I think the west will fall and we should not want Gallia to join it."

There were disgusted looks on the council members' faces, a few angry shouts and scattered hisses.

"Then let us vote," said Lord Eventide. "Let those in favor raise their right hand."

And all hands were raised, all hands but Gastreel's and the Lady Fiona's.

The matter was agreed to, and Gallia, for better or for worse, would go to war.

Chapter Fifty-Nine: Freedom

Xan killed the men, and he killed the women. He killed the young and he killed the old. The wicked men, those unlucky enough to stand in stunned silence as their former leader turned against them, had been met by a storm of steel that rent their frail bodies to pieces.

And when his butterfly blade was dripping blood from both sides, when corpses lay all about him, hacked and slashed and motionless on the forest floor, Reev found he could say nothing, for his mouth was bound in cloth.

Xan was panting, but bloodlust remained in his eyes. As the survivors ran into the woods, he turned and gave chase. His face was speckled with blood, he called out curses and angry shouts.

Reev, sitting amid the carnage, began to struggle, trying to find a way out of his bonds. And as he struggled, he thought, and he wondered if Xan could have merely scared them off, struck a few blows then sent them running. Or did these wicked people deserve death?

Carnage was all about him, blood in every place. And Reev felt sick to his stomach. These men and women who said they were from "Ur," had not known Xan had been freed from Lothan's slavery. But a new spirit had replaced it, the spirit of Xan, now thirsty for revenge and desiring nothing more than the destruction of Lothan's forces.

Xan's shouts were rising in the distance... then more shouts.

Voices Reev recognized.

~

Reev had wormed his way out of his bonds and untied the cloth from his mouth. He was walking unencumbered through the woods, and the leaves were crunching under his feet. A trail of bodies was scattered across the forest floor like a trail of breadcrumbs to follow.

And Reev followed this trail beyond the woods, down into a slight valley, a place of open grassland before a great wheat field.

And Fortunato was there, Fortunato of Ríva, and there was a bow in his hands.

He was picking off the fleeing men of Ur one by one with his arrows.

Wrinn was there too, and Xan was crouching on the ground, exhausted, covered in blood.

"Reev!" Wrinn shouted. "There you are… Reev!"

And Reev walked up to them slowly, still dazed by the carnage he had witnessed, sickened by it, even. The men of Ur had unwittingly invited their greatest enemy to their camp—they had invited Ivan Xandrast, an angel of death.

And that angel of death had brought along Fortunato, and he had brought Wrinn. And Reev was breathing free, and there was no wound on any part of his body. They had failed to cut him with Serpentax. Perhaps they had known Lord Calion was gone, and that it would have been impossible for Reev to find healing.

But they had failed, and they had brought their destruction upon their own selves.

Reev was drawing near Fortunato, Wrinn, and Xan. Fortunato loosed the last arrow in his quiver, and it struck home, striking the tall man from before in the back.

Reev stood in the sun's light. "Fortunato… Wrinn… Xan… let's go to the city together. I… I have a feeling."

~

Xan had washed as much as he was able, but his tunic and trousers were still splattered in blood. Fortunato and Wrinn had just a little blood on them. Only Reev was clean. They walked down the Royal Road together, the great dirt thoroughfare that connected east and west. Some looked at them curiously as they walked as one.

And at the gate, Reev was stunned to see the Lord Chancellor Eventide, and a man he did not know, a man in a scarlet doublet, black breeches, and a hat.

Eventide's eyes widened. "Reev Nax," he said. "You are safe. Alive. And in one piece."

"I am," Reev said, "but I won't return until Fortunato and Wrinn can come with me."

"You drive a hard bargain," said the Lord Eventide, "but laws are laws."

"No," said the man in the doublet, "let them in. A fine fighter is this elf, and a mighty warrior is this man.

"You might have need of them in the coming conflict."

The diplomat, Armande, departed the city just after he had said those words.

Reev looked up at the Lord Eventide. "Will you? Will you welcome back my friends?"

The Lord Eventide's gaze seemed to soften.

Chaper Sixty:
The Tables of the Law

"The sentence of exile has, according to our laws, always been irrevocable," said the Lord Eventide in the light of the Galiope Town Hall.

Fortunato and Wrinn were standing in the center of the room, surrounded by the lecterns and the gathered noblemen, among them Gastreel. Reev looked on.

"In fact, it is in the Tables of the Law," said the Lord Eventide, "that anyone so sentenced is not to ever have his sentence lifted. The crimes of these two were serious, for it involved matters of state. They assaulted a foreign emissary, risked his death, and perhaps wider war if a blow had been placed in a more inopportune place, and Armande had succumbed…"

"I can vouch for Fortunato's character," said Gastreel, "as can Reev Nax, and many gathered here. Valiantly did he fight in the Battle of Galiope, when the city was endangered, when the rokahn threatened to destroy us all."

"The Tables of the Law are not something to be changed," said another man, red-haired and pale, dressed in black. "For if it is changed in the Tables of the Law, there is nothing protecting this council from becoming a den of tyranny. If we overrule this ancient custom, even for men like Fortunato and Wrinn, there will be no limit on the laws this council can pass, and woe betide the people of Gallia."

"A small change, Alden," Gastreel said to the red-haired man, "for an asset in the coming war. And we will not regret it. The law, writ on stone tables, can be overruled by unanimous vote.

"We will need to bend reality, bend rules and the way of things, if we hope to overcome an enemy many times stronger than ourselves. The Empire has overrun nations much stronger than Gallia, and now we have risked their wrath."

"What says the son of Simeon?" said a bespectacled woman with gray hair.

Reev stepped forward. "My lady," he said.

"Call me Llewyn," she answered.

"My lady Llewyn," he said, "I spoke the words I meant outside the city gate. If you will not lift Fortunato and Wrinn's exile, I will not return to the city. I will depart with them. And where I go, there is no telling."

The Lord Alden's eyes gleamed.

"To some it may seem an empty threat," said Reev. "But Gastreel and others, and many much wiser than I, have said I am the Prince of the Dawn, the Sage, the one promised to defeat Seymus. Perhaps, you should consider my departure in light of that, with war threatened at our doorstep."

The council grew hushed. Dozens of somber faces rung Wrinn and Fortunato, all around.

"The Tables of the Law," said the Lord Alden, "or the extinction of our people. That is what the son of Simeon implies is the stakes of our choice. But nonetheless, there is a wit of wisdom in his words. For Fortunato is indeed a mighty warrior, and this Wrinn his protégé overcame Armande, after all."

"There is something else," Wrinn, at last, spoke. "A Blight that had spread across Gallia. You will not know of it, except in rumor, and that is because of us. It turned the South Weald to desert, and the trees to death. It is our doing that it no longer threatens the city."

The council's faces, to Reev's eyes, seemed unmoved by Wrinn's words. Yet their silence to his heart felt encouraging. And he had spoken the truth; wherever Fortunato and Wrinn went, he would go, and not without them.

"I move," said the Lord Alden, "that we change the Tables of the Law just this once. An exile's sentence may be revoked, in times of war. And a second motion, to revoke the sentence of exile for Fortunato of Ríva and Wrinn Finnis, and purge their exile from the record books. All in favor?"

The men and women of the council raised their hands one by one, starting with Alden. To Reev's wonderment, Gastreel raised his hand last.

"The sentence of exile is revoked," said the Lord Alden. "Welcome back to the city, Fortunato and Wrinn. So great was our love for you, the law was no object."

Reev was glad at the sight, but his heart stirred him. There was a storm within himself, and a storm quickly growing in the world outside.

Chapter Sixty-One:
Grave Petitioner

The Tower of Pythor was in front of Bala, and even if he craned his neck, he couldn't see the top. Mr. Gastreel had found him at Dada's house and brought him here, and he had dressed him in a little robe of ash gray. Then Mr. Gastreel had gone into the tower, and he had left Bala here, alone.

The tower looked spooky from where he stood, and the skies overhead were cloudy. It was cold and Bala wanted to go someplace warm, where he could sit inside and have something to eat, and maybe some milk to drink.

Gastreel was walking out from the open doors of the tower, and he was holding something in his hands, a bowl carved out of mortar.

"Bala Rabaam," he said, "it is a big day for you, a big day indeed. You have advanced from hopeful to the status of 'grave petitioner,' and I have it on good authority that you will be apprenticed soon."

He put the bowl in Bala's hands.

"And then what?" Bala said.

"And then you will learn the art of magic," Gastreel said. "You will learn to wield it like a painter wields his brush, or a scribe wields his quill.

"And you will use your powers for good, Bala.

"I am sure you will use your powers for good…"

~

The night they returned to Galiope in safety, Wrinn was at his bed in the Dragonpaw, thinking, remembering, reminiscing about what had occurred, what had happened. To him, it still felt like a dream, and at times, he wondered if Lord Calion and Nenré and the elves were just figments of his imagination, and if seeing the elves of Alonar was just a vision he had. But the quarterstaff, made from red yew "from the forests of Doncalion" and covered with a layer of lacquer, was leaning against his bedpost. It was the only sign that what happened had not been a dream.

Reev was sleeping across the room from him; Bala was nowhere to be found. Ambrass the serving girl had not been at the Dragonpaw today.

But in the midst of the silence, there were whispers in the back of his mind, whispers he could hear if he truly cleared his thoughts and shut his eyes.

"Thank you," the whispers said. "Thank you, Son of the Forest. Thank you…"

Chapter Sixty-Two: That Night

Fortunato was walking down the street when he saw it, the sight of Ambrass, his former love, locked hand in hand with Nocturne Rabaam, and as he drew near they were unaware of him, and they kissed.

He would kill the bastard. He would kill him, he swore. And he began to shout curses, to shout things even he was not in control of or aware of, and Nocturne stepped in front of her protectively, and she had gone a shade of white.

"I told you not to take what is mine, Nocturne," Fortunato said. "I told you! I told you!"

"She is not yours, not yours anymore," said Nocturne, that devil, that bastard, that cur.

"And you…" Fortunato said, fixing his eyes on Ambrass. "You! You harlot!"

And some of the whiteness in her face faded, and there was even an indignant look in her eyes. "I thought you were dead! I thought you were dead, Fortunato!"

"And so you thought I was dead, and so you went after this devil?"

Tears were welling in Ambrass's eyes. "Were you so faithful?" she said. "Were you so virtuous?"

Her voice had grown soft. "Who was it? Who was it that tied that white cord around your wrist?"

And he looked at that white cord, and beside himself, turned the other way.

~

In his upper story room, Fortunato upturned tables and chairs. He swore to kill Nocturne, to wring his neck or cut him down with his sword.

And there was a knock on the door.

His angry energy spent, calmer than he had been in many hours, he answered the door. It was Wrinn there. Wrinn.

~

At the Green Girdle in Middletown, they both had ales, tall ales, and the ale bubbled in the glass. And this dirty watering hole was now filled with people, for it was night, and the night was young.

"I will kill him," Fortunato said again, to Wrinn this time, but by now even he did not believe his words.

"And get thrown out of Galiope again?" Wrinn said. "I hope you'll let me come with you, like the last time."

"Perhaps," Fortunato said, "Galiope is not the place for me. Perhaps I should return to the Empire. Maybe I belong there."

"That's silly talk," Wrinn said, a grin on his face.

Wrinn was looking at the white cord around Fortunato's wrist. Fortunato laid his arm on the table, and stroked the fine fabric. It was elvencloth, the finest fabric known in the world.

"Ambrass is your love," said Wrinn, "not Nenré."

"Ambrass and I?" Fortunato said. "No. That story is no more."

The night wore on, ales were drunk—more ales than was wise—and Fortunato found his mind drifting, drifting to that night on the battlements when Ambrass had sent him away.

"Never again," he said, delirious from drink. "Never again…"

Chapter Sixty-Three:
A Drop of Blood

It was autumn full and true. The skies were steely gray, and the trees outside the city walls were arrayed in bright colors—red, gold, and yellow. Ambrass was still working at the Dragonpaw, and lately her body had become distended and uncomfortable, and at times she would find herself falling into spells of delirium. Nocturne would be here later this night and she was in the great hall, sweeping diligently, and the floorboards were so clean you could see every contour of the wood. Supper today was cottage pie and a salad of apples and pears and vinegar, but though the nightly menu changed, each day seemed to blend into the next, and every day, her body felt more distended, and every day her spells of delirium seemed to grow.

That night on the battlements, in the dark of night, the moon had been a pale sliver, and Fortunato had been holding her hands. His eyes seemed to water, though Ambrass had seen little outward emotion in him before. "I love you," he had said, again after her dismissive words. "It seems I cannot help it."

Ambrass looked outside the windows of the Dragonpaw. She was still sweeping, but now, it was to keep herself busy, for the booths and tables were empty, and there were no patrons to serve. She could not get comfortable, whether she sat or stood, whether she lay in bed or stretched her arms and legs. She was beginning to miss her old life, her life among the gypsies.

That night, the Dragonpaw was busy, and the great hall was filled with music. Ambrass busied herself as a good worker would, giving the patrons whatever they needed. She had worked so hard over the summer, she had amassed a large stash of coins. Yet her body was so stretched, and the spells of dizziness were getting worse.

That night, she dreamed it was spring and the trees were green and blooming with flowers, and the grass was verdant with life. She dreamed she was in a little house in the woods in the midst of this vernal paradise, and that she was in a rocking chair, and that Glenda was by her side.

And at her breast was an infant, an infant whose skin was as white as the moon. It was small but it was beautiful in its own way, a tiny little thing, pale and glorious. And as it nursed there was a sharp and terrible pain, and a single solitary drop of blood ran down her skin.

At that moment she wept, and Glenda walked over to comfort her, but there was no comfort for her left in the world. No comfort, for she was alone. No one was there to rescue her.

Chapter Sixty-Four:
The Hand of the Gods

It was autumn, and the air was cold. A wind was blowing, and Reev Nax, standing on the city battlements, could see that the trees had turned all manner of brilliant shades of red, yellow, and orange. The air was brisk and he knew that winter would soon be on its way, winter with its drifts of snow, its icy gale.

Behind him stood the wizard Gastreel, and below them the young men of Gallia were departing the city in a line ten men deep. Ten thousand of them had been sent to war, ten thousand sent to fight the Empire. There seemed to be no end to their number as they walked down the Royal Road. They were dressed in green and longbows and quivers filled with arrows were strapped to their backs. Longswords were at their sides, and as Reev stood there, it seemed there was no end to them, that he might stand here for hours, days perhaps, and not see the end of their marching down the Royal Road.

"Do they go to their deaths?" Reev said softly.

Gastreel placed a hand on his shoulder. "Let us hope not," he said. "Let us hope the council has not decided on folly."

The soldiers were marching, the yeomen soldiers. A trumpet pealed and a chorus of trumpets followed. A young man walked by pounding a kettledrum, and the army marched to its beat.

All these people had been sent to fight the Empire, all these people, these young men with lives ahead of them, families perhaps but no more. How could the Gallian League beat back the Empire where every nation had failed, when ancient and venerable nations crumbled before it?

"I fear it is," Reev said. "I hope it is not folly, but I fear it is."

And it struck Reev at that moment that he was an Imperial

citizen, and that Fortunato was, too, and that these yeomen soldiers, mustered from the Gallian freemen, were going to war against their own country, against the land of Reev and Fortunato's birth.

"Why did they do this?" Reev asked. "Why did they decide on this course of action?"

"Kindred feelings," Gastreel said. "Good feelings among the nations of the Northern World... a belief, erroneous as it is, that the Zarubes and Gallians are brothers, that an attack on one is an attack on all."

Was this what Gastreel meant when he spoke of trouble in the west? Was the Empire laying waste to the cities of the west? Was the Empire the reason why the west, in Gastreel's words, was crumbling?

"I fear..." Reev said. "I fear they will all die, or be scattered. And then I fear, after they are defeated, that all of us in Gallia will pay a terrible price."

"For all our sakes, I hope you are wrong," said Gastreel. "But your words are portentous. They are wise. You seem to have a keen eye for things such as this."

And there was silence for a little while, and the yeomen soldiers continued to march, in their tens, in their hundreds, in their thousands. And Reev could see that the sun was getting low in the sky, that the day was growing late.

"I've been thinking of everything that's gone on," Reev said. "Of Lord Calion. Of Nenré. Of the wound I was dealt. And..."

"And what?" Gastreel asked.

"How will I defeat Seymus?"

"By the gods' help," Gastreel answered.

"And how will I do it?" Reev said. "What must I do?"

"Much remains to be learned," Gastreel said. "I went back to the library a little while ago. I scoured every shelf. I looked in every room. I spent three days in the Library of Dendérion, three days, and so many hours I lost track. I tried to find the lost prophecies.

There was no trace. They must be in the Elven World somewhere, in the keeping of Nenré's father, the king."

"And will we go there? Will we go to where Nenré is?" Reev asked.

"No," Gastreel said. "Not now. The way is too dangerous. We cannot risk it. Gallia—"

"—isn't safe, either," Reev said.

"No," Gastreel replied. "No, it is not entirely safe. But for now, we are here. For now, we remain…"

There was another pause, and Reev was shivering despite his thick winter cloak.

"Gastreel," he finally asked, "what sort of name is Reev Nax?"

It was a silly question on its face, but in truth it was a meaningful question, and important.

And Gastreel, despite himself, smiled, and there was a little light in his eyes. "The Nax family…" Gastreel said. "I do not know much of their history."

"Aunt Ramona said she and my father grew up in a town called Winter Ridge," Reev said, "up in the Dragonteeth, up in the mountains. She said I had a grandfather named Kal and that he is still alive. He might know."

The last of the yeomen soldiers exited Godsgate. Their forms were like dark shadows moving down the breadth of the Royal Road.

"The mountains are troubled, and never more than now," Gastreel said. "There are rokahn… And in the Dragonteeth's caverns, there are nameless things. The uplanders have always been hardy, but I cannot imagine the state of their towns and villages now. There have never been so many rokahn before, spawning from their holes."

The sun was edging closer to the horizon and Reev could see it was about to get dark.

"It is almost night," Gastreel said, "and for an old man like me it is a long walk back to Rosetree Manor. I confess I look forward to resting in my own bed."

It was hard to remember, sometimes, that though Gastreel was a mighty wizard, he was still a man, and getting on in years. Where most old folk would be napping in their rocking chairs at his age, Gastreel was still moving, still acting as if he were in his prime.

"Will you come with me?" said Gastreel.

"No," Reev said. "I guess I'd like to be alone for a little while."

"Very well," Gastreel said. "I will see you tomorrow."

And Gastreel the Archwizard turned and disappeared into the night.

Reev remained alone on the battlements, thinking, pondering, praying.

And as he stood there, there was a wind, and he sensed someone approaching.

He turned to see Xan there, Xan with his butterfly blade. His eyes glinted with moonlight. "Reev Nax," he said, "the one who rescued me."

And Reev found he was still uncomfortable in Xan's presence, and still there was a worry in the back of his mind that Xan would turn on him and dash him to pieces with his butterfly blade.

"Xan," Reev said. "Hello."

A smile appeared on Xan's face, a smile illumined by the city lights. "I was thinking," Xan said, "about how some say you are the Hand of the Gods. And I remembered that I was once a Hand as well, the Hand of Lothan. And I thought, Master Reev, that I could be your Hand, the Hand of Reev Nax."

"No," Reev said. "No, there is no need for that, no need at all. But you can be my friend, my companion. We can fight at each other's side."

"That sounds good as well," Xan answered. "As for you rescuing me, I owe you a debt I cannot easily repay, but I will try to repay it."

"There is no need," Reev said. "Consider the debt canceled."

The words did not seem to comfort Xan, and for a brief moment his smile vanished, but then it returned. "A friend then, a friend and a companion."

And Xan turned, and into the darkness he disappeared, and Reev again was alone. He turned to face the city and its lights. His eyes looked toward the mountains.

Much remained to be done. Many things were left to be accomplished. But for now, the Empire was not here. For now, Lothan's work had been thwarted.

Yet war was coming, war between the nations and other kinds of war. Somehow, Reev had a role to play. Somehow and some way, the role he would play was vital. Somehow and some way, he would crush Seymus underneath his feet.

THE END

Continued in Book Three, *The Iron Mask*...

Glossary

Vardic Calendar	Julian Calendar Equivalent
Albos	January
Kaldsil	February
Primrane	March
Tidusca	April
Brenua	May
Aurelios	June
Odens	July
Sextil	August
Harona	September
Brightleaf	October
Anthanos	November
Candlebright	December

ELVEN PHRASES

Sí quilenthi: "I am an elf-friend."
Dra'datsi: "Outsider." Used of elves born outside the Elven World.
Illunitari: "The Radiant One."
Indoren Hannen: "Kings of the River."
Indoren Sirot: "Kings of the Forest."
Riven Velatoren Drasoren: "Books of the Outer Princes."
Alonar: An ancient Elvish term roughly corresponding to Gallia and some surrounding lands.
Té veli: "He is handsome."
Bet inié indoren granaras dus héan?: "Will the daughter of the king degrade herself so?"
Bet el?: "What's that?"

Adada ié: "Aid me!"

An: "Go!"

Nibollen: "Dwarfs."

Parda: "Leave!"

Ananda: "(You all) go!"

Velati Sonoren: "The Prince of the Dawn."

Gallian Coins

Penny: The standard coin, silver.

Shilling: A thick silver coin, worth twelve pennies.

Crown: A gold coin, named for the crown on one of its faces.

Terms

Accromancy: Magic of speed and increase. Accromancers can grant themselves and others powers of speed and quickness, as well as increased strength.

Adamant: A blue-colored metal, hard enough to pierce stone, named after Emperor Adamantus.

Almania: A grand duchy south of Gallia, considered part of the kingdom of Zarubain. Its strong military is renowned in the region.

Archwizard: The highest-ranked wizard. His duties include presiding over meetings of the Council of the Twelve and overseeing the maintenance of the Tower of Pythor.

Black wolves: Large, intelligent wolves of the Dragonteeth Mountains. They are often captured and forced into the service of rokahn. They are one of the three divisions of great wolves, along with white wolves and brown wolves.

Brill: Also called Brilium, a large town in the Imperial province of Gad, north of Norwood.

Cathedral District: A large district of Galiope just north of the main gate, Godsgate. It is home to the city's churches and cathedrals.

Council of the Twelve, the: The ruling body of wizards, consisting of the foremost members of the twelve orders—Green Robes, Blue Robes, Gold Robes, and so on—and presided over by the archwizard. They meet in the Tower of Pythor once or sometimes twice a year within the walls of the city of Galiope. Most of the ruling wizards live apart from the city, but many have a home in Galiope.

Dark iron: Called *malirion* in Elvish, a metal first fashioned by the Dweorg. Weapons forged of it wound the soul. A wound of dark iron is considered impossible to overcome; death follows in hours, days, or for the strongest, weeks.

Dark One, the: A name for Seymus, the enemy of the gods, the king of the Abollaren, or demons.

Doncalion: A forested region in the north of the Elven World.

Doomblade: One of the original *estirion* blades, first called *Pelladrimas* ("Flame of Fire") and wielded by the elven warrior prince Camlon in the First Shadow War. Through many names and owners it eventually made its way into the hands of the human Simeon Nax.

Dragonpaw Inn, the: A large inn of Galiope, owned and run by the half-elf Glenda.

Dragonteeth Mountains: Large snow-capped mountains, stretching from Gallia in the east to the ocean in the west, forming the border of the Northern World and the lands of the elves.

Druen: Elvish for "night people," a term for the cursed elven tribe known as vampires.

Elf-friend: A term of legal and cultural weight according to the elves, it is granted to non-elves who have proven themselves steadfast allies and trustworthy friends of elvenkind. Elf-friends are allowed to dwell in the Elf Lands and participate to a lesser extent in elven society.

Elven Quarter, the: A district of Galiope in the northern edge of the city, home to elves, mostly those of the Lamen tribe, or High Elves. It is known for its cleanliness and elven architecture.

Elves: Long-lived beings whose kingdoms and settlements lie in the north of the world. They are divided into several tribes, including the Lamen, the Umen, the Lonen, and the Nurnen. In recent years, the Lamen kingdom lost a war to the Kingdom of Zarubain and untold thousands of elves were brought into forced servitude.

Elvish horse: A kind of warhorse bred by the elves for speed and bravery. They are known by the bony horns that grow on their noses.

Empire, the: A vast state composed of seven provinces, ruled by an emperor and the Imperial Council. It is considered the foremost military power in the world.

Estirion: "Star-iron" is the hardest and sharpest metal known to man. The means of the making of star-iron swords are lost to history. They were said to be forged by Danthelon, the so-called "Wonder-Smith." Only twenty are known to exist, and are considered priceless.

Forest Realm: A term for the elven territories belonging to the Umen tribe. Most of the Forest Realm is contained within a vast forest that stretches hundreds of miles.

Galiope: A large city of the Northern World, called by those that love it the Great Queen of the North.

Gallia: A region east of Zarubain and west of Kardir, a place of mixed forest and farmland. Its greatest city is Galiope.

Gallian League: A league of towns in Gallia that band together in times of war.

Godsgate: The south-facing main gate of Galiope, serving as the major exit and entry point.

Greenwater: A district of Galiope built low to the ground, known as a place where sewers empty into the River Galios. It is known for its squalor and poor sanitation.

Gypsies: A wandering folk who traditionally roamed the world in colorful wagons. In recent years, they were welcomed by the Gallian government and allowed to settle in Galiope.

Hawk's Keep: A keep in the center of Galiope, its last defense in time of siege. It also serves as an armory for the city.

Horn Keep: A fortified keep in the western quadrant of Galiope.

Imperial: To those outside the Empire, a citizen of the Empire. To those within the Empire, a man or woman originating in the coastal provinces associated with its founding.

Imperial City: The largest city in the known world, the capital of the Empire.

Kav: A state southeast of Almania. In recent times, a wall was built around its entire border.

Lonen Elves: A tribe of elves known for their atheistic beliefs and their advanced technology in war. They are often black-haired and pale in complexion.

Lonen Town: A district of Galiope in the city's western quadrant, home to elves of the Lonen Tribe. It features Lonen architecture and is almost homogenously elven.

Market District: A large district of Galiope, north of Middletown, known for its shops, mansions, and financial institutions.

Mekara: A region of forest and plain north of the Empire, home to warring barbarian tribes.

Middletown: A district in Galiope just north of the River Galios. It is home to many shops and market squares.

Necromancer: A sorcerer with power over death and withering.

Noricum: A small region in the center of the Imperial province of Gad, named after the River Nor. Its administrative center is the village of Tancreda.

Norwood: A small village in the region of Noricum in the Empire, in the province of Gad.

Odynomancers: Wizards with power over pain and torture.

Old Wood, the: A forest east of Galiope. The ancient Gallians thought it sacred.

Ratlings: Furry humanoids with rodent-like features. They often live on the fringes of human society, in walled-off ghettos in human cities and in isolated communes. They are naturally athletic and, in the Imperial Army, are often used as spies and skulks.

Rokahn: Humanoid creatures known to dwell in the Dragonteeth Mountains, considered creatures of shadow. When their population swells, they will often raid the lowlands for food. Breeds include kehrad, toltar, and the standard species simply known as rokahn.

Saré: A dark head-covering common to married elven women of the Lonen tribe.

Selwyn's Parish: A large district of Galiope named after Saint Selwyn, an ancient Gallian renowned for his piety. Decades ago, a fire swept through the district, destroying most of the buildings. Around the same time, the gypsies arrived in Gallia and were welcomed. They rebuilt and settled the district.

Servants of Seymus: Six beings in service of the Dark One. They wear iron masks and are clothed in black.

Sindomas: A white flower renowned for its healing properties. It blooms in autumn.

South Weald, the: A large forest just south of Galiope.

Starstones: Shards of crystal, infused with magic to the point that they steadily give off light.

Strathbrad Gate: A gate of Galiope leading northeast in the direction of the town of Strathbrad.

Tower of Pythor: A tall tower in the center of Galiope, walled off to the outside world, where the wizards have their base of operations.

Unlife: The energy of undeath; the necromantic force that gives animation to dead flesh and bones.

Vampire: In Elvish, *druen*—a tribe of elves cursed in ancient times with a thirst for blood.

Wall, the: A large wall forming the border of the Empire in the north. Only one gate allows northward or southward passage.

Wizards: Powerful magic weavers of the Northern World. They are governed by a council and have their own nation-state within the walls of Galiope.

Wizard's staff: An implement of magic that wizards use. Without it, their skill at magic weaving is weakened. The first task a wizard who has achieved full rank undertakes is the fashioning of a staff. They are constructed of crystal and certain types of wood.

Wodenscross Court: The richest district of the city of Galiope, built on a high, flattop hill. Its large mansions are passed down and usually remain within families; they are never for sale.

Woodsmen of Brill: A group of hunters and rangers who dwell around the town of Brill in the Empire. They are said to know the tongue of birds and beasts.

Zarubad: The largest city of the Northern World, far west of Galiope, by the sea, the capital of the Kingdom of Zarubain.

Zarubain: A large kingdom of the Northern World, west of Galiope. Its legal ruler is the king of Zarubain, who dwells in the capital city of Zarubad. Outlying regions are governed by dukes (duchies), counts (counties), and barons (baronies).

APPENDIX 2: FORTUNATO OF RÍVA

Born 1121 Sextil 23 in Ríva, Anthania Province, Empire, to Petro and Alessa; Petro a fisherman, Alessa a mother, of no family name or illustrious family history. Telantine blood comes from Alessa, who many generations past had a maternal grandparent from the Isle of Serpents.

Biography: As a child and into his teen years, Fortunato got into trouble. He fell in with bad characters and had numerous brushes with the law. At age 12, he—with his friends—was caught stealing apples from a farmer's field, and it was the last straw for his father Petro, who beat Fortunato and demanded he never the leave the house without his supervision. Fortunato, that night, ran away from home. He eventually found his way northwards into the province of Gad, and acquired a familiarity with living off the land. At age 12, Aurelios 1134, he was abducted by the Woodsmen of Brill for intruding on their territory. His skill with the sword and bow were noted, and the Woodsmen gave him a chance for life. He began his training and for two years learned the art of living in the wilderness, becoming a novice member of the Woodsmen.

The Woodsmen were allies against the forces of darkness growing throughout the world. Under their care and supervision, they—without the knowledge of the Imperial government—aided the transport of Reev Nax from Gallia to the town of Norwood. Fortunato was among that party, and there he met Gastreel, with whom he had an instant connection. Gastreel sensed something great in Fortunato and convinced the leader of the Woodsmen that Fortunato was needed in the North. Fortunato made his journey to Galiope the day after Reev was securely settled in Norwood.

For eleven years, Gastreel and Fortunato corresponded via letter. Fortunato became entrenched in the affairs of the North, and would report to him anything alarming or concerning.

At age 19, in spring of 1141, war broke out between the rokahn and the Gallians in what would become known as the Wars of '41 and '42. Fortunato fought in a battalion with Nocturne Rabaam and others. In Sextil 1141, during an excursion in the mountains where they were clearing a rokahn dark-hold, Fortunato discovered a litter of Black Wolf puppies, all but one of them dead, and the survivor malnourished. He called her Tyra Jade and raised her to health. She became a strong adult. Fortunato's habit of riding her as if she were a horse became famous throughout Galiope; but others heard of this, too.

In Harona 1142, the Wars of '41 and '42 ended. Fortunato, now 21, was approached by a woman calling herself Raena. His riding of a Black Wolf was noted by an order of warriors whose origins began in the Elven World, the Arlom Riders—a band of fighters who ride on unusual beasts. He was inducted into the Order of Arlom Riders, and spent the next two years of his life wandering the Northern World in Raena's company. He saw this as part of the mission Gastreel had given him, gathering intelligence on the northern kingdoms; he continued to correspond with Gastreel via letter.

Eventually, Gastreel returned, having left Reev Nax in the care of the ratlings Skreek and Neek, and he and Fortunato reconnected in Galiope.

About the Author

Cursed at birth with a wild imagination, Andrew Cooper spent his youth dreaming of worlds more exciting than Earth.

He is a graduate of the Odyssey Writing Workshop. His stories have appeared in Morpheus Tales, Fear and Trembling, Residential Aliens and Mindflights, among others.

He is also a graduate of the Creative Writing program at Western Michigan University.

Visit **www.aj-cooper.com** to sign up for the newsletter and stay up-to-date on new releases.

Find him on **x/Twitter** @ajcooperwriter.

www.ingramcontent.com/pod-product-compliance
Lightning Source LLC
Chambersburg PA
CBHW050809190726
48285CB00005B/1846